The Collector

R. Allen Chappell

Dedication

This series is dedicated to those *Diné* who still follow the *Beauty Way*—and while their numbers are fewer each year—they remain the well from which the people draw strength and feed the *Hozo* that binds them together.

Acknowledgments

Again, many sincere thanks to those Navajo friends and classmates who provide "grist for the mill." Their insight into Navajo thought and reservation life helped fuel a lifelong interest in the culture, one I once only observed from the other side of the fence.

Graphics and layout by Marraii Design

Cover art by Daniela

Author's Note

In the back pages, you will find a small glossary of Navajo words and terms used in this story, the spelling of which may vary somewhat, depending on which expert's opinion is referenced.

Table of Contents

1

The Trader

There was quite a line waiting for Clifford Johnson to open his trading post, some eager to pawn jewelry, others desperate to rescue family heirlooms teetering on the edge of redemption. The *Diné* are, for the most part, an even-tempered people; a thousand years waiting around for something to happen has provided them an extra measure of patience. Still, as the sun lifted in a near cloudless sky tempers rose. Everyone has their limit and the Navajo are no different.

It started with a muted grumbling at the back of the queue. Then several went to the barred window to peer inside and curse. Shaking their heads in disgust they returned to their place in line, scowling, and muttering dark threats.

Tommy Nez, determined to pawn his ring for Saturday night beer money, made so bold as to bang on the door and yell out, "Open up you crazy old bastard! I know you're in there…your truck's out back."

A snaggle-toothed woman at the back of the queue cackled and called, "Hey you, Tommy…maybe he's hurt in there…maybe some robbers got him like last time… Maybe you should just kick down the door." The old lady, still drunk from the night before, was ignored. Her husband, also tipsy, was the only one thinking the idea had merit but even he drew the line at kicking down doors.

As the sun warmed to its work, a customer known only as 'Bad Eye' thought of the corner phone booth; borrowing a quarter and straining his one good eye he looked up the number to call the trader's wife.

Almost shouting, he complained, "The store's still not open! Where the hell's Clifford?"

On the other end of the line a surprised Louise Johnson glanced first at the clock and seeing it half-past nine immediately hung up in the caller's ear and dialed Tribal Police. The woman had ample reason to be alarmed.

~~~~~~~

In his twenty-three years in the business Clifford Johnson had only twice failed to open the store by eight o'clock of a Saturday morning. The first time, nearly ten years previous, he'd hit a cow on his way in to work. The ill-fated bovine stepped out of the brush without warning and paid the price. Cliff's new truck was totaled, pinning the trader unconscious in the cab. The local rescue unit got there quick enough, but after seeing what appeared to be an exposed kidney, took an inordinate amount of time prying him out of the wreckage. Clifford was barely regaining his wits as they pulled up to the free clinic. The volunteers jostled the stretcher inside to find the new intern on duty.

The resident physician had taken a couple of hours off. A fishing crony had called to say the Browns were filtering down the Animas to the confluence. The fish were reported milling about—unwilling to risk the muddied waters of the San Juan—easy pickings for a fisherman who knew his business.

The excitable young Navajo intern fresh from his schooling was about to call Farmington for an ambulance when he discovered the gore didn't belong to the trader after all but to the unfortunate cow. Cliff, for his part, had suffered only a dislocated shoulder. The intern grinned as he jerked the ball joint back into place, saying, "You got lucky this time, Trader."

Regaining the power of speech with a stifled yelp, Clifford focused on the kidney in the pan beside him. The young doctor nodded his head and laughed, saying Cliff was welcome to take it along as a spare if he liked;

noting the rescue team had already divvied up the better parts of the cow.

The second time the trader missed an opening was four years later when surprised by burglars waiting in the darkened back room of the store. The desperados ordered him at gunpoint to empty the safe. Cliff, not easily intimidated, initially refused and was so severely beaten for his trouble as to be left a little whopper-jawed—his speech permanently affected—a distinct disadvantage for a man who makes his living dealing with the Navajo.

On this particular Saturday morning, however, Clifford Johnson was not nearly so lucky.

2

The Crime

Thomas Begay hung up the receiver and stared first at the phone, then through the kitchen window and across the sage flats to the blacksnake ribbon of highway— already shimmering and undulating in the morning heat.

Well, I'll be go to hell... Thomas had no idea what to make of the call.

"Who was on the phone?" Lucy Tallwoman, busy at her loom since dawn, didn't bother getting up or raising her voice. This was the most productive part of her day and she didn't like disruptions. Still, she was curious. They didn't get many calls. She'd spent most of her life without the luxury of a telephone and figured now that they had one she had some catching up to do. The notion of missing even a single call was unsettling. She'd heard the phone ring, and Thomas talking, but couldn't make out who the caller might be. The second time she asked she made it a good bit louder and got an answer.

"It was Billy over at Tribal Police. He says he's on his way out here to take you in."

Lucy murmured, "Yeah, right," and grinned in spite of herself. Thomas *would* have his little joke in the morning. She listened for more and when it didn't come grew testy, "Who was it really, and what did they want? Was it Sue Yazzie? Sue don't usually call this early." And then thought to herself, *Sue knows I'm working by now, she wouldn't call.* Lucy Tallwoman didn't have many close friends; should Sue Yazzie be taken out of the mix there wouldn't be any. Lucy's growing renown as a weaver had caused many in the craft to shun her...some out of pure jealousy alone.

From the other room, Thomas made no further effort to identify the caller—offering instead only a muted curse against a background of kitchen noise.

Then, too, there was this business with Thomas Begay. In a society where *any* contact between a man and his mother-in-law is a serious taboo—Thomas taking up with Lucy Tallwoman was a moral thorn in the side of the entire community. Traditionally minded though she was, Lucy nonetheless refused to give up Thomas Begay. They'd stuck it out a long time now hoping people would eventually forgive, or at least forget. So far that had not been the case.

Totally exasperated Lucy turned to the door with a scowl—only to find her husband standing there holding two steaming cups. Thomas pursed his lips causing his own frown to tighten. "No, I'm telling you—it was my nephew and he's coming to take you into the FBI's office this morning."

Lucy studied his face for a moment and was convinced he wasn't fooling around. She shook her head and asked, "Did he happen to mention why?"

"What he said was…" and here Thomas tried to recall exactly what Billy Red Clay had said. 'The FBI wants to question Lucy about a murder that happened this morning. I'm going to have to bring her in." Thomas gave a lift of his chin in her direction. "That's about all he said."

With a lowered eyelid, Lucy regarded her husband for a long moment. "A little strange don't you think?" Her hands kept the shuttle skittering back and forth through the vertical warp, pausing only to pat down every few inches of weft with her mother's old white-shell comb. Finally, at the end of the run, she gave a sharp tap with the long-board to lock it in. The cedar loom was her mother's own design, built by her father back when he was young. No one else had one like it. Not that it was better than anyone else's but like Lucy Tallwoman herself, it was just different. "The FBI must think me a witch if they believe I know anything about a murder in town this morning. I haven't been off this place in over three days." So foolish did the notion seem she almost smiled…almost.

As Thomas set her coffee on the low table by the loom, Lucy noticed a slight tremor in his hand. *No, her husband did not in the slightest take his nephew's message as a joke.*

Thomas sucked in his breath and moved to close the kitchen door. "Don't ever say that...about being a witch, I mean... that's all we need, people thinking like that again. It's good your father didn't hear...you'd be on your way to the sweat lodge this morning."

"He hasn't come in yet?" The words were hardly out of her mouth when they heard the door creak open as Old Man Paul T'Sosi fumbled his way through the mudroom on his way to the kitchen.

Thomas cocked an ear at the door and shook his head. *It wouldn't do to upset the old man this early in the morning...that could make for a long day.*

Paul's mental state seemed a bit improved these last months—possibly due to the new diet and vitamin regimen his doctor suggested—not any sort of a *real* cure to Lucy's way of thinking. She'd pestered the physician to continue searching for a more definitive answer to her father's bouts of mental confusion. The GP admitted there could be other contributing factors but assured her *that* would be a long shot. "It would be rare to see any significant improvement at this stage of the game no matter what we do."

She got a second opinion, but that clinician, too, thought it just the natural progression of old age, and declared there was probably nothing further to be done for it.

Lucy Tallwoman was not one to be easily dissuaded and remained convinced medical science could go some better. Making an appointment with a specialist in Farmington, she was in turn referred to a well-known authority in Albuquerque. That appointment would be coming up soon, and she intended to see it through regardless of the cost or final diagnosis.

Still concentrated on her weaving Lucy pushed her chin toward the highway, "How long do you figure… before Billy Red Clay gets here?"

"I'm thinking forty-five minutes—if he don't get sidetracked." Thomas knew his nephew wouldn't hesitate to deal with some deserving traffic offender along the way and God help one so foolish as to be driving under the influence. Billy Red Clay missed being out on patrol in the same way a chained up dog would miss chasing cars. "Why do you ask how long before he gets here? Are you thinking of making a run for it?" That would be Thomas's solution. For him, it had always proved to be the best course of action.

Lucy frowned at the thought. "Billy didn't say anything else? You know…just something between the lines maybe?" Lucy tried sounding unconcerned, but knew her husband saw right through it.

"Not that I could tell, he didn't. Billy's pretty much a straight talker, but he's always been closemouthed when it comes to his work with the FBI. He's...reliable...I guess you would say. That's probably why he was picked for the Bureau's Liaison Officer in the first place. There were others that had the seniority on him, you know...loose-talkers...every one of 'em."

Thomas Begay was not fond of Tribal Police, or any other law for that matter. It had been a while now since he and Tribal had last hooked horns, and while he had proven to be less than law-abiding in the past, even Tribal conceded he had mellowed. That was the opinion of Harley Ponyboy a kindred spirit back in their wilder days. Harley had seen Thomas in his prime, and it had, indeed, been something to see.

Lucy Tallwoman couldn't help thinking it was her husband's past reputation causing Tribal to send his nephew on any call in which Thomas Begay might play even a minor role.

The old man's voice was heard from the kitchen, barely discernible through the closed door. "Where do you suppose the damn cream and sugar's being kept these days?" Paul said this in the manner of a person recently accustomed to talking to himself. He didn't really expect an answer.

Lucy Tallwoman shook her head, narrowed an eye at the door and whispered, "Right where it's been since we built this house…" And then louder, "It's right there, on the cabinet beside the stove, Dad."

Thomas called to his father-in-law, "I might have left something in front of it Paul… You'll have to look."

~~~~~~~

Billy Red Clay, when he finally came rolling in, pulled up to the front of the house and beeped his horn. On the reservation even close friends seldom come directly to a person's front door without warning. Disregarding such protocol could, in fact, be dangerous.

Fortunately, Old Man Paul T'Sosi had already returned to his *hogan* behind the big house. The old *singer's* hearing not being what it once was, he remained unaware Billy Red Clay had arrived. That was probably a good thing. Paul getting involved in this would likely lead to some serious pushback should he learn of the young policeman's mission. He and Thomas Begay seldom aligned on *any* course of action, but when they did, they were formidable.

"Can you believe that big-nose cousin of Elbert Sosi?" Billy was incensed. "He comes whipping past me like a house afire, and when I pull him over he's three-sheets-to-the-wind already! Lucky for me the patrol officer was on his way back into town and took him off my hands." Billy snorted, "I'd like to see Elbert's clan try to get him out of this one… I don't care if his cousin is on the Council." The young officer slung his head in contempt and was about to curse, but seeing Lucy at her loom, only smiled sheepishly and sent a weak little wave her way.

Thomas got right up in the lawman's face. "So what the hell's up, Nephew?" Thomas Begay didn't parse words when it came to family being carted off by the law…even if that law was family, too.

Billy being related, and of the same clan as Thomas, was himself a man of few words. The young officer hesitated, looked down at his boots, and was reluctant to answer. "I'm not sure how much I can say just yet, Uncle." Seeing the expression on Thomas's face forced him to reconsider. "What I *can* tell you is that Clifford Johnson was found in his store this morning dead as a rock." He sighed and admitted, "Just about everyone in town already knows that much I guess." Gazing back down at his boots he frowned at the dust. The boots were new and Billy intended to keep them presentable as long as possible. He had his own office now and thought it high time he tried to look like somebody.

Thomas didn't back up an inch or say a single word, just waited for his nephew to continue.

"Aww, hell, Uncle, I may as well tell you… The trader was slumped over his desk with a unfinished note in his hand." The young lawman considered how far he should go and again hesitated. Finally, he sighed, "The only thing he'd written was 'Lucy Tallwoman' and then it just sort of squiggled off the paper, not really readable." He glanced at the pair and shrugged. "Old Cliff had taken a pretty hard hit to the back of his head; whoever did it probably left thinking him dead. Later, he must have come around enough to drag himself to his desk...tried to use the phone from the looks of it. There was a bloody trail halfway across the room. Agent Smith said there was no way a man should have been able to make it that far in his shape...but he did. He must have been a pretty tough old bird." Billy said this with a trace of admiration.

Lucy Tallwoman, shocked and unable to speak for a moment could only sit hands to her mouth in horror. She had known Cliff Johnson since she was a girl. The trader had been her mother's agent when *she* gained prominence. After Lucille's passing, Lucy's work had become collectible in its own right, her fame eventually surpassing even that of her mother's. Lucy Tallwoman had in fact reached the enviable position of selling mostly at private treaty—much of her work spoken for even before it was off the loom. Nearly everything went to one or another of a very short list of private collectors—a secretive bunch virtually unknown even to each other. It took Clifford Johnson a good many years to put that list together and he made certain no one knew who was on it...not even his wife.

Some locals thought Lucy Tallwoman's prices unwarranted; her good fortune became the root of more than a little conjecture and jealousy in the community. For a while there were even a few of the more agitated who slyly suggested—she might be a witch.

Lucy's mind was a flurry of questions, *why was my name on that note...how can I possibly be connected to Clifford Johnson's death? This can't be real?*

Her husband was wondering along those same lines and was quick to point out to his nephew, "Lucy's been right here for days now, Billy. She couldn't have killed no one this morning."

The two watched silently as Billy Red Clay shined his boots on the back of first one and then the other pant leg. After a final critical glance at his footwear, the Tribal cop straightened and raised his eyes with a frown.

"Well, hell, Uncle, we know *she* didn't kill no one. Fred Smith never thought she *done* it." He held up a hand and waved a finger. "But, Cliff Johnson *was* her agent. And with Lucy's name being the sum total of his last words, it's only natural the Bureau should think she might have *some* clue as to who did do it." Billy's swarthy face turned a shade darker as he shook a forefinger at the pair and raised his voice for the first time. "It took some determination on Clifford's part to scratch out that note! Agent Smith just wants to know why *Lucy's* name?" and then added, "He made it clear he wants to talk to her before anyone else does. I'm not really sure why being *first* to question her is so important, but he seems to think so." Billy softened his tone. "That's why they sent me out here to bring her in this morning." He touched the brim of his hat in Lucy's direction, and then gave his uncle a pointed look. "They thought otherwise *someone* might put up a fuss." He turned again and signaled his apologies to Lucy. "Fred Smith would have come but he's stuck with the forensic people and couldn't get away. He said to tell you he was sorry he couldn't make it out here in person this morning."

Lucy Tallwoman, still not fully recovered from the news, had only one thing to say, and she said it in a most determined way. "I think we'd best be calling Charlie Yazzie."

Thomas nodded his agreement. "Time to lawyer-up I expect—Fred Smith, or no Fred Smith."

Billy Red Clay grinned for the first time and bobbed his head at his uncle. "I already called Charlie on the radio. He was on his way into Farmington anyhow, him and Harley. They'll be waiting for us at the Federal Building."

"What's Fred Smith going to think about you calling Charlie in on this? Having Lucy show up with a lawyer before he even has a chance to speak to her might make him a little unhappy...wouldn't you think?"

Billy smiled. "I doubt Fred will say a *damn* thing. No one talks to the law these days without a lawyer...and Fred likes Charlie. He'd rather him be involved than some shyster. Just be glad Charlie keeps up his *bona fides* with the bar association." He doubted Thomas knew what *bona fides* were—waited for him to ask—and was disappointed when he didn't. Billy just heard those words himself the day before and was laboring under the impression they projected some semblance of credibility.

Thomas was obviously pleased his nephew had taken it upon himself to call in legal aid. Whatever *bona fides* meant, he took it as a good sign Charlie Yazzie had some. He was now inclined to see this clan nephew in a kinder light. Thomas liked Agent Smith well enough, but one couldn't be too careful when dealing with any kind of law…especially not government law.

"Nephew, you did good." Thomas, grinning himself now, was encouraged to think there was at least this assurance they would get a fair shake. "I guess I'll just follow along behind you into town, that way you won't have to bring Lucy all the way back out here. We need to do some grocery shopping in town anyway." He glanced over at his wife. "We better get the kids out of bed to keep an eye on Paul and take the sheep out. This might take a while." He scowled in the direction of the bedrooms and the sleeping children. "Those two are getting bad about laying in of a morning." He clucked softly to himself. "We were going to dock lambs before it got so hot the flies were out. I suppose that will have to wait now."

The family's utility flock had increased significantly these last few seasons and so had the problems that entailed. There was no end to the work involved in raising market lambs and docking tails wasn't on Thomas's list of favorite pastimes. Lucy Tallwoman's bunch of wool-producing Churros, on the other hand, pretty much took care of themselves.

~~~~~

Legal Services Investigator Charlie Yazzie, along with his friend Harley Ponyboy, were on their way into Farmington with the intention of picking up a few odds and ends for a project they'd been coerced into. Charlie's wife Sue was of the opinion some sort of roof over the back porch was long overdue. She figured the time had come to make that happen. "We could use a little shade out there in the heat of the day," she'd said, "and they are calling for rain later on, too," but then grudgingly admitted, "Rain don't look likely to me. That radio has been saying rain for a week now...I'm tired of hearing it." Sue had not been in the best of moods the last few days and Charlie had no interest in making matters worse.

Harley, gazing happily out the window as Charlie's truck breezed through the smaller communities along the way, couldn't help smiling at the day's prospects. Ever the optimist, Harley Ponyboy figured they should be able to finish the job by noon, and hoped they might then be able to go look at a horse a friend had for sale. There is little the *Diné* enjoy more than *horse-trading*. Its long been a favorite form of entertainment on the reservation—in a similar vein to horse *racing*, another favorite pastime—but without the specter of financial ruin. Even Charlie occasionally found himself caught up in a horse deal. His own grandfather had made his living dealing in horses and had expected at the time that his grandson would someday follow along in the occupation. The old man hadn't counted on the boy's grandmother who, as it turns out, had other and very different plans for him. It was at her insistence and encouragement that Charlie eventually worked his way through UNM to become a lawyer. Which is not so different from being a horse trader as one might think.

3

The Heat

Senior Agent Fred Smith's office was on the second floor of the Federal Building in Farmington, not far from the reservation, relatively speaking. Charlie Yazzie's official truck was already in the parking lot when Billy Red Clay pulled in with Thomas Begay not far behind, a black plume of diesel smoke trailing in the wind. "That's why these trucks are called coal burners," he often said.

Lucy Tallwoman took her time getting out of the cruiser...waiting for Thomas...and eyeing the Federal Building. A shadow of uneasiness had fallen over her on the way into town despite Billy's best efforts to set her mind at ease.

The three Navajo entered the big double doors together and then made their way up the stairs to the second floor. Charlie Yazzie and Harley Ponyboy sat at the far end of the foyer, which served as a waiting area for several associated offices. Smiling reassurance, Charlie motioned them on back. Harley Ponyboy, peeking around the investigator, didn't smile but gave a quick lift of his eyebrows in greeting.

The receptionist had already informed Charlie that Agent Smith was in a meeting but should be out shortly. That information was passed along to the late arrivals. In the short interim that followed, the five *Diné* chatted back and forth. Charlie, too, did his best to calm Lucy's lingering case of nerves.

It was only a few minutes later that the big mahogany door swung open to reveal a well-dressed trio, two of whom might have passed for local businessmen, if not for Thomas Begay's whispered determination they were Federal Marshals. No one could offer up anything to dispute this and their attention turned to the equally impressive third person, an attractive woman in her mid-thirties, impeccably and tastefully attired. She spoke to the receptionist and was duly pointed toward the restrooms. As she passed, the woman nodded pleasantly to the group seated along the wall, but seemed to hesitate for just an instant at the sight of Charlie Yazzie. Harley Ponyboy caught the look and elbowing Thomas leaned closer to whisper, "Did you see that? Looks like Charlie's still got it all right." He nodded to himself. "Yep…he's still got it…"

Agent Smith followed the others out and stood in the doorway smiling at everyone but indicated only

Lucy Tallwoman and Charlie Yazzie were to come with him as he turned back into his office.

Billy Red Clay frowned and looked over at his Uncle Thomas in a way there could be no doubt he was disappointed.

In the office, Fred Smith ushered Lucy and her newly acquired legal council to seats at the moderately sized conference table, and then took a place just opposite the two. Fred being from that part of the country, and knowing the protocol, first asked about everyone's family then offered some small talk before approaching the real business at hand. It was what Navajos would expect from one of their own, and hearing it from a white person pleased them, especially coming from one of Fred's caliber. The Federal Agent soon had Lucy Tallwoman smiling and chatting about the children, giving her his undivided attention until interrupted by a soft knock at the door. The receptionist stuck her head in to announce the same woman they'd seen earlier in the foyer.

Fred looked up and smiled as she entered. "This is Agent Carla Meyor, a Bureau Specialist in our Art Recovery Division out of the New York office." The woman immediately came forward to take Lucy Tallwoman's hand, commenting on her traditional dress, which she obviously admired. When she turned to Charlie and offered her hand it was with a quick tilt of her head. "I understand you are a lawyer now, Mr. Yazzie...Legal Services I believe?"

Charlie said that was so and couldn't help feeling there was something he was missing about the woman. Carla quickly picked up on this and laughed. "I thought I recognized your name in an earlier conversation with Fred. He said you might be here today. I was in one of the groups you tutored at UNM...but that was a long time ago. I wouldn't expect you to remember."

Try as he might, Charlie could not place the woman yet made the appropriate affirmation that he did.

Carla doubted this, but accepted this attempt to acknowledge he did, with a smile and a nod.

Lucy Tallwoman, who at first avoided looking directly at the female agent, now studied her more closely, drawn to something in her appearance or manner, or a combination of the two...something so elusive she couldn't think what it might be. She hadn't known many white people on a one-to-one basis and had little to compare this person with. Still, there was something...

Carla noticed but said nothing.

Fred Smith appeared thoughtful and listened to them chat for a moment before adding, "Carla by the way, does have a law degree from UNM but later changed career paths. She earned her Master's in Art History at Brown, where she concentrated on Native American collectibles. Her dual degrees attracted the attention of the Bureau, which fortunately was able to recruit her to our Art Recovery team. She's only recently come onboard officially. She *had* previously been involved as a consultant in several high-profile federal cases." The agent paused and gave a wave of his hand toward the door. "The two gentlemen you saw earlier are investigators currently assigned to the same unit."

Charlie, tongue in cheek, remarked, "Ah, well, Thomas Begay will be disappointed, he figured them for Federal Marshals."

An odd look flitted across the FBI Agent's face. "Actually, Charlie...they were *both* Federal Marshals before coming on with us." And then looking across at Lucy Tallwoman, smiled quizzically. "How could your husband possibly know that?"

Now it was Lucy Tallwoman's turn to smile. "It's a gift, I guess—I don't think I've ever seen him be wrong when it comes to identifying lawmen."

Fred Smith exchanged glances with Charlie, who shrugged but didn't pursue the remark. The agent pulled himself back to the matter at hand. "Charlie, you're probably surprised at the attention the New York Bureau is affording a local case like this, but it may be bigger than you think. The two agents you saw earlier were wrapping up an investigation in Santa Fe, but flew down when the circumstances of Mr. Johnson's death became known. Ms. Meyor, here, drove up from

Albuquerque this morning—only arrived an hour or so ago, in fact. We have reason to believe this case may be related to similar ones the Bureau's investigating in both New York State and Santa Fe." Fred directed his gaze in Lucy's direction. "Is there anything you can tell us that might explain why Clifford Johnson made so desperate an effort to leave your name on that notepad?"

Lucy looked at Charlie who, smiling, nodded she should answer, causing Fred Smith to smile as well.

Her voice hardly above a whisper, Lucy leaned forward across the table. "I have been thinking about this since I first heard this morning... I have no idea why he would write my name. I'm working on something for him right now...supposedly already spoken for...but Clifford didn't say *who* the buyer was. He did say, though, that the gentleman was from New York. New York the city, I mean." She paused to collect her thoughts and went on. "A few years back Clifford's wife, Louise, sent me a clipping from one of those interior decorating magazines featuring one of my earlier *Rainbow Yei—Yei Bi Chei* pieces." Lucy used the old Navajo phrase, *Yei Bi Chei,* for spirit helpers instead of the more common singular "*Yei*" denoting the actual God. She went on to mention the figures were depicted as Corn Dancers, a style that later became so popular she began to portray nearly all her *Yei Bi Chei* pieces as such. "I guess you could say I have become identified with them. That and my *Chi'ihónit't* or spirit release, they are now my signature on a piece."

Carla didn't bat an eye at any of this, which led Charlie to believe she might have been more familiar with his friend's work than they had imagined.

"Lucy, would you have any idea what your work is selling for in some of the New York galleries…or even those in Santa Fe?" Fred was doodling on a pad as he spoke and pushed this over to Carla.

Carla glanced at the paper and then, not looking at the agent, addressed Lucy Tallwoman directly. "Lucy, are you aware some of your early work has recently changed hands at some rather large figures?"

Lucy's mouth tightened. "I'm not sure what you mean by 'large figures' Clifford Johnson has always handled the business end for me. I know my work brings more than most of the other weavers; that's been a sore point locally for a while now." Lucy frowned. "None of it's my doing, that's for sure, I never let out what I'm paid for any of my stuff." She shook her head. "I wouldn't have any idea what something brings once it leaves the reservation. I only know what I have been told by my agent." She quickly corrected the statement, "Was my agent, that is…" and her voice faded to an awkward silence.

Carla stood ready to pursue the subject. "Would it surprise you to learn, Lucy, that some of your pieces have brought as much as fifteen thousand dollars—just in the past year or so? There are avid collectors bidding up the prices of anything of yours that appears on the market." She paused a moment as though looking for the right words… "Everything in the Native American market has gained value of late but it is your work that stands out at the auction houses and by a considerable margin, I might add.

Charlie Yazzie's eyebrows shot up and for a moment he appeared speechless. He'd had no idea Lucy Tallwoman was so well known, or her work so valuable. He was aware she and Thomas had been doing well of late, building the new house and all, but this latest information was totally beyond the realm of anything he might have imagined. He and Thomas Begay had been close friends since school days and kept relatively few secrets from one another. He was nearly certain Thomas didn't know what sort of money his wife's work was bringing, at least not beyond what Clifford Johnson paid her. He probably had no clue as to what those pieces ultimately brought on the open market. Everything went through the trader. It was no secret he handled all of Lucy's business affairs.

Carla Meyor went on. "Word has it you are now considered *the* definitive weaver of traditional Navajo textiles. Collectors all over the world are becoming interested." The agent slowly nodded her head, as though mentally qualifying the statement. "No one else is producing their own wool from old-line Churros;

very few of those sheep are even left now…not to mention the hand carding and spinning. And fewer still are dying their yarn with locally found plant and mineral dyes—that knowledge alone is nearly a lost art." Carla paused to let this sink in before adding, "My sources consider your work to be quite remarkable and confirm prices at auction are approaching record highs and will probably go even higher in the future." The agent was nearly breathless when she finished and sat silent, staring at Lucy as she would an enigma of the most unusual sort.

There was something else in that look that no one but Charlie caught, but even he couldn't figure out the significance of it. He turned to the bewildered weaver to ask, "Lucy, I'm assuming Cliff Johnson has been sending you a running account of your earnings…along with some sort of periodic written summation, for tax purposes if nothing else?"

Lucy turned to the investigator with so blank a look on her face he was momentarily taken aback and could only cock his head in surprise.

"No, he has never done any of that. He seldom told me who the buyer was for any particular piece, unless I happened to ask…which I almost never did…most weavers prefer to leave all that to someone who knows that end of the business and just concentrate on their next piece. It's important to leave the finished piece behind to ready their mind for a new work. That's why we make the *Chi'ihónit't,* so our spirit can find its way out of the old and allow us to move on to the new. Clifford said there was really no need for me to know who his buyers were. He considered his client list private and for obvious reasons, I suppose. I've never begrudged him that; when my work is finished and in the trader's possession I'm paid immediately. His bookkeeper takes care of that. I'm paid what Thomas and I think is more than fair, judging from what others make.

Agent Smith looked up. "His bookkeeper? And who might that be?"

"Cliff's wife Louise, at least that's who signs my checks and takes care of my taxes." Lucy cleared her throat and made certain she was understood when she said, "My mother had complete trust in both Clifford and Louise Johnson." The weaver glanced around the table and observed what she perceived to be doubt on the faces of these admittedly more sophisticated people. Even Charlie Yazzie raised an eyebrow. Lucy visibly drew back. "Are you people saying the Johnsons haven't been honest with me?" Color rose to her face making her embarrassment even more evident. She gazed into the faces of those around her, *is it possible they are right and my family has been taken advantage of all these years?*

No one spoke for a moment, causing Fred Smith to take the opportunity to interject, "One of our agents out of the Albuquerque office is a forensic accountant. He's on his way out to the trading post this morning for a preliminary look at their records. If he finds anything out of the ordinary, now or later on, you will be one of the first to hear of it. I expect to learn more later this afternoon. In the meantime I can only suggest we not jump to conclusions; at least not until the facts are in." He waved a hand in Carla's direction. "Ms. Meyor intends to be around for several days yet and will keep you updated on any developments on her end of the investigation."

Charlie ran his tongue along his upper lip and raised a finger. "Just one other thing Fred. Do you or Carla have any reason to think Lucy's safety should be a concern—in respect to Clifford Johnson's note, that is? The trader obviously meant to make it clear he had some sort of concern in regard to Lucy, and possibly even meant his words as some kind of warning."

Fred Smith pursed his lips in thought then scratching the back of his head, spoke saying, "As I mentioned, Charlie, we are bending every effort to sort this thing out, and do have some of our best people on it…as you already have seen. There *is,* obviously, the question of why Lucy's name was in Johnson's mind at the time of his death. *Was* that meant to be a warning of some sort? Unfortunately, we're unable to say at this time. I would, of course, advise ordinary caution going forward, but I'm not currently aware of anything to be overly concerned about in that regard. Again, we will keep you both posted."

Charlie nodded his understanding.

Fred then turned his attention from the Investigator and directed a final remark to Lucy Tallwoman herself. "Should you recall anything…anything at all you feel might prove helpful…do not hesitate to call me personally regardless of the hour." He passed her a card with his home number scrawled on the back. "Any time of the day…or night." Then sitting back and smiling at them both, the agent wound up the meeting. "I hope this little get-together this morning has not overly inconvenienced either of you and would ask you both to keep anything you've heard or said here in the highest confidence." As Fred rose from his seat, he reached across the table to shake hands with them both. "I thank you for coming and will most definitely be in touch."

Carla began gathering her papers but looked up for a moment. "Lucy, I know it's a lot to ask, but I wonder if I might drop by your place in the next day or so. I've become fascinated by what I've learned of your work and would love to see it in progress…but only if you can find time of course…and just for a few minutes, I promise." And then Carla too, after writing her number on the back of a card, passed it over to the weaver. "Nothing official you understand, just an honest interest in your work from a purely personal view, nothing more, I can assure you."

Lucy took the additional card, looked at it briefly, then nodded and said, "I'll call you." Later, in the truck, she showed Thomas the card and told him the woman seemed genuinely interested in her weaving.

"Humph…" Thomas was instantly suspicious. "What did Charlie have to say about that?"

"He said it was fine. He mentioned he has more confidence in Agent Smith than any of the past Agents here on the reservation. And then, too, Carla Meyor seems to have his respect. She does know an awful lot about my work. I think that's interesting—who would have thought a woman in New York City would know so much about an ordinary person like me out here on the reservation."

Thomas gave his wife a sidelong glance and said in a firm voice, "You have never been ordinary," then watched as she turned away with a dubious smile. "I noticed Charlie was still in the office when we left. I imagine he might let us know more later." Thomas didn't sound confidant that they would be made privy to much of that information.

~~~~~~

Harley Ponyboy didn't say much on their way to pick up the materials for the Yazzie's new back porch. Charlie, too, was quiet, apparently deep in thought over the morning's meeting.

Harley frowned over at the investigator; it had already occurred to him there wouldn't be time to see the horse this day. The disappointment caused the little man to look away finally, to concentrate on the dark line of clouds building to the Northwest—tall black thunderheads, towering thousands of feet above the western edge of the Colorado Plateau. At least there was the promise of rain. Later, coming out of the store, Harley felt a few drops. "Rain," he murmured. "Rain, by God...rain." It was a magical word for most in that country.

Charlie, still lost in thought, appeared not to hear as they loaded up and pointed the truck back toward Waterflow and home. He still had not said more than a dozen words since they left the lumber company.

Finally, Harley turned from the window and casually mentioned they would be lucky to get the tarpaper on the newly built roof of the back porch before the rain would be on them, assuming those thunderbirds held course in their flight south.

Only then did Charlie seem to take notice of the fast approaching weather system, and with a backward glance at the clouds increased their speed. "What...? I guess I wasn't paying attention." Charlie again glanced in his rearview mirror and watched as the gathering storm sent a powerful gust of wind to scout its way south across the canyons. "I guess I've been so caught up in this thing with Lucy and the Johnson murder that

I'm not paying attention to much of anything else." He knew, of course, what Harley's main concern was and turned to him with a smile. "I expect that *horse* will still be there in the morning, Harley. We'll try to get by there a little earlier tomorrow."

Harley nodded back, obviously still unconvinced. Lucy Tallwoman's problem might well delay their horse-trading beyond what his friend thought. Charlie was the only one with enough money to make any credible attempt at negotiating a trade. Harley did, however, know it would do no good to press the investigator. Charlie Yazzie was a stickler when it came to his job and generally gave full priority to whatever that might entail.

As the others left Fred Smith's office that morning, Billy Red Clay was called in after them, and *still* was in there as they left the building. Harley thought this curious but Billy, of course, was not prone to divulging secrets either. They stopped at the Co-op for the small roofing nails they'd forgotten in Farmington.

Harley was still pondering what might have gone on in the meeting when they started up the Yazzie's driveway and saw Billy's cruiser in front of the house.

Charlie came to a stop as the policeman, not making any other sign, got out and walked to the back of the truck to begin untying the building materials. Without a word, the three men began ferrying the items to the back of the house. Sue Yazzie came from the back door to check that the colored metal for the new porch matched that of the roof. She immediately noticed something was up with the three men.

"I expected you back long before now," she declared as she watched her husband from the corner of an eye hoping to catch some clue to the reason Billy Red Clay might be there. She thought it odd the young officer had been wrangled into helping with a building project when he was obviously still on duty...and he was wearing his good boots, too.

Charlie turned to her. "There's been a murder in town, and Lucy Tallwoman needed a little help at the FBI office." Charlie didn't say anything further and Sue could see he didn't intend to either, at least not in front of the others. She put down the box of roofing nails and went directly into the house to call her closest friend.

Billy Red Clay eased up next to Charlie and whispered, "Agent Smith let me in on what's going on." Thinking this half-truth might bring the investigator to expand on what else, if anything, *he* had been told by the FBI agent.

"That's good," Charlie murmured, doubting Fred had said very much beyond what he himself had been told. He figured Billy would eventually be filled in...he was the Liaison Officer after all...something Billy often pointed out.

Harley watched from the other side of the truck and took some satisfaction in hearing Charlie as close-mouthed with the Navajo cop as he was with him.

Sue returned to the porch just as the men were covering everything with a worn plastic tarp, in anticipation of the coming rain, she supposed. She stood a moment on the back steps arms folded, giving Charlie a final look; a look that let him know she wasn't happy.

"The kids are watching cartoons...I'll be back," and then as an afterthought, "There's a stew in the refrigerator. Heat it up." Her husband took this to mean she might not be back for a while.

Harley Ponyboy nodded as she left and then turned to Charlie while pointing at the door. "I'll just step inside with the kids and see what they're watching...not all of those cartoons are fit for kids to watch these days, you know." Harley loved cartoons.

Billy Red Clay waited until they were alone, hoping the Legal Services Investigator would take advantage of this last chance to add something to what little he'd been told in Fred's office.

Charlie, clearly not intending to be forthcoming in that regard, thanked the policeman for the help and said he would get up with him first thing in the morning.

Billy looked down for a moment and seeing his boots had once again gathered dust, wiped them clean on the back of his pant legs for the third time that day, and blurted out, "I'm telling you, Charlie, I'm the damn

35

Liaison Officer down there now, and I deserve better than being shut out of everything."

Charlie silently nodded his agreement, then watched pensively as the policeman drove off in a huff. Billy really did deserve better, and as much as he liked Fred Smith, he thought he would have a word with him concerning the young officer when next they met. *Men like Billy Red Clay don't come along everyday...not out here on the reservation they don't.*

As he sat the stew on the stove Charlie glanced through the open door to the living room. Harley Ponyboy and the two children sat wide-eyed at the antics of Wile E. Coyote and his nemesis, the wary and devilishly clever Roadrunner.

Joseph Wiley Yazzie had somehow come to identify with the coyote and often cheered him on—much to the consternation of his adopted uncle who was well aware of coyote's true nature.

Joseph agonized over each new escapade and nourished the hope the outwitted and befuddled creature would eventually find a way to get even with the bird. He was unaware, that in his own culture, it was Coyote who would have the edge.

Harley Ponyboy, for his part, couldn't imagine the people who made these cartoons not understanding about Coyote. But then, Harley often was puzzled by the disparity between cartoon life and the real thing.

Sue Yazzie, as the children's mother, felt Harley's influence—adopted uncle or no—was occasionally a little out of sync with the modern mores she and Charlie were trying to instill in their children. That aside, she knew Harley to be good-hearted and trustworthy, and knew he could always be counted on in time of need. The children could do worse for an uncle.

When the phone rang the three watching television didn't even look up.

"Yazzie here." Charlie took calls at home just as he would in the office, and when the caller identified himself, he relaxed. "Yes, Fred...?"

Agent Smith didn't bother with the usual niceties. "I just had a call from our people in New York. It looks like the Bureau may have another related case on its hands up there. Here again, there seems to be some pretty obvious ties to Lucy Tallwoman." The agent didn't wait for Charlie to catch up. "One of Lucy's most ardent collectors was found beaten senseless last evening in his New York penthouse. He's hospitalized and still unconscious at last report. The housekeeper who happened to be out at the time, said one of Lucy's wall hangings was pulled away from the wall only the label on the back was missing. That's one of the few clues they have going for them right now. It's not your average home invasion, that's for sure."

Charlie finally interrupted the agent, "Is the man expected to recover?"

"They think so, but he's quite elderly and that could have a bearing." The Federal Agent paused for emphasis "There's no indication who might be involved at this point. I've already contacted the Begays and advised a bit more caution might be warranted, at least until the killer of Clifford Johnson is found. There may well be more than one person involved and, while it's possible *our* killer could still be in the area, I somehow doubt it. This doesn't have the earmarks of a random act or one perpetrated by a local. Johnson's wife said nothing was missing as far as she could tell and there was no evidence of any serious kind of search being made." The agent paused, but not long enough for Charlie to interject a comment. "I'm still waiting to hear from our Santa Fe office, they've been talking to various galleries up there to see if any of Lucy's work is scattered around the tonier establishments." Fred finally paused to catch his breath waiting in silence, thinking he might have been cut off… "Charlie?"

The Investigator, bombarded with more information than he could process, was suddenly at a loss for words, rare indeed for Charlie Yazzie. "I can't imagine Lucy Tallwoman being the cause of all this. It just doesn't seem possible. I wouldn't have thought her known outside the reservation."

"Well, apparently, she is. And there are several high-dollar players scrambling to lay hands on her work." Fred Smith seemed to have something else in the back of his mind and that, too, worried the investigator.

Charlie let his gaze wander through the door to the living room—to Harley and the kids watching television. Wile E. Coyote was once again in trouble, hanging at the edge of a cliff with a lop-eared, hopeless look in his bloodshot eyes. Joseph Wiley had a hand to his mouth wide-eyed and certain this time the jig was finally up for the conniving canine.

"Charlie, there is one other thing… Charlie?"

"Yeah Fred, I'm here. I figured there might be something else…"

"A number of years ago, when I was first posted to the Albuquerque office, there was a fairly well-known southwestern artist out of Taos whose work suddenly began to attract an inordinate amount of interest—and out of the blue began racking up impressive sales—far beyond what his work usually brought. When the artist later died a rather mysterious death local law enforcement was baffled. The Bureau was called in to do the forensics and though it could not be proven back then, there was a very strong suspicion he was poisoned. In less than six months all his work skyrocketed in value. Like a stock bolstered by insider trading."

"You're saying he was deliberately killed to increase the value of his paintings."

"Art is like oil, Charlie, or any other commodity for that matter; when the supply is limited or the source no longer exists, the price goes up." Smith paused. "A young and inexperienced investigator posed that theory to his superiors at the time, but as I said, nothing could be proven. Nearly ten years later, the artist's wife, on her deathbed, admitted she'd gradually poisoned the man. She died a very rich woman"

"What brought this to mind, Fred?"

There was a slight pause as the Federal Agent cleared his throat. "I was the inexperienced agent who posed the theory, Charlie. But no one ever saw fit to mention my report outlining those suspicions...so I'm mentioning it now."

"You don't mean to suggest this could be the reason behind the Johnson murder, do you? Surely you aren't serious."

"The operative word there would be *suggested*. It's just something to keep in mind going forward. It might well be as far-fetched as some thought the first time, I offered it. But I've covered a lot of ground since then and have, for damn sure, seen stranger things in this business."

Charlie thought about it, but was forced to conclude the operative word might better be *far-fetched*. Still, out of a sense of propriety and personal friendship for the agent, Charlie didn't say so. "I guess we'll just have to wait and see, Fred...but I hope you're wrong."

"Me, too, Charlie...me too."

As the investigator put supper on the table he looked and saw the cartoon was ending. He called that it was time to eat. Amid loud protests the television shut down. If there was one thing Harley Ponyboy liked better than cartoons, it was eating.

4

The Factor

Percival Vermeer was old money and in New York old money has its privileges. With that as a given, there were certain standards even Percy was compelled to adhere to. The scion of an old and well-embedded financial family, his people dated back to the days when "Wall Street" referred to an actual wooden wall, built by the Dutch to repel Indian attacks...and others. In Percy's strata of society, it didn't hurt that his lineage was rumored to include the famous Dutch painter, Johannes Vermeer, whose self-portrait was said to bear an uncanny likeness to Percy himself. Though the painting's authenticity was never verified that did not prevent it being hung in the great hall of the Vermeer's Hampton estate.

As a family, the Vermeer clan had long been blessed with an intuitive understanding of human nature, including its nearly universal propensity toward greed.

Percy, in particular, seemed willing to take advantage of that particular failing in all its many forms. People who could afford to avoid the man (and there weren't many) preferred doing so, on both a business, and social level.

One of Percy's peculiarities, strange as it seemed even to those close to him, was the pursuit and acquisition of American Indian antiquities. This unlikely interest eventually evolved into a near passion for traditional Navajo weavings and it was not long until he was the acknowledged motivating factor in that particular segment of the market. Percy was not in it for the money; he already had plenty of that. His obsessive-compulsive nature demanded he have the best. He was not only dedicated but was also ruthless in adding to his growing collection. His agents were everywhere—from the far reaches of isolated Southwestern trading posts, to exclusive New York galleries and auction houses.

His baser foibles notwithstanding, Vermeer did have his charitable side, including the sponsorship of many deserving causes. Not the least of these admirable pursuits was his involvement in funding educational grants and scholarships for disadvantaged students: some of which were designated for tribal peoples...chief among them, the Navajo. Students considered it quite a coup to snag one of these grants as several of the recipients were singled out upon graduation for lucrative positions in Vermeer's own far-flung enterprises.

There were those people, of course, who belittled Percy's philanthropic efforts, alleging them more tax-deductible displays of self-aggrandizement than any true upwelling of the human spirit. Even so, various political advocacies thought his good works might be worthy of higher aspirations. Some even wondering aloud if the man was not suitable for public office.

"Archibald, I want to know where the woman lives and I don't mean just the general area of the reservation; I want to know the exact location. And I want to know what she's currently working on as well—as soon as possible if you please." He lifted a brow in Archie's direction. "I assume you're investigating that list of collectors who own her work?" Vermeer lifted a finger in warning. "I've recently been informed that another faction is interested in her and could become problematic going forward. It's important no harm should come to our artists out there. I trust you'll see to that?" He lowered his voice to a whisper, "As usual, Archie, it's important no one know of my part in the project."

Blumker nodded his head and smiled. There was no need to mention anonymity, and yet Percy never failed to do so. Archie and his employer were of a kind, and despite their dissimilar stations in life, each sprang from the same Dutch roots. Whether that had anything to do with it or not, each man seemed to have a deep and intuitive understanding of the other. Archie knew quite well what was expected of him.

"Oh, and Archie, how's that other thing we discussed coming along? Any word yet on how that's working out? Has your man been in touch?"

Archie had hoped he wouldn't ask. He never told the man less than the truth and the truth was he didn't know. This was not what Percy would want to hear, but it was honest nonetheless; that had to count for something.

"Ah, that...well as it stands right now, I'm still waiting to hear. But I have no reason to think things aren't progressing as they should." Archie's operative in New Mexico was late reporting in. That could mean nothing of course, but he now thought it prudent to fly out there and see for himself what the matter might be. His operative was still due a considerable amount of money and though there was an intermediary who acted as a buffer, one couldn't be too careful.

Archie Blumker required few things of an employer and they were, for the most part, quite simple. Chief among them was that he be treated with at least some modicum of respect, and this was what he admired most about Percy Vermeer—the man took great pains to treat people with dignity and respect, no matter their position. Be that respect sincere or not was uncertain, but just the perception was quite enough for Archie. From the people he himself employed, regardless how valuable their skill set, he demanded a strong sense of duty, and reliability. A lack of either was cause for censor in one degree or another.

The two men spoke for nearly an hour before Blumker left the house patting a fat envelope in his breast pocket. For propriety's sake, he took the back road out of the estate. He sighed as he pulled up to the barrier, then got out to drag open the ancient and unwieldy affair. *Why is there not a modern gate with an electronic opener as at the front entrance? It isn't like the man can't afford it.* Archie shook his head and smiled to himself for thinking such thoughts, *Bite your tongue Archie...* No, Percival had been very good to him and he intended to repay that kindness by doing the very best job possible. The work was not easy and carried some inherent risk. Still, it was interesting, even exciting at times. He was a company man in the truest sense of the word.

Percy, always generous to a fault, seemed to have little regard for cost or expense once he sat his sights on a thing. All his employees said so. His chosen people were given cart-blanche in pursuit of their tasks. No accounting for expenses was required and no questions were ever asked in that regard. All in all, Percival Vermeer was as near the ideal employer as one could wish.

What was bothering Archie at the moment, however, was the lack of word from his operative out west, a growing concern he couldn't reason away. The person was a professional, sourced through a trusted intermediary. This particular operative was the go-between's first choice for the job and thus would be that person's responsibility. Ultimately it was he who would be made accountable.

Uppermost in Archie's mind was that Percival Vermeer be kept isolated from the mechanics of the business. A man in Vermeer's position couldn't risk the slightest hint of such a connection. That was Archie's responsibility; it was up to him to make sure Percy never had reason to regret that trust.

After deliberate consideration, Archie decided not to fly out of JFK even though that would be easiest. There were several nonstop red-eyes from New York to Albuquerque and it was early enough he would probably have his choice. His other alternative, the more discreet itinerary, would take considerably more time and effort. For Archie, however, the peace of mind was worth the trouble. He was a man who believed the devil was in the details, ultimately that could make the difference between success and failure...

~~~~~~

It was a long drive to Baltimore, fighting rush hour traffic the first part of the way. Archie was then left with a short layover for a flight out of BWA.

Being told there was only one seat left in "economy" hadn't helped, he was pretty sure which seat it would be, and he was right. The most undesirable seat on the aircraft—in the tail section—and backed up tight against the bulkhead of the food service module. Seat adjustment would be minimal at best. Despite the lack of a meal being offered in Archie's section there still was plenty of galley noise and the constant bustle and clatter of flight attendants with their drink carts carrying assorted small bags of unappetizing snacks. Now, he was exhausted and hungry and meant to do something about it. He thought fleetingly he might better have abandoned his ironclad rule and flown first class. But that might have drawn attention and left an impression in someone's mind that could well be a problem later on. No, staying under the radar was the proper way to go about it.

When he stepped onto the main concourse at Albuquerque's International Sunport, it was with an aching back and growling stomach.

This was one of his many flights to New Mexico's international hub, and he had long ago learned his way around the terminal. Striking off toward the car rental counters he noticed an elderly Hispanic woman with a gaily decorated food cart featuring a southwest favorite. "Green Corn Tamales," the sign read, and then in smaller letters, "Just like your Mamacita used to make!" Archie considered himself more of a gourmand than gourmet, but the smell of the steaming tamales was enticing enough he surprised the woman with what she considered a large order. Archie, for his part, was taken aback at how small the little corn-shuck wrapped delicacies proved to be. He sighed, appraising the first tamale with a skeptical eye. He had hoped for something more substantial yet found them, in fact, to be so delicious he made a mental note to have them again on his return.

At the counter, Archie listened patiently to the car-rental agent as he described what was available—and then without hesitation selected a four-wheel-drive Chevrolet pickup. He wanted something generic enough to blend in, yet capable of off-road use. Where he was headed this tan Chevy should fill the bill. Leaving the rental agency's desk, he found an open-front phone booth affording some small protection from prying eyes. He sucked down a tamale as he dialed the number.

"Mondé?"

"Raul...please."

"Raul? *Si*..."

In only a moment another phone was picked up and a man's voice...brisk, educated... came on the line.

"Yes, this is Raul."

Archie thought the man sounded harried from what he remembered of their previous sessions. In previous conversations, Raul exuded a calm self-confidence with a self-deprecating sense of humor that made Archie smile. He hoped the man wasn't stressed on his account. That might indicate something had gone awry.

Raul Ortiz ran one of the largest American Indian art galleries in the city, a business he inherited from a father who had fingers in many pies. It had fallen to Raul to carry on the Ortiz family tradition. Though educated in art and business, the man's real specialty was procuring talented and trustworthy people for difficult and sometimes clandestine assignments. Raul was not unknown to Albuquerque authorities.

"Have you heard from our friend?" Archie asked cordially enough.

"No, I haven't. He may have run into something …if you get my drift."

"No… I do not get your goddamned *drift*." Archie's voice remained perfectly calm. "He's overdue, that is already a problem." Archie purposely let the phone go silent a moment. "I'll need to know something within the hour." He leaned into the booth and partially covered the mouthpiece. "…Or I'll find him myself…and you along with him." With that, he hung up and nonchalantly plucked the last of the tamales from the paper bag. He slipped off the shuck wrapper and stuffed the entire thing in his mouth, chewed with bulging cheeks, and thought to himself, *I wish my Mamacita had known how to make these things.* He crumpled the empty paper bag and placed it in a

receptacle marked in both English and Spanish—
Trash/*Basura.*

Archie picked a motel on the outskirts of town, not overly expensive, but respectable enough to avoid undue attention. The manager himself was at the desk and after receiving his key Archie eyed him for a moment before leaning across the desk to murmur something. The manager smiled then nodded and Archie passed him a twenty-dollar bill.

Archie woke after exactly fifty-nine minutes, looked at his watch, then redialed the number.

"Yes?"

"Raul?

"Yes, I've been waiting for your call."

"And?"

"It's complicated…"

"Oh… How so?" Archie felt a tickle run up his spine.

"Our friend has a broken leg…" There was a nervous little laugh Archie didn't like the sound of.

"Ah, I see, and how did that come about?" Archie's voice still friendly enough, almost pleasant should one not know the man.

"I don't know how it happened exactly…he said he stepped off a curb and the leg just went out from under him…fractured a femur when he hit the pavement." Raul hurried on as one might logically do when trying to convince someone of an illogical occurrence.

"What…is he eighty years old?"

"No, no, only in his thirties I would say. Trust me… it was just one of those one-in-a-million accidents…you know?"

It was one of Archie's cardinal rules never to trust a person who thought it necessary to ask that you *trust* him. He found it an immutable clue to a person's character. To discern such things was one of Archie's more remarkable abilities—possibly learned in his early years as a cop. Some thought it a sign of paranoia…and they were right to think so. Archie, however, felt ten years of looking up society's rectum was enough to give anyone a shitty outlook.

Raul waited, the palms of his hands sweating, making his grip on the receiver uncertain. He cradled the phone with his chin while drying the hand on the chair's brocade. *Given Archie's reputation, it might be wise to take some measure of his thinking before pressing him too far.*

Neither man knew where the other was located or what they looked like, but Archie's ability to find people was legend—he'd found *him* originally, hadn't he? That had been several years ago and though Raul thought their relationship mutually satisfactory, they had never actually met in person. This thing with the operative, however, had the potential to change all that, and should that be the way of it there would, most assuredly, be consequences. No one wanted that.

After a desperate silence and despite the sinking feeling in the pit of his stomach, Raul pressed on. "Uh... I was told to ask about the rest of the money...do you have that with you?" A considerable portion of the operative's final payment was Raul's cut and he felt he would be remiss should he not at least mention it.

Archie, on the other end of the line, remained silent.

Raul himself was a person of some reputation thereabouts, and it galled the man to think this arrogant New Yorker should cause him to doubt his own abilities. His resources were, in fact, considerable. And in the face of this, there *was* always the chance this man's perceived reputation was in itself unwarranted. Should push come to shove Raul dared think his own people might be up to handling such a person. Being from New York didn't necessarily make him any smarter or more threatening than someone from Albuquerque. There were some very dangerous men in New Mexico—some of whom Raul knew personally—any one of them might be happy to do him the favor.

When Archie finally did speak it was almost in a whisper, "You...you want the money...?" and then more briskly, "Does this mean the assignment has been completed as we asked—the information in hand?"

"I assume so," Raul's tone became slightly more assured. Despite feeling the game might be slipping away he plucked up his courage and plowed on. "The man's a professional after all; I would assume he has an understanding of what's required."

Behind the bravado, Archie thought he caught some slight hesitation in Raul's manner, a hint of fear perhaps. This registered somewhere at the back of his mind and he didn't like it…he didn't like it one little bit.

"Well, in that case," Archie went on, "and since he has that fractured leg and all, I assume I will have to go to him. I can manage that."

"Oh, no, you needn't bother, we've caused you quite enough inconvenience already. I can send one of my people to pick up the information, and bring it to you…you can just pay the courier what's owed…where did you say you're staying?"

A little alarm sounded in the back of Archie's brain and he hung up the phone.

Raul knew then he'd made a terrible mistake and had no idea how to go about rectifying it. Archie had been a generous and reliable client and he hated to lose him, but that, of course, was the least of his worries now.

5

The Party

It was just past eight o'clock that night as Lucy Tallwoman, hoping she hadn't waited too late to call, dialed Carla's hotel. The desk clerk let it ring; causing Lucy to think the woman might be out to dinner or in the shower. But in fact, it was only a few minutes later that Carla called back. Lucy immediately apologized for the hour.

"Oh, not at all, I was just coming back from the restaurant. I still have a load of paperwork to attend to, before I can even think about bed."

The FBI Agent sounded happy enough to hear from her so Lucy lost no time inviting her to the little cookout they had planned for the next day. "Charlie Yazzie and his wife are coming, and one or two other friends might show up...not too many...we should have plenty of time to talk."

This seemed to please the woman as she immediately accepted, "How exactly would I find your place?"

"Charlie already thought of that. He and Sue will be picking up some things I need in Farmington and can swing by your hotel...you can follow them out if you like."

"Hmm, well that was certainly nice of the Yazzies. Yes, that would be great! Please tell them I appreciate it."

"Good then. They should be by about four o'clock. That should leave us plenty of time to eat and talk, and for you to get back to town before dark. It's hard to see those cows on the road at night."

Lucy thought the conversation went well enough. When Thomas came in from the corrals and heard she'd invited the FBI agent, he seemed proud of her bold approach to one in so important a position. His wife didn't have a lot of experience with whites, not on a social level, and certainly not one of Carla's caliber. Her friend Sue Yazzie was the one who was good with white people, often urging Lucy to be more open to the idea as well.

Lucy Tallwoman's early experiences with white people at her boarding school had not always been pleasant ones. Now, however, she was beginning to think her friend, Sue, might be right. Maybe it *was* time to be more like her. Sue's stint as Office Manager at

Legal Services had lent a whole new perspective to *her* outlook on social engagement and she was obviously convinced her friend would also do well to become more involved with her patrons; it was those people's support, after all, that made up the bulk of her income.

The next morning Lucy was up early, as were her husband and the kids. Thomas was determined to get some work done on the sheep and it looked like it would be a nice cool day for it, with perhaps a shower or two should the weatherman be right. That might hold the dust down, he thought.

Most of the preparations for the cookout would fall to Lucy Tallwoman and her father, old Paul T'Sosi, and she wondered if he would be helping out at the grill. Before he got sick he had insisted on being in charge of all outdoor cooking. Now she didn't know if he would feel up to it or not.

Just as Lucy was having these thoughts, her father came in from his *hogan* grousing that it was way past time to eat "Where's lunch?"

In the old days, it was common for elderly people to refer to any meal as "lunch." Paul seldom used the term in that way anymore, but it was still in the distant corners of his mind and surfaced more and more these days. When Caleb and Ida Marie thought some of the things Paul said were funny, they would smile and exchange secret looks, though both children remained very fond of their grandfather. This morning he seemed especially lively and talkative, almost his old self and Lucy was left to wonder what caused these obvious swings in mental acuity.

"How are you feeling…?"

"Okay, I guess, I am getting hungry though. You know it's way past time to eat?" The old man looked over at Thomas. "What's for lunch?"

Lucy sighed, "Yes, we know. Dad, I was just on my way to the kitchen. Is there anything special you might like?"

Paul T'Sosi rubbed his chin in thought. "Well, we haven't had fried rabbit for a while. Isn't Caleb going hunting anymore?" He snorted, "Why, when I was a boy we almost lived on wild cottontails. Nothing sticks to the ribs like *Gah*."

Thomas turned from the window where he had been looking down at the corrals and the children working the sheep through the chutes. They were checking for ticks. He disliked the thought of filling the old cement long-tank with sheep dip and spending hours running them through. They hadn't had much trouble with ticks in the last couple of years, but he knew it was the season and that it's always wise to catch them early.

"Caleb knows it's not time for rabbits to be good yet Paul, we really shouldn't mess with them this late in the summer. They might still carry the fever now. I expect it will be a while till we have rabbit again."

The old man frowned. "When I was a boy we ate *Gah* anytime we were hungry. The jackrabbits got *warbles* this time of year, that's true, but the cottontails were still good to eat. People are too damned picky these days." Paul got a faraway look in his eye as he gazed out the window and across the sage flats. "I bet I have eaten a pickup truck full of rabbits in my day and look at *me*." The very thought of all those rabbits made the old man shake his head. "There were plenty *Gah* back then; they were everywhere, and a damned good thing, too. The government was making us cut back on the sheep and without those cottontails we'd a gone hungry a lot of the time. We sheep people were hell on coyotes back then and had them thinned out pretty good I guess. That made for lots of rabbits."

Caleb and his sister, also thinking it time to eat, had come up to the house and unnoticed slipped into the room as the old man was talking. Caleb was all ears— he thought just about everything Paul said was interesting. He didn't think the old man was losing it at all.

The boy slipped up beside his grandfather. "How did you thin out those coyotes? *Acheii*, I haven't been seeing many rabbits lately. I think they are all about eaten up now. People say it's hard to get a shot at a coyote, but I still see them every once in a while. I think it's time I had a bigger gun; that .22 doesn't hit hard enough for coyotes."

Paul T'Sosi turned to look at his self-adopted grandson and gave him their secret smile. He kept his voice low so only the boy could hear, "Back in the old days we had *Coyote gitters*—that's what the government hunter called 'em." Paul searched his memory and finally ran across a fleeting image of that old reprobate hiding there among a tangle of unrelated synapse. "Now, there was a rough looking old white man for you, all he ever did was hunt varmints and drink whiskey, and the government paid him to do it, too." Paul chuckled, "I expect that was about all he knew how to do…but he was good at it. I never doubted that. The government paid him for each coyote's scalp he brought in, kind of like they used to do for some Indian scalps in the old days."

The boy's eyes widened at this unknown bit of information.

Paul brought his mind to bear on how things were back then. "That old man was so lazy…and almost never sober," he laughed. Oh, he'd set a few traps in the culverts under the highway; that was easy enough. He could run those in his truck, but mainly he just handed out *gitters* to us sheep people here on the reservation and we did the real work."

Trying to think further back, Paul shook his head for a moment. Though once considered to have a photographic memory, that ability had faded with time and the old fellow had to tap the front of his head to jumpstart his memory. He thought that helped.

"Those *gitters* looked like little steel pipes that could be set in the ground, near an old sheep carcass maybe. It had a cyanide capsule with a blank .22 cartridge under it. A little strip of cloth came out of the top that you put coyote pee on. That was the trigger. When *Ma'ii* came along and pulled at it, the .22 shells would fire the cyanide gas right into their face, and in just a minute, no more *Ma'ii*. No one was supposed to have those *gitters* except the government trapper. Still he would pass them out to us sheepmen for free—all we had to do was bring him the scalps." Paul was on a roll—having one of his "good" days.

Caleb found it hard to believe anything was ever thought wrong with him. His *Acheii* was a "Singer" with dozens of complicated ceremonies stuffed in his head; maybe his brain was just filled up?

The others, not listening to the old man's talk, started for the kitchen, Paul holding back a little to catch Caleb as he passed. He reached out and plucked at the boy's sleeve as he watched the others file out of the room. The old man squinted one eye at the boy and motioned him closer; putting a finger to his lips he whispered in the boy's ear. "That old trapper is dead now but his son is still alive. I have been knowin' *him* since he was little. His mother was *Diné,* a friend of my wife's, they died only a year or so apart." Paul dropped his head to think on that for a moment, and when he looked up there was a glint of moisture in the old man's eyes. "The last time I saw that boy he was a grown-up man. It was at the Co-op and he told me he still had a sealed case of his father's *gitters*. He mentioned he would give me some should I ever need 'em." Paul bobbed his head at the boy and grinned. "Who knows if they are any good anymore…but maybe?"

Caleb couldn't help smiling to himself as he watched his *Acheii* follow the others to the kitchen. He was thinking how much fun he and his grandfather would have thinning out a few coyotes—some now so bold they were coming to the corrals at night, hoping to steal a lamb, or take a bite out of an unwary goat.

~~~~~~~

Young Ida Marie Begay was the first to spot the Yazzie's pickup truck coming up the road. The thirteen-year-old watched with interest as the car following them parked in front of the house. *So this is the FBI woman that has such an interest in Mama Lucy's weaving. She is certainly pretty enough—in her designer jeans and expensive sneakers.* Ida Marie was unabashedly bold in her assessment of people and decided she would stay close to this New York woman, maybe pick up a few pointers on city ways. *Not that I have money for any fancy clothes right now…but someday maybe…*

The girl and her brother spent a portion of each summer at their white benefactor's ranch near Cortez and were becoming well tutored in white ways. Aida Winters had been their natural mother's self-appointed guardian even before they came along. She loved the young Sally Klee as a daughter and later couldn't help having a strong interest in her children. Aida had stood by Sally even after she ran off with Thomas Begay, back when he was a drunkard. He had carried the girl off down country to the *Diné Bikeyah*, where they lived a somewhat sketchy sort of life near Farmington. Thomas was either drunk or in jails much of that time making for a more or less pitiful existence for the young Sally Klee.

Aida had no children of her own and intended to someday leave Caleb and Ida Marie Begay a portion of her considerable estate. Already she had set aside money to help with their education. In fact, the children only recently returned from their vacation stay with Aida and were home and with the usual array of sturdy no-nonsense school clothes their benefactor insisted they have. The two thought of Aida as their grandmother and so did Aida. Some people around Cortez thought it a strange sort of thing, a well-off old white woman taking in Indian kids and all, but that was the way of it. After a while most came to accept the relationship...more or less.

Thomas Begay opened the door for the Yazzies, Carla Meyor following close behind. Everyone was introduced in turn, but Old Man Paul T'Sosi hung back and studied the white woman for a few moments before coming forward.

"I hear you study *Diné* weaving and have heard of my wife?" the old man said and in so serious a manner the woman stopped to think before answering.

Looking directly at Paul, Carla smiled and put out her hand. "That's right, I do know of her, and I'm somewhat familiar with her work as well. And you are a *Singer*, am I right?" Paul acknowledged her with a curt nod of his head.

It perturbed the old man to think this woman from New York knew who he was, and even more so, of his long-dead wife. He hadn't expected that and shook hands in a somewhat hesitant manner, barely able to return her steady gaze. There was something about the woman that bothered him, and it wasn't because she was white. No, it was something else; something that was eluding him for the moment. He backed away and took to his favorite chair; watching, he thought to himself *it might come to me by and by…there's something about this woman…*

Later, Thomas, seeing the old man had drifted off to sleep, went outdoors without waking him, and took over the grill, arranging the blazing wood to suit himself. Charlie joined him and only moments later

Harley Ponyboy came around the corner of the house. The three of them began laying cuts of lamb to braise over the glowing coals. The men stood back as the meat sizzled and popped. Harley raised his nose, sniffed, and smiled as he smacked his lips.

Thomas sneaked a glance at the Legal Services Investigator and then lifted his chin in the questioning gesture so familiar to those who know the *Diné*. "So…Charlie, have you heard anything new on Clifford Johnson's murder? I'll bet the FBI knows more than they let on, huh?" Thomas was forever poking and prodding for information he thought unavailable to the general public.

Harley looked over at the lanky Navajo and grinned. "Charlie's not going ta tell you nothin', Big Boy. You'd be better off waiting for your Nephew ta come…he's invited ain't he?"

"Billy said he'd be here but might be a little late." Thomas was still looking for Charlie to reply and when he didn't, frowned down at the grill and murmured, "Billy Red Clay probably knows something."

Harley snorted at this, "Ha! Billy's worse than Charlie, here, when it comes ta letting out any 'privileged information' as he calls it. I wouldn't expect much from him."

Charlie, silent during this exchange, picked up a long fork and poked at the end cuts on the grill. "Why don't you two ask Carla Meyor? I *would* like to hear what she has to say."

Thomas smiled. "Well, then *you* should be the one asking her. Harley thinks she has an eye for you."

Harley chortled, "I'd be careful not ta let Sue see you paying too much attention ta that woman. I think she's already a lil' jealous."

Charlie frowned at the pair. "You two better not get anything like that started... I think Sue's curious enough about her as it is. Lucy must have told her something about the meeting yesterday—none of which, by the way, she was supposed to mention." He grinned when he said this but meant it as a friendly warning as well.

Thomas didn't deny any of this but was quick to defend his wife. "I doubt Lucy told her much...she knows better than that." It wasn't unusual for the three of them to get into an argument over some little thing, but this particular subject might turn into more than that.

Charlie wasn't up for that and changed the subject. "Doesn't look like Billy's going to make it?"

Thomas looked down the road and silently nodded agreement. "Something must have come up, it's not like Billy to be late to the table."

Carla Meyor and Lucy, still in the house, headed for the living room where the loom was set up. Lucy beckoned for Sue Yazzie to follow. She had hung back, not certain if it was meant to be a private conversation.

Sue was pleased to be included and chatted along with them as they passed the still sleeping Paul T'Sosi. Lucy smiled at her father and shook her head. "When he dozes off, he doesn't hear a thing. We won't be disturbing him."

Carla glanced at the old man and some odd thought flickered across her face, but no one caught it. They followed the weaver over to the loom. The piece was less than half-finished but was clearly another *Yei* blanket; so far, only the five Yei-Bie-Chies legs were showing beneath the first few lines of their skirts, each of them in different earthen tones.

Carla knew the market for these *Yei* weavings was insatiable and didn't wonder that Lucy had now specialized in these to the exclusion of geometric patterns or other more common designs.

It was as though Lucy was channeling the FBI Agent's thoughts. She admitted the *Yei* pieces were bringing two to three times more than her other work. "We still owe a little money on the house and until that is paid off, I'm concentrating on what I know will sell at a good price."

Carla Meyor was quick to agree with this assessment of the market and thought Lucy's plan going forward to be smart business. She touched the weaving, almost reverently, noting the smooth but firm melding of warp and weft. It took finely drawn yarn to allow that. Carla was amazed at how cleverly the work was crafted.

It was no wonder this woman was considered one of the finest weavers on the reservation. Carla's admiration for the piece was both effusive and genuine leaving Lucy Tallwoman at a loss for words, her face almost glowing in the light of such praise.

Sue Yazzie was smiling at her friend as she put a hand on her shoulder and said, "Yes, we are all very proud of what Lucy has accomplished these last few years. And we think she has an even brighter future ahead of her—there's no one more deserving."

Carla nodded thoughtfully. She had many technical questions to ask and the three women talked on about dyes and carding and the many other things she was curious about.

Sue Yazzie eventually left the pair to check on Joseph Wiley and little Sasha. She'd left them helping out in the kitchen alongside the older children. She suspected her younger daughter might be proving more of a hindrance than help. Like her brother she was proving to be a headstrong child, and at two years old not everyone could handle her. In the next room, though, she was pleased to find the girl under the apt tutelage of Ida Marie Begay who had taken charge of the younger crew. Thomas's oldest child had fallen into the predictable Navajo pattern of assuming responsibility for those smaller than herself.

The earlier winds had died to a gentle breeze and it was decided the meal could be served outside in the brush arbor or *summer hogan.* The men set up a long plank table with boards resting on firewood stumps for benches. Thomas had run electricity off the house to the shelter and now in the quiet of evening it made a fine place for a meal.

Lucy Tallwoman made it a point to seat their guest at her side, with Thomas on her other side, and the children scattered here and there as they pleased. Charlie and Sue sat just across the table and Paul T'Sosi and Harley Ponyboy began carrying over platters of still sizzling lamb. Before seating himself at the head of the table, Paul offered a few quiet words in old Navajo thought to be thanks for the meal. But only Thomas and Harley were close enough to hear and understand what he actually said. Harley turned and raised an eyebrow at Thomas but was quickly warned off with a frown.

"So, Carla, how long will you be with us here on the *Dinétah?"* Sue's tone was warm and friendly, and she smiled as she canted her head to catch the woman's reply.

"Oh, not long I'm afraid, I have a few loose ends to wrap up and then some reports for headquarters. That's about it...only a few days at the most."

Lucy joined in, "I hope you get to see some of the sights here on the reservation before taking off."

Carla laughed. "Oh, I know... I've seen a good many of those sights growing up. I'm from Durango originally; my father was with the Bureau of Indian

Affairs for years and worked at several reservation schools—for a while he was even at the Navajo boarding dorms over in Aztec."

This surprised everyone. Charlie, Thomas, and Sue had all attended the boarding facility on the Aztec High School campus. The three searched mentally for a memory of the man but none could actually recall anyone who might be Carla's father.

When Sue looked her way, Lucy Tallwoman had an odd expression on her face, something secret and hidden that might have escaped anyone else.

A speculative glance from Sue Yazzie caught her friend Lucy off guard as she passed a platter of lamb Carla's way. "Well...a Four Corners' girl, huh?" Sue said smiling.

"Yes, I suppose that's where my interest in Navajo art came from, though it took me long enough to get back to it." Carla nodded again as though thinking about it. "I misspent a few years, I guess, before I settled on art. But in the end, I think it's what I was meant to do."

Sue laughed, "Well, it looks like the FBI was a step in the right direction for you." Then she changed the subject to how famous Paul T'Sosi was for his grilled lamb.

Paul himself had also noticed the look on his daughter's face but acted as though he hadn't. He gave no notice he'd heard any of the conversation and passed the other platter around the table in the opposite direction. Thomas took a generous portion noting the blank expression on his father-in-law's face, a look he'd seen before. He wondered if the old man was having a relapse.

6

The Operative

There is, in every scheme-gone-wrong, a time when it becomes excruciatingly clear the plan has come undone, is broken, and probably unfixable. Raul Cortiz realized now how little he actually knew about the man who would come for him—only that he was a professional who would kill him if he could. This was a given, but not the part that most bothered him. He himself could run, hide and stay hidden. His family, on such short notice, would remain vulnerable and he knew there was no help for that now. He could save himself...or he could save his family...that's what it came down to. It was no more complicated than that.

Hard man though he was, Raul wasn't prepared to leave his family to so uncertain a fate. He tapped the fingers of his right hand on the polished mahogany of his desktop, determined to remain focused and in control. There was the razor-thin chance he could negotiate his way out of this mess—though he knew the chances of it were highly unlikely. An agreement with a man like this, once made, was seldom negotiable.

~~~~~~

Less than ten minutes had passed since Archie hung up the phone. He changed into a golf shirt and tan Khakis before moving to the window to gaze across the parking area. It was beginning to fill up. All of the more desirable close-in spaces had already been taken. His tan rental was midway back, in the shade of a poorly manicured tree…an ash he thought…its drooping branches, along with a scraggly line of shrubbery, almost hid the truck from this angle. That parking place was worth what he paid for it. It wouldn't hurt the manager's car to spend a day in the sun. He scanned the lot. *Well,* he thought, *this might work out after all. There had been fear in Raul's voice and that was always a good sign.*

He picked up the phone and redialed the number. When Raul answered, Archie apologized. "I'm sorry, I must have been cut off before; the connection seems fine now. What I was about to tell you was, yes, of course, go ahead and send your man. I'm at the Bella Vista on 528 North. I'll be waiting in the lobby." Archie thought a moment. "Tell your guy I'm in a blue suit and grey Stetson."

On the other end of the line, Raul realized he had been holding his breath and let it out in an embarrassing gasp. "Ah...yes... I thought something like that must have happened. It will take my man only a few minutes to run by the operative's place and then he'll be right over." He was careful not to mention the money still owed. The person he was sending was more than capable of taking care of that little detail.

Archie suppressed a smile, hung up the phone, and gathered his things. After checking out of the hotel and settling himself in the pickup he opened the sunshade, which had come dear at the airport gift shop. Archie was not frivolous with his money, or Percy's either for that matter, but neither was he willing to skimp on necessities. He arranged the sunshade in the windshield leaving only a little slit to peek through. He sipped at the tepid bottle of water left in the truck and watched from half-closed eyes as arriving guests filtered in, while others left for nearby restaurants. Some of these same diners were already beginning to return by the time the black Lincoln pulled into the lot...cautiously at first...tentatively, as though the driver was aware he might be watched. Archie knew at once it was him.

The big sedan took one of the open spaces at the far end of the hotel. Two or three minutes passed as the driver assessed his surroundings. Finally, a large man, casually dressed in Levi's and a button-down shirt, got out and ran an eye along the upper floor windows, then again turned his attention to the parking area. Tucked away in the shade, the tan pickup with local plates caught his eye almost immediately—the manager's truck, he guessed. People who live in Albuquerque know what the sun will do to a vehicle. Shady parking spots are like gold. A higher-up always takes these choice places for themselves. Apparently satisfied with the situation the man strode toward the covered entrance.

Archie, canting his head to watch through the tiny opening in the sunshade, noted the measured stride and confident air...*a man who knows what he's about.* He smiled at the elegantly thin brief case dangling from one ham-like fist. *A cop,* Archie figured...*or rather an ex-cop, like himself.* He watched the man's every movement, how he carried himself, his awareness of his surroundings, all with the unblinking interest of one whose life might depend on what he learns. The man, with a final glance around, disappeared inside showing an obvious certainty in his ability to handle whatever might be waiting. Archie knew it wouldn't take him long to figure things out.

He swallowed the last sip from the plastic bottle and tossed it behind the seat. He had been hoping Raul would come along or send some goon that might be tailed back to him. But this was clearly not the case. Trying to follow this person would be pointless, possibly even dangerous.

He studied the Lincoln, and then stepping down from the truck, sighed at the twinge in his back. *I should have taken something for this earlier,* he thought. Reaching in his pocket for the coiled steel wire, he fiddled with it for a moment, adjusted the rubber coated hand loops and then plucked the little set of picks from his waistband…it was time to earn his money.

7

Time & Trouble

Lucy Tallwoman watched from the living room window as the last of her guests followed the glare of headlights through blowing clouds of dust and up onto the highway. A stiff breeze had come up after sundown sending a fog of powdered red clay across the flats. Carla Meyor was last in line.

The woman had hardly left Lucy's side the entire night asking about this and that, nothing of any great importance but over a short period of time she'd learned a great deal about Lucy Tallwoman and her family. After dinner, the agent had been quick to jump in and help clean up, even took a few minutes to talk with the children.

Once or twice, Lucy caught her father looking over at her, no more than a glance each time, but knowing him as she did, she found it significant enough to make a mental note. In the morning she would ask what he was thinking...if he could remember what he'd been thinking.

Sue Yazzie seemed preoccupied with the FBI Agent as well and studied the woman when she thought no one was looking…following her every nuance with a calculating gaze.

That was understandable in Lucy Tallwoman's view. She was pretty sure she knew what was going on in her friend's mind and regretted telling her what Harley Ponyboy said in Fred Smith's office—about Carla seeming to know Charlie from their college days. *Sue was the last person in the world that should have any worry in that regard…*she shouldn't have mentioned it…but it was too late to fix now. She had only jokingly referred to it but was sorry now she'd said anything at all.

Beyond the barest social niceties, Charlie Yazzie paid Carla Meyor little attention, directing his interest, instead, toward the men's conversation, which leaned heavily toward the murder of Clifford Johnson. He also had to listen to Harley Ponyboy lament his missed chance at a good horse. Harley's friend had sold the gelding that very morning before Harley could even make an offer.

Charlie did glance across the table at the FBI Agent now and again—the act caught each time by his wife, which caused him to color and quickly look away. His view of Carla Meyor was becoming complicated. He truly could not recall the woman at UNM—this though she clearly seemed to remember him. She was not a woman any man would be likely to forget. He wondered what could be so different with her now, that he couldn't remember anything at all about her. *When Professor Custer gets back in town next week, I'll ask him if he recalls anything about the woman.* There was little chance of that, probably. He knew his former professor had no reason to remember a law student not interested in the science of archaeology. Charlie had been one of the few that fell into that category. It was a big school with a lot of students, he doubted anyone would remember very many of them.

In the pickup going home, Sue seemed preoccupied, unusually quiet, only occasionally glancing at the children asleep in the back seat. The two youngsters were worn out from playing with Caleb and Ida Marie. Joseph Wiley had decided Thomas's daughter had become a little bossy these last few months. He did, however, pay particular attention to her brother Caleb and all that he said or did. Joseph Wiley's sister Sasha, of course, idolized the older girl and tried to emulate her every move.

Nearly halfway home, Sue finally broke the silence. "So...that Carla seems very nice; Lucy certainly seems to have taken a shine to her. It's high time she mixed a bit more with someone like that...it will be good for her I think, and good for her business, too." Then she waited...

"Hmmm." Charlie figured there was more to come and guessed what direction it would take. When he finally answered, it was with more than a little trepidation. "I guess so. She's personable enough, that's for sure, and she seems to have a real interest in Lucy's work, too." He looked down at the speedometer and backed off the accelerator just a touch. "Carla may just be putting her together...she's very good at it from what I hear...it's what she does."

"That's not a very nice thing to say..."

Charlie shrugged and peered through a veil of wind-blown dust. "I didn't really mean it that way.

She's an Investigator. Investigators are always investigating...that's all I meant."

"Does that go for you, too, *Investigator*?"

"Sometimes..."

"You still don't remember her from the university?"

"Not really."

"You've always had a good memory for people... faces. Your Aunt Annie says you never forgot a face, or even a voice...even when you were a kid."

"Well, I don't remember *her*. Those were some pretty large groups they had us tutoring back then...and it was a long time ago. I can't remember everyone. What I do remember is how hard it would have been without that extra money the tutoring brought in."

"She's very pretty, don't you think?"

"I suppose..." He smiled over at her. "But she might not have been pretty back then."

"So, you're saying that's why you don't remember her? She might not have been pretty enough?"

"No, that's not what I said." *This could get ugly,* he thought. "I'm just saying I don't remember her back then... That's all I'm saying." *Yes, I know exactly where this is headed. She doesn't usually focus on something like this; something has set her off—Lucy's been talking all right.*

There was something about Carla Meyor that made her different, not just for Sue...but for everyone. Charlie shot a glance at the rearview mirror to see if the woman was still behind them and knew instantly that was a mistake.

"Still back there?"

He sighed, "Yes, she's still back there...I'll bet her ears are burning too." He attempted a smile but couldn't pull it off. His wife was frowning now. *She isn't going to let this go.*

"You've never told me if you had any white girlfriends at college. Why is that?"

"Well, that's probably because I never had any."

"How about Indian girlfriends...or Mexican?"

"I went out with a few girls...no one special...I told you that a long time ago."

"I don't remember you saying..." Sue's voice trailed off, now remembering more than she wanted to.

"Well, it's a little late to be asking about it now isn't it?" Charlie looked back at the kids. "Why don't we finish this little conversation tomorrow morning...after we get some sleep...and maybe a better perspective?"

Sue crossed her arms and looked out the side window where there was really nothing to see beyond the darkness with its windblown ghosts of things that may never have happened.

~~~~~~~

Charlie left early for work the next morning, anxious to see if there was anything new in the Clifford Johnson murder...at least that's what he told himself.

Billy Red Clay was sitting in the parking lot at Legal Services, busy writing something in a notebook. He looked up as Charlie backed into the spot next to him and rolled down his window.

"What's up, Billy? You been waiting here all night? We missed you at the cookout by the way. Your Uncle Thomas called your place but didn't get ahold of anyone."

"No." Billy said, "I haven't been here all night. I called Sue a few minutes ago and she said you were on the way into work. I figured to catch you before you got tied up." The policeman shook his head. "And I couldn't make it last night for the cookout. My mom fell and hurt her head. I had to take her to the clinic. She's all right this morning. She's going to be fine, they said."

"Well, I'm glad to hear she's going to be all right." Charlie looked up at the clock. "So, what's on your mind Officer?" He watched as Billy finished whatever he was writing in the little notebook and remembered the first time he'd referred to the new recruit as "Officer." It was on the young man's first day on the job. It was his birthday, and Billy had stopped by on his lunch hour to let Charlie know he'd made the cut. The investigator had never seen him happier, or prouder, even when he was a kid trailing around after his Uncle Thomas during summer vacations.

Billy looked up from his pad, and Charlie could see there was something serious troubling him.

"Charlie, I thought you'd want to know: Louise Johnson turned up missing last night. She was supposed to call Fred Smith back about some information he wanted, but by nine o'clock he still hadn't heard from her. Fred called several more times, still no answer. He finally went to her house to make sure she was all right. The house was unlocked. No Louise. Her car wasn't in the garage and still hasn't been located."

Charlie felt weak in the stomach. "What? The woman just disappeared... No one saw anything?"

"They questioned everyone in the neighborhood that they could lay their hands on. Nothing."

Charlie had a lump in his throat, barely able to get the words out. "Sue and I just saw Louise at the grocery store yesterday. We talked for a minute about Cliff and when the service would be...that sort of thing. She followed us out of the parking lot and on out of town towards Farmington. We turned off at our place and she went on toward her place in Kirtland. At least we supposed that was where she was headed. That's the last we saw of her. There wasn't much traffic; she beeped her horn and waved as she went around us." Charlie put a hand to his forehead and rubbed that little spot just between his eyes, where the headaches usually started. "That's the last we saw of her."

"Well it doesn't look good Charlie. Fred's pretty upset. The FBI has another shitload of people on their way up here now." Billy glanced around the lot a time or two as though afraid someone might recognize his unit. "Captain Beyale is jumping up and down, saying Tribal needs to get moving on this; we need to get involved, he says... FBI or no FBI. He wanted to know all the particulars, and when I told him the FBI hadn't released everything as yet, he blew a gasket, wanted to know why we weren't in the loop. He said as Liaison Officer I should be made aware of what's going on at all times." Billy, frustrated, shook his head. "The Captain thinks Tribal should be made privy to everything the Bureau has in a case like this." Billy glanced around again. "I told him, the Feds never send *everything* down to the local agencies. They always keep an ace in the hole." Billy sighed. "Then he really went ballistic. He wanted to know why I hadn't called him last night. I told him about my mom...her falling and all—but by then he wasn't even listening." Billy looked down at his notebook. "Charlie, I'm beginning to think this is partly my fault for not speaking up to Fred."

Charlie rolled his eyes. "Billy, the FBI has their guidelines on this sort of thing. It's no reflection on you." Charlie hated to see the young policeman beating himself up over something he had no control over.

Billy nodded half-heartedly. "Every agency in the state has been notified. Fred is heading up a meeting this morning for local law enforcement. Nine o'clock sharp at the FBI office. He said everyone should be there. He specifically asked that your office be notified." Billy sat there a moment. "I was just working on my report when you drove up. Hell of it is, I'm not sure what all I should include, I'm not sure Fred wants what little I do know to get out until he okays it."

Charlie gave the policeman a conspiratorial wink and looked away still trying to absorb the news of Louise Johnson's disappearance. The reservation was no stranger to crime, but this added twist to an already complicated case was something no one saw coming.

"Charlie, can I use your machine to get a copy of this report? I want to keep a personal record of everything as it goes down."

"That might be a smart move. Come on up to the office Billy. I have to call Sue anyway, and probably should talk to your Uncle Thomas as well. I doubt they've heard about Louise. That should leave us just enough time to make that meeting with the Bureau."

~~~~~~~

It was almost noon before Billy Red Clay followed Investigator Yazzie out of the Federal Building, both men disappointed in the little they had learned beyond what they already knew.

"Well, that was pretty much three hours shot all to hell," Billy Red Clay was looking at his little black notebook as he said this, and sure enough, there really wasn't much there.

Charlie shook his head. Billy was right, there wasn't much to say about a meeting like that, he thought. It seemed to him the FBI was holding back, anxious to hear what everyone else might know but reluctant to make a full disclosure. That was just like the Bureau, but it wasn't like Fred Smith. Charlie thought he could see a guiding hand from a higher-up in Albuquerque.

Charlie was halfway down the stairs to the parking lot before he looked up to see Thomas Begay and Harley Ponyboy sitting on the tailgate of Thomas's truck. Thomas had somehow squeezed the big diesel pickup in between Billy's unit and Sheriff Dudd Schott's cruiser. The pervasive animosity between the town Indians and Schott went back a long way. Early on, as a deputy, Dudd had earned the distrust and disgust of the entire Indian population of San Juan County both on and off the reservation. The Indians still referred to him as Deputy Dawg and considered him nothing more than a joke. Charlie knew Dudd was none too well thought of by whites either. No one could figure out how he became Sheriff in the first place...but there he was.

Billy smiled, "How the hell did they get those truck doors open far enough to even get out?" He broke into a chuckle. "Thomas might be skinny enough to squeeze out the driver side, but Harley would play hell getting out the passenger side."

Charlie couldn't help grinning. "He let Harley get out before he pulled in. They've done it before …anything to yank Dudd's chain."

The two miscreants, Harley and Thomas, were hoping Dudd would come out first and go into his usual tirade. The two were counting on Charlie and Billy to intervene. It was a spur of the moment plan and might have ended badly, had their friends not got there first.

"What do you two think you're doing?" Charlie tried to wipe the grin from his face but there was enough left to encourage the pair further. Harley, jumping down off the flatbed, gave a double lift of his eyebrows, it had become his signature greeting, and no one could figure out where it came from—he smirked and gave the Investigator a thumbs up.

Billy used his official voice, "Better get that truck out of there, boys. I don't think I can even get *my* car out until you move yours." It wouldn't look good for Fred Smith to come out and see an argument with the sheriff going on right here in the parking lot.

Charlie was staring at a door ding in Dudd's car and hoped it wasn't Thomas's doing. He sighed knowing he couldn't rule it out. His friend had a long history with Dudd Schott.

Thomas lifted his lanky frame off the tailgate. "Anything you officers say. We don't want any trouble here." He sucked in his belly and wedged his way up the narrow passage; as he opened the door Charlie saw the edge fit perfectly with the long ding in the sheriff's car.

Frowning, the Investigator pointed out the damage to Billy Red Clay. "You going to give your uncle a ticket for that?"

Billy shook his head and grinned. "You know I don't have the authority to cite him off the reservation...but I'm sure he's hoping someone's going to *try* giving him a ticket."

Harley came up and stood beside the two lawmen as they watched Thomas ease the vehicle out, nearly hooking the sheriff's bumper in the process.

"I told him this was a bad idea." This is what Harley usually said when one of their plans didn't work out. Charlie sniffed, and didn't bother looking his way. He'd heard it all before.

Dudd Schott came down the steps to stand, hands on hips. He didn't speak, nor did anyone else. The Sheriff glared suspiciously around the group for a moment, then throwing up his hands went directly to the driver's side of the cruiser without noticing the door ding. The grim set of his jaw changed to surprise as the engine backfired in an explosive report.

The Navajo lawmen remained impassive but were thinking the same thing; *Thomas stuffed a potato in Dudd's exhaust pipe!*

The Sheriff sat quite still for a moment, then with a death grip on the steering wheel glared back at Thomas in the rear-view mirror before restarting the car and driving off as though nothing had happened.

Charlie watched as Thomas hung his head out the window, laughing. He turned to the man's nephew. "He's going to wind up paying for this eventually, you know."

Unable to keep from laughing, Billy went around to check his own exhaust before getting behind the wheel. Looking through his open window he said, "I know...sometimes, he just seems to get in these moods and then doesn't know when to quit."

"He's actually gotten better than he used to be," Charlie admitted. "Hard as that may be to believe right now."

Back at Legal Services the men gathered in Charlie's office and the conversation quickly turned back to the meeting. Thomas wanted to know what went on and if anything new had come up. He said Lucy was at wit's end when told of the disappearance of her old business associate's wife. "This coming on top of Cliff Johnson's murder has really affected her and you know she's not one to be easily upset."

Harley, quiet until now, blinked and turned to the two Navajo lawmen with a questioning look. "I hope you two aren't going ta tell us it's all privileged information? I'm getting tired of hearing that same old excuse every time someone around here asks a simple question." He put on a frown and directed it toward Tribal Policeman Billy Red Clay who he thought would be more likely to let them in on some little something.

Billy sighed and studied the little man for a moment. "Harley, in this particular case I can truthfully say we don't know a damn bit more than we did before the meeting. Isn't that right, Charlie?"

The Investigator didn't even have to stop and think about it before nodding his head. Then Charlie caught them all off guard by saying, "Fred Smith may be holding out on us...he's keeping something back, that's for sure." When the Tribal Police Officer didn't agree, he insisted, "Why do you think that would be, Billy? You're the Liaison Officer?"

The policeman flashed him a surprised glance, which quickly turned sour. "I don't know why you would ask *me* Charlie. I'm generally the last one to know what goes on over there." Billy was proud of his recent advancement but had, of late, felt the Senior FBI Agent wasn't all that concerned what *he* thought. "I guess Fred's under a lot of pressure from the top on this one, and just doesn't want it screwed up by the locals— maybe that includes us. It's not every day two white people come to such an end here on the reservation." He then said exactly what was on his mind, "...and on Fred's watch, too, not that there was much he could have done about it...still, it has to chafe him a bit." Billy looked down at his boots stretched out in front of him and frowned. *There is just no way to keep boots polished in this country.* "Maybe he was just so focused on Cliff's murder that the wife's disappearance threw him for a loop. He's as upset about this as anyone—I can tell you that right now."

Charlie felt the Tribal cop might be right, but also knew that didn't make it any easier for him to swallow. He remembered what he'd been meaning to ask the policeman earlier. "Did you see Carla Meyor at the meeting? I didn't notice her in there—I know there was a crowd, but Carla's hard to miss. She's FBI and on the case, I would have thought she would be there."

Billy thought about it then shook his head. "I don't recall seeing her either...could have overlooked her I guess..."

Charlie looked around the group. "Just between you and me, I still don't remember ever meeting the woman—back at the university, I mean. Every time I think about it, it seems like there might have been someone or other like her all right but somehow, Carla Meyor, just doesn't fit the picture."

Thomas and Harley gave one another a sidelong glance. It wasn't like Charlie Yazzie to be uncertain about *anything*.

The receptionist brought in a tray of fresh cinnamon rolls, saying, "My mom sent these over a little while ago from the school cafeteria. She thought you gentlemen might like one."

Thomas jumped right up and took the tray, carefully setting it on the edge of Charlie's desk closest to him. Harley, instantly at his side, nodded thoughtfully at the rolls. "That's my great-aunt that sent that over," he informed everyone, thinking it might give him some prior claim on the goods. "She does the baking over at the school lunch place now. Her husband died a few months ago over at Leupp, and she had to move back over here where she has people."

Billy Red Clay gazed admiringly at the rolls. "What made her think of us?"

"Well," the receptionist said, turning color, "...in all honesty, she got a ticket this morning from Officer Hastiin Sosie. She hoped maybe one of you boys could help her with it."

"What was the citation for?" Charlie asked.

The woman reached in her sweater pocket and pulled out a folded summons. "It's for parking in front of that fireplug across from the Co-op."

Billy Red Clay moved to take the ticket with a skeptical look in his eyes. "She didn't know about parking in front of fire hydrants?"

"Oh, she knew…she just didn't think there'd be a fire in the five minutes she meant to be in the store…and she was right, too. But Hastiin Sosie didn't see it that way. He read her the riot act and then got around to asking her what clan she was. He's single you know. She told him she was of the Autumn Clan, and he said he didn't know there was one." The receptionist held up her hands and looked surprised. "My mom only moved back over here from Luepp about a month ago to take this job; she'd have never got a ticket over there. She said they're not so particular where people park over there. That's what she told Hastiin, too. She told him she couldn't afford no ticket."

Charlie grinned over at Billy Red Clay. "Why don't you see what you can do about it, Billy?"

The young policeman glanced at the ticket, looked over at the rolls, and then the receptionist. "I'll talk to Hastiin. Maybe he won't be able to make the court appearance. You can tell your mom she'll hear from me in a day or two—just tell her not to send any money until I say."

Only then did Thomas reach for a roll and sat back down with it. It wouldn't be right to eat a person's gift rolls if nothing could be done for her. "Well, God love her," he said, munching away. "It looks like her heart's in the right place anyhow."

Thomas had every confidence in his nephew's ability to help the woman. He knew Billy's soft spot for poor people and old ladies and such, and felt he would most likely prevail. Thomas had already reached for seconds when Harley, still on his first, frowned at the disappearing pan of rolls and moved them more his way.

8

The Price

The garrote had barely touched Big Ray Danson's throat when he raised his hands and spread them in an instant declaration of submission. There was no question who his assailant might be and as a professional himself, was quite aware how delicate his situation was. Pinned to the back of his seat with virtually no way to reach this man, Big Ray was essentially defenseless. The ex-cop had been perfectly set up. His only option now was to remain perfectly still and listen. This assassin obviously intended some sort of conversation or *he* would already be dead—that alone offered a thin ray of hope.

Archie whispered, "Good morning," as he rose from the luxurious depths of the Lincoln's rear carpet. He spoke directly into the big man's ear as he reached across and took the man's sidearm. "I'm sorry I missed you inside...but then our sort of business is better conducted in private, wouldn't you say?"

The big man showed little fear—there was that to be said of him. But then he knew any show of emotion would be lost on his assailant. He was certain of that. The wire was already on the verge of bringing blood. He didn't bother berating himself for falling into the situation. His only thought was that he must be getting old; that was about the size of it, he guessed.

Archie was always amazed how tenuous a thread a man might cling to, even when teetering on the brink of eternity. Always, it seemed, they divined some fragment of hope no matter how desperate the situation. He loosened the wire slightly that the big man might catch his breath and perhaps answer a few questions should he be of a mind.

Ray Danson, still barely able to breathe, felt a wave of relief even at this small concession. He gasped and blinked and was finally able to regain some small control of his vocal cords. But when he spoke, it was little more than a squeak, "All right then…what do you want?" He seemed surprised he could get the words out at all, the thin wire still hidden in the flesh of his neck—just there, below the lump of his Adam's apple—all but precluding any sort of normal speech even as close as they were.

"A little information is all I really want. The right answers might put me in a more charitable mood." Big Ray knew this was a lie. They were of a kind, the two of them. No, there was probably only one way this could end.

Archie snugged the noose just a hair for emphasis then quickly eased off, but only slightly. "There then…a little more comfy? Not too tight, I hope? It's been a while… I don't ordinarily do this sort of work anymore."

The ex-cop heard the smile in Archie's voice but didn't mistake it for more than it was…personal satisfaction in a game well played.

This big ex-cop was not a person to trifle with, and Archie was well aware the slightest mistake on his part could be a game changer. The whole thing might just as easily have gone badly from the start—become more complicated, dangerous certainly, given the sort of man now at his mercy.

If it hadn't been for the seat back between them Ray Danson might have considered making a fight of it. As it was, he was trapped and without any reasonable kind of option. The big man remained silent, conserving his breath, clinching his hands…hope already fading. He let his gaze wander up and down the sidewalk. Deserted. Across the long hood of the Lincoln there was something…a flicker of movement, just there…in the upper branches of the hedge. He blinked, and a small yellow bird blinked back, seemingly unafraid. The tiny creature appeared to be singing, though no sound could be heard inside the Lincoln. With the windows rolled up things were wonderfully quiet. Ray doubted he could hear a train go by should there have been one. And certainly no one could hear him call out. *The thing now is to prolong this last precious snapshot of life,* he decided, and still there was a small voice whispering…*there is always a chance…*

Over the years Big Ray had come to realize being a stand-up guy was highly overrated. Even among his own kind it was seldom more than a myth. *"Honor among…" People will do what they do when up against it. In the end, it really doesn't matter.* He intended to tell this man whatever he wanted to know and take as long as possible doing it.

Archie felt the man relax and knew they had come to a mutual understanding. He eased up on the wire another smidge as an incentive.

"There's nothing in the brief case...is there?" Archie was fairly certain there wasn't.

"No, there's nothing."

"And my operative?"

"There is no operative."

"I see...Raul had you kill him?"

"No."

"Then...what?"

"I was the operative. There was no one else. Raul couldn't come up with anyone he trusted." Big Ray tried craning his neck slightly, thinking to ease the wire further, but only made it worse. "The thing is, I was sent just to reason with Clifford Johnson, offer him money and possibly, in some way or another, bring him to some point of negotiation."

"He was not amenable I take it... I'm not surprised."

"He was already dead when I got there." Ray said this matter-of-factly with not so much as blinking.

Archie, though surprised, was inclined to believe him, and mulled this new information over, turning it this way and that in the light of common sense. After thinking on it there was little doubt the man was speaking the truth. There was no reason to do otherwise at this stage of the game.

Clouds had rolled in almost as soon as the sun came up, but despite the increasing overcast it was growing warm in the car. Albuquerque is like that in the latter part of autumn. The nights are cool, but things heat up quickly after first light. Sweat beaded Ray's brow and traced a path into one eye. His natural reflex was to wipe it away but through willpower alone he was able to resist the impulse.

Archie couldn't help admiring the man's fortitude. "So...then, Raul sent you to deal with me?" Archie pretty much knew where this was going now but thought a little conversation might keep the man's mind right until he heard what he really wanted to know.

"Yes, Raul felt that would be best...he's not very good at this part of the business you know. You would think he would be, but he's not. He assumed you wouldn't believe him...his story about your contact...I mean." That's the second surprising thing about Raul...he's a poor liar when dealing with anyone of any intelligence and he's usually smart enough to know it." Big Ray attempted a chuckle, choked, and coughed a little despite the lessened tension. He thought the wire had already done some damage at this point, not that it really mattered now. Trying to clear his throat succeeded only in a red-tinged spittle appearing at the corner of his mouth. Nonetheless, the very effort of speaking seemed to make the process easier as he went on. "Raul thought I might be able to retrieve the final payment should you have it with you...he said it was a lot of money." Ray thought this was something that would interest Archie and perhaps shift a little blame from himself. He was sweating now, as big men often do under duress, his shirt grew dark around the collar and underarms.

"Ah, well then, Raul must not be as smart as I supposed...."

"Well, no...Raul really isn't that smart, but he knows people and has a handle on what most will do in a given situation...he's very good at that...usually."

This was a lot of words for one with a garrote snugged beneath his Adam's apple. He took a shallow breath, bringing with it an involuntary strangling sound. He waited, hoping this might cause Archie to ease the wire even further...but no. As he went on Big Ray kept an eye on the rear-view mirror, "You might want to know...Raul has someone else interested in Clifford Johnson's list. Big-money people from across the pond, they intend to control the better part of the market." In the mirror, Ray noticed a hint of curiosity at this. He hoped it might buy him a little additional time and was quick to take advantage. "They're foreign...from somewhere in Europe, according to Raul." The ex-cop spoke as clearly as possible now and chose his words carefully. "Raul seems to think the best collections in this country are in the hands of only five or six people—unaffiliated collectors, and all of them frequent clients of Clifford Johnson."

Ray blinked and seemed to be having trouble seeing. Thinking it due to the increasing cloud cover he tried harder to focus through the heavily tinted windows of the Lincoln. He concentrated on the hedge, and again caught sight of the small yellow bird, a piece of straw in its beak this time. The bird seemed confused, going on instinct maybe; at this juncture it didn't seem to know exactly what to do with the straw. Ray thought it might be considering building a nest. A second, even smaller bird appeared, this one with a bit of string in its mouth. It had only a small spot of yellow on the breast... *Ah, that would be the female* Ray thought. He had no real experience with birds but wished now he had taken more of an interest in such things. As he studied the pair of little creatures it occurred to him they might be beginners at this. His own perception of the situation was that this might be a poor place to build a nest. Everything was growing dark; he could hardly follow what was going on with the birds now.

Archie, caught up in Raul's traitorous involvement with this other faction, didn't realize he had inadvertently tightened the garrote. Seeing the big man was fading he quickly loosened the wire and raised his voice to refocus his attention.

"So, you do understand... I will need to know where I can find Raul?"

"Yes," the big man answered dreamily. "I figured you might want to know that..."

~~~~~~~

Archie Blumker washed his hands in the lawn sprinkler and threw a glance back over his shoulder at the Lincoln. The man at the wheel, chin resting on his chest, appeared to be only dozing in the warmth of a cloudy afternoon—someone's grandfather, perhaps, waiting patiently for a dawdling family member.

~~~~~~~

Raul Ortiz had not been nearly so agreeable to deal with. Archie hated it when someone wouldn't take their medicine like a man.

Raul had at first denied Big Ray's confession—tried to talk his way out of the situation and when that failed began to whine and grovel. Finally, Raul caught his breath as though awakening at last to the reality of the situation. Then between involuntary sobs, admitted there had been no operative stepping off a curb...no fractured leg...and most importantly no information. He confessed he had made the story up fearing repercussions. He had, of course, been correct in that assumption, but horribly incorrect in the severity of the consequences.

Raul now admitted Ray's part in the thing. But swore the ex-cop had been instructed there was to be no killing—not under any circumstances. He warned the man that could only bring in the FBI and was to be avoided at all cost. Based on Ray Danson's final report Raul was convinced he had not killed Clifford Johnson and declared the trader's death must have been from some later incident.

When Archie picked up a picture of Raul's family from the desk, the man began to cry. He blubbered incoherently until Archie found it necessary to backhand him across the face then—slap him with an open palm. *People like this shouldn't be in the business*, he thought. *When things come to a fine point, they really don't have the 'cojones' for it.*

Archie's entire take-away from this tense and disjointed "interview" with Raul was that Big Ray's effort to obtain Clifford Johnson's client list, and possibly the man's own private collection which was known to be considerable, was poorly thought out from the beginning. He could see that now. When questioned about the other operatives, Big Ray had offered the thought that Archie was being played off against highly motivated foreign interests, but didn't know who they were. When Archie mentioned this to Raul, the man shuddered uncontrollably, pulled a small book from his desk drawer and handed it over before falling completely apart.

Archie was very good at getting at the truth in such situations and eventually felt both Raul and Big Ray Danson had come clean. He was now certain Ray Danson was not responsible for the trader's death and had been smart enough to cut his losses and leave the trading post after only a cursory search of the file cabinets. Someone else was responsible for the death of Clifford Johnson and probably his wife as well. Raul Ortiz, on the other hand bore the burden of treason should one go so far as to use that word. He had violated the code and had reaped the reward for such treachery. There might have been further repercussions had Archie had time; he was fairly certain there might one day be attempts by the Ortiz clan at vengeance. This would have been the time to nip it in the bud had there been time. He hoped that wouldn't come back to haunt him.

~~~~~~~

Archie had hoped to remain completely insulated from the Clifford Johnson affair. Percy Vermeer himself had said it wasn't his job. Now that was impossible.

Not only were his aspirations of an easy fix dashed, but he was afraid even more desperate people might be waiting in the Four Corners. And he hadn't a clue who they might be. He doubted the little black book of Raul's would be much help in the short term.

On his way out of Albuquerque Archie clicked on the radio and hummed along with some melody he was unable to identify.

"*KOB-FM* radio" the announcer crooned when it ended, "*93.3*—the sweet spot on your radio dial." Archie had, from the time he was a child, preferred radio over television. Now, he occasionally toggled the receiver between stations—back and forth between FM music and AM—to catch the news. KOB, the most powerful radio station in New Mexico was always his first choice when traveling in the *Land of Enchantment.* He was almost never out of range of one or the other of the two frequencies.

He stopped in Bernalillo for fuel, a sandwich, and several bottles of water. He was careful to stay hydrated in this arid land; neglecting that could affect a person's thinking.

Mysteriously beautiful as New Mexico might appear to the uninitiated, Archie had long felt there were secret elements at play. The clarity of atmosphere coupled with magically subtle whimsies of light make for mood changing vistas. Somber dark canyons and soaring snow-covered peaks overwhelm those from lesser places. A person might easily be fooled into thinking this country more benevolent than it really is. "The Land of Enchantment" label was more indicative than most might think, but in ways they couldn't imagine.

The truth is, New Mexico has always been a hard and sometimes treacherous country with more violence over the centuries than almost any other part of the Southwest. From Paleolithic times on, humans seemed drawn to something so irresistibly pervasive they became forever marked by it. Later, when the Spaniards made this country the frontier of their colonization efforts... Well, that's when things really heated up.

As he angled north toward Cuba, Archie took note of the pueblos along the way. There were quite a number of them. Zia was one and just a bit farther up the road, the turn off to Jemez. Amazing to think these were some of the oldest continuously inhabited towns in North America. On a working vacation he remembered once catching a trout near Jemez Springs; the only trout he'd ever caught. Just the thought of it made him smile.

He crossed the dry bones of riverbeds, counting them milestones in a desolate and boring run to the northwest. The clay hills and eroded valley bottoms gave little evidence of the verdant, sometimes lush mesa tops to the north and east. Archie had, over the years, inveigled connections all over this part of the state—all in the service of Percy Vermeer and his insatiable quest for the finest in Native art and artifacts. He had never fully understood it himself, but seldom did he fail Percy. This time he had been dealt a poor hand, yet remained determined, confident even, that he would ultimately prevail.

This *Conquistadors* route up from Mexico, even today, waxes interminably long at times. Only the diversity of the land and fleeting shadows of forgotten peoples kept Archie's mind engaged.

He stopped at Nageezi for a cold soda and carried it outside where he sat on a bench in the sparse shade of a *ramada*. The sketchy brush shelter, barely able to fend off the heat of the day, offered little reprieve from the afternoon sun. An old Navajo man, enjoying a drink of his own at the other end of the bench didn't look up or take any notice of the newcomer.

Archie smiled to himself, knowing it difficult to draw these older people out. Still, it might be something to pass the time.

"It's a hot one today, isn't it?" Archie said this peering off into the distance, as if speaking to himself.

The old man didn't turn or acknowledge the remark.

Archie shrugged his shoulders and stretched. "It seems like I've been driving all day. I'm tired…"

Still the old man didn't answer, only took a sip of his drink—remained staring straight ahead without so much as a nod.

"I don't know how you people got around in this country in the old days. It must have taken forever to get anywhere."

The old man gazed out across the country with only the buzzing of a fly to break the silence.

Archie drained his soda, set the bottle beside the bench and half-rose to go.

The Navajo, inscrutable as ever, made a tiny noise in the back of his throat, his shoulders shook a little, and the noise became a chuckle.

Archie settled back down to wait. If he had learned anything about Indians over the years it was to have the patience to wait them out.

The old man began to speak, but in a voice so small Archie had to lean toward him and cock an ear just so to understand. "A rider," the old Navajo said, "one time rode a horse from Bloomfield to Cuba in only twenty-four hours."

Archie edged a bit closer.

The old man sniffed, "I guess with this new highway that might be over a hundred miles…maybe even more. Back then a rider probably would have gone cross-country in some places…saved a few miles…but not too many. It was still a hell of a ride." The old man turned toward Archie but as would any *Diné* with good manners, he looked aside and never directly at him. "He was a young white man, too." He said this smiling to himself as he watched secretly to see Archie's reaction—thinking this white man might take some measure of ethnic pride in so laudable an enterprise. "It was a hot summer, too, like this one." He said this more or less, Archie thought, to perk up his interest, and possibly incite empathy for the young horseman.

Archie finally nodded. "There's no telling really, what a person can do once they set their mind to it." Then, sensing this wasn't enough to suit the storyteller, he began rubbing his jaw as though thinking more about it. "There should be some sort of memorial, I suppose, to that rider—right along the highway here—so tourists would know how wimpy they are zipping along in their air-conditioned automobiles." Archie said this to see if he could get a rise from the old man. He thought to himself *once an old Indian like this has his dander up he might say all sorts of interesting things.*

This particular old man, however, let the comment pass with no indication he agreed…or even heard. Then he grimaced and went on, "I doubt there is a horse or man alive today capable of such a ride across so torturous a stretch of country in that heat."

Archie knew very little about horses, or what sort of animal it would take to accomplish such a feat, but he did know something about men, and having just covered a good portion of that route by pickup truck he was inclined to agree; it would take an extraordinary man to make such a ride—even back in a time when there was no shortage of extraordinary men.

The old Navajo, seeing Archie's appreciation of the achievement, did not want to leave him with the impression that only a white man had the gumption for such a business. He was thus encouraged to tell yet another story. This one from an even earlier time, a story, he said, that was told him by his grandfather which in turn had come from *his* grandfather before *him*. The old man being quick to point out neither grandfather was known to lie.

Archie was inclined to show a greater interest this time, certain he would learn something of historical value if nothing else.

"There was," the old man began, tapping his brow with a forefinger as though to awaken the tale, "a white soldier carrying a message…just over there…beyond that big stretch of flats." The Navajo pointed with his chin toward the Jicarilla Apache Reservation, barely visible in the distant haze to the northeast. Nothing more than a blue line of mesas and mountains, all jumbled together, none discernable one from the other.

"That soldier was tired, his horse moving at little more than a walk, when he came to the attention of an Apache Indian; a young Jicarilla warrior returning from a raid down country. His party had separated, splitting up to confuse a posse of Mexican ranchers." The old man seemed uncertain how much of the tale would be interesting to this white person so decided on an abbreviated version. "That Indian was taking a rest from the heat, just off the trail, hidden in the brush. His own horse had died of wounds and exhaustion leaving the Jicarilla afoot. After watching the soldier for a few minutes, the Indian thought it would be nice to have that Bluecoat's horse. Even a worn-out horse is better than no horse at all." The old man paused to steal a glance at his listener and seeing the man's attention lagging, decided to dredge up even more exciting details. "Falling in behind the soldier, but staying well back, the Apache saw by the horse's tracks it was unsteady on its feet. Knowing there was no water in that direction, the Indian was thinking the animal would pretty soon give out. He was careful to stay out of sight so as not to cause the soldier to go faster...or maybe turn around and take a shot at him. He soon saw he was right about the horse. It was clear the animal was starting to stagger." The old Navajo took a swallow of his orange drink, grimaced and spit out an insect swimming valiantly for its life. He cleared his throat took a deep breath and went on with his story.

"My Grandfather said the soldier surely must have looked behind him a time or two, but he never saw that Apache. In those times, Apache were good at being sneaky. They were like coyotes; you wouldn't see one if he didn't want to be seen." The old Navajo thought for a time, making certain he had all the elements of the story in order before continuing.

Archie waited, sneaking a look at the old man and thinking he had drifted off in the warm sage laden breeze.

From the corner of his eye the storyteller guessed what the white man was thinking. He coughed and shook his head before recovering his place in the tale. "Just at sundown the Jicarilla caught up...and under cover of the coming darkness…eased up on the soldier…shot him low in the back with an arrow. The blue-coat was already worn down I guess—that one arrow killed him pretty good from what my great-great-Grandfather had to say."

Archie could see the white soldier was not to be the hero of this story. He suppressed a frown; not so much because of the soldier's bad luck or that he was white, but because the story was making him thirsty again.

The old man smiled. "That horse," he said, "never even moved when the soldier fell off. Just stood there with his head down, all spraddle-legged and lathered up." The old *Diné* blinked a time or two and spared the white man another glance to see how he was liking *this* tale.

Archie knew the old man was trying to get his goat. He smiled inwardly and bent forward to show an even greater interest.

"Well," the Navajo went on, nodding again in the direction of the place it surely must have happened. "That Jicarilla stripped off the horse's saddle and other gear to lighten him up a little. After eating what little there was in the soldier's saddlebags and drinking from his canteen, he gave the horse the little sip that was left from the palm of his hand and jumped on that animal. He goaded it north for another twenty miles at least. He would have to pinch its ears or reach back and twist its tail occasionally to keep it going." The old man gazed over at Archie, wrinkled his brow and nodded knowingly. "I won't tell you what else he did to that horse, as I know white people are softhearted and can't stand to be thinking about such things." He stopped a minute to let this sink in. "Back then, Apaches knew a

lot of tricks to use against horses...and people, too."
The old Navajo, after inspecting the contents emptied
his drink in a last swallow and set the bottle down on
the bench between them.

Archie gave him a look, more of a grimace perhaps
that the storyteller must have mistook for sympathy for
the horse.

The old man spat in the dirt.

"When that horse went down for the final time the
Indian stepped off and shot his last arrow through its
throat so he could drink a little blood. Then he made a
fire and cooked some strips of horsemeat, you know, to
carry along with him. He walked the last thirty miles to
his *wickiup* in a night and a day." The old man smiled at
the incongruity of his next statement. "None of his
people that heard the story thought it anything out of the
ordinary." The old man didn't think it so unusual either
but was equally certain white people would.

"A Navajo woman, who was later carried off by
that same Jicarilla and kept as his wife, was the one
who told my great-great-Grandfather this story," the old
man smiled into the past and drowsily recalled. "That
woman got loose finally and came back to us. She was
my great-Grandfather's mother so that means *he* might
have been half Apache himself. I don't know. Among
the *Diné*, if your mother is Navajo, you are Navajo and
that's all there is to it." The old man, thinking back over
what he had been saying, blinked as though surprised to
find himself part of the story.

Archie shook his head at the tale. "I guess they
don't make 'em like they used to?"

This caused the old Navajo to laugh outright, "I
don't know about that, some of those Jicarilla are still

plenty tough bastards..." He cocked his head to one side. "Our people never like to go fight them Apache, not if there is any way around it." He turned to Archie and looked him up and down. "I hear there are whites these days who are saying those Apaches are cousins to the Navajo—that we were all the same people once—somewhere up north I think." The old man nodded his head in that direction. 'It's true a lot of the Apache words are almost the same as ours... But we still never liked 'em much..."

~~~~~~~

It was coming on dark when Archie pulled into Farmington and took a room at the Crestview. The motel was nearly new and though he seldom stayed at the same place twice, he liked the Crestview well enough to make it the exception. Oil field hands made up the bulk of the motel's regulars and they generally stayed to themselves. He'd noticed a good many work-over rigs on his way into town, and several mud-splattered fracking units were parked just to the side of the building.

There might be some drinking and loud behavior later that night but tired as he was he doubted it would bother him.

Archie retrieved a pint flask from his bag and had a long pull—wondering if he should call Louise Johnson, or after the note he'd sent, just wait for her to contact him? He hoped for her sake she hadn't sold him out...she would regret it if she had.

9

The Discovery

Lucy Tallwoman was at her loom early but hadn't touched the shuttle in more than twenty minutes. She was thinking. And she had a lot to think about. The piece on the loom still unfinished was no longer a priority and was now afforded little thought. If her suspicions were correct and her client records were no longer available—misplaced, missing or stolen—the Begays might soon be in a financial bind. They wouldn't be the only ones though. Trader Johnson had an enviable collection of craftsmen under his guidance, in both silver and textiles. He controlled more of the region's market than most realized. Without the trader's carefully curated list of buyers they would all be left with few options and none of them fast fixes.

Clifford Johnson had been wrong when he said, "It's not important that you know who the buyers are. We'll take care of all that for you."

She knew her work would still be as valuable as ever—probably more now that she knew how she had been manipulated, and her mother before her as well. It was the time involved that worried her. They had virtually no cushion, nothing in reserve. Everything had gone into the new house as it trickled in, and there were still plenty of bills left to pay. Building a new customer base would take time, and she would need help doing it. This time she intended to be part of that process. She would never again entrust her future and that of her family, to someone else. For now, the logical person to turn to might be Carla Meyor. She had the expertise and possibly even the gallery connections needed to put a marketing plan together, and that, along with a strong interest in her work put Carla first on the list, in fact she was the only person on the list. *Yes, Carla is the one I should call first.*

Thomas came up from the corrals with two tired and dirty children in tow. Dipping sheep is hard, grungy work but without it, life for the sheep man would be even harder, and far less profitable. Ticks, lice and flies make life miserable for the sheep and can affect the entire operation.

"I'm glad that's over with. The kids have been dreading it for weeks now, and so have I."

Lucy turned and nodded. "I should have been down there helping—I just can't seem to get into my weaving right now. I didn't realize how much I had come to depend on Cliff and Louise. I don't even know how to start with finding someone else...I'm thinking about calling Carla Meyor. She's the only one I can think of who might be able to help."

Her husband shook his head. "I'm not sure that's a good idea just yet. Charlie might have some ideas. Old Man Paul seems to have something going on in his head about that woman, too. Maybe it would be better to just concentrate on your weaving for now and then when everything settles down, we can figure out where to go from there. Everything will fall into place eventually."

In the corner, Paul T'Sosi brought his recliner upright with a start, still foggy from his nap, and only catching the part about the sheep. "What? You were dipping sheep? Why didn't you call me to help? I don't mind getting a little dirty." He snorted. "And it's not like I can't do that kind of work anymore."

"I know, Paul, we just didn't want to wake you; it sounded like you might be having a dream, you were talking in your sleep, too. It's bad luck you know, waking someone who's talking in their sleep. They could be speaking to the Holy Ones or lifting a curse on someone."

"What was I saying?" Paul didn't think he talked in his sleep; *it might not have been me doing the talking at all. It might have been the dream talking to me.* This was something he wasn't about to acknowledge and he changed the direction of the conversation. "So how did the dipping go—did those Suffolk bucks give you any trouble?" They were big bucks, leased from the Extension Service's program and not to be bred to Lucy's ewes: the ones kept for wool. The Suffolk cross produced a larger, more delicately flavored lamb for market, but it also insured the wool would barely merit carpet grade. The Suffolks were meant expressly for their expanding market lamb flock. "Well, we don't want them mixed into our Churros. Those Churros need to be kept as they are."

"Yes, Paul, we know that." Thomas tried to keep the frustration out of his voice. "We kept them separate all right. It's not time yet to put those bucks in with any ewes. The Churros won't take a buck yet anyway. They won't come in heat till later on when the weather cools."

Paul knows all this better than anyone; he must be having an off day, or maybe he's still half-asleep.

Caleb sidled over beside his Grandfather and when he thought no one was watching, leaned down and asked, "Did you ever get in touch with that old trapper's son...the one who has the *coyote gitters*?" He was fascinated by the thought of the banned coyote control devices.

The old man looked up at the boy and had to think a moment before answering. When it finally came to him, he laughed quietly and patted the boy's hand. "Harley's taking me into town shopping tomorrow and I'll be meeting the trapper's son at the Co-op. Lucy found his number for me and after she went to bed last night, I talked to him on the telephone." He gave the boy a conspiratorial wink. "I'll see what he has left; I know he'll let me have a few. And if he's not too proud of them we might just as well try to buy them all. We should have got us some of those things years ago; they are just going to waste where they are now. That man don't care nothing about coyotes. We can put 'em to good use around here this fall."

The boy smiled back at the old man. "That will be great *Acheii*—I know exactly where I'm going to set 'em too."

Thomas, on the other side of the room, looked up from talking to Ida Marie. "What's that I heard about getting coyotes?"

"Oh, nothing Dad. Me and Paul, we're just thinking we need to get after these coyotes around here, you know, sort of thin 'em out a little."

Thomas shrugged and turned back to his daughter and their conversation about the possibility of some New York style clothes for the coming school year.

Paul smiled at Caleb. "I wouldn't say anything about those *gitters*. Your father might think you're not old enough to be messing with them." He snorted and tossed his head. "But I think you are...I know I was at your age. We'll just keep it between you and me." He watched as the boy went to wash up for lunch, *That boy's plenty old enough to learn about coyotes; he and his sister both have sheep of their own now and it is time they learned how to protect them.* Traditional though Paul was, he had long ago taken a different and more realistic attitude toward the mythic coyote and its constant drain on their flocks, *Coyote is what he is...and that is all that he is. It won't hurt to thin them out a little.*

10

The Gitters

Harley Ponyboy took one hand off the steering wheel and pointed to the cardboard box in Paul T'Sosi's lap. "What ya got there, Paul?" Harley had dropped the old man off at the Co-op to meet a friend while he ran a few errands. He had only been a few minutes, but when he returned, Paul was already sitting on the bench outside holding a small carton. "That didn't take you long, not much to catch up on, huh?"

"No, just a few things someone's son had been keeping for me. He had to get back to work. I doubt these things will be worth the trouble." Paul, knowing Harley's insatiable curiosity, thought it best to just show him. He doubted he would know what they were anyway…they were from another time. He flipped open the flap on the carton and held it so his friend could see inside.

Keeping his attention on the approaching traffic Harley cut an eye at the box. "Don't look like much ta me. "

"Naa, just some old tools. He wanted me to have them, he said…they were his dad's." Paul's voice sounded thin and far away as he closed the box and glanced out the side window. When his grandson got home from school he would be excited to have a looksee at these things. Caleb would want to know all about them—what they would do and how they did it—if they still could do anything at all. Paul's face turned grim as he looked out across the country; there was more to it now than just coyotes. But he was the only one who knew that. The old man's vision was not what it once had been, but it was good enough to know what he saw up there on the ridge behind the house.

Later in the day as Paul sat outside, he watched Thomas Begay returning from Shiprock where he'd been working on a man's car—he had been gone all morning—longer than he expected. The truck pulled up in a cloud of dust which the wind grabbed, carrying it up in the air where it hovered a moment and then just disappeared.

Thomas got down from the truck, and noticing his wife's pickup was gone, paused to wonder where she could have gone. Eventually his eye went to the sheep pens. This had been his morning to take them out and he was late. He'd fed them their supplement at daylight before he left, but knew that wouldn't satisfy the old man. Now he would be in for a chewing.

Paul came toward the truck, appearing unconcerned. "Don't worry about those sheep," he called. " I already took 'em out for some greens this morning."

"Paul, I thought we'd talked about this. You are supposed to wait for someone to go along and help with those sheep! I know I'm late this time, but you should have got Lucy to go with you, or just waited for me."

Paul snorted, "Lucy was working, and I didn't want to take her away from it...she has had a hard enough time getting back into her weaving as it is." He gave

Thomas a look. "I only took those sheep up the ridge behind the *hogan*. I been saving that new grass up there. I thought this would be a good time to let them in on it—we're trying to finish out them lambs, aren't we? They need a little fresh grass right along. That little bit of feed you been giving them from the Co-op isn't enough." The old man said this forcefully enough Thomas thought it best to take a step back.

The younger man made a conscious effort to remain calm. "The County Agent says it *is* enough, Paul." He took a deep breath. "Where did Lucy go? She's not supposed to go off by herself either, not until they find out who was behind the Johnson murder. We don't know yet that she's not in danger, too. She's to stay close by…that's what we decided."

"She just went into town to meet with that female FBI. She should be safe enough with her wouldn't you think?"

Throwing up his hands, Thomas headed into the house to wash up. "We should just stick to the plan…that's all I'm saying, Paul… Just stick to the plan." As he passed the old man Thomas thought he might have seen a smile but he refused to notice. They had been on good terms for a long while now, but it could just as easy go sour again.

The old man, left to himself, gazed out across the sage and greasewood flats thinking of his morning on the ridge. Someone had been up there on the point spying on them. This was the family's camp—they were the only ones who had any business up there. Thomas would need to know when the time was right. *He had a right to know. He was after all, the man of the house now.* Paul and Thomas had grown closer over the years, not that he ever let on he thought so. His son-in-law would understand later why he hadn't said anything. There were a few loose ends to tie up first. He had to get it straight in his mind first—how he was going to go about killing these people.

11

The Rogues

By midmorning Charlie Yazzie was absorbed in the latest report from the Bureau, most of which he and Fred had already discussed. He had no doubt the reports sent out to local agencies were censored to some extent. He was therefore pleased, when the receptionist buzzed through to announce the agent himself was on the line.

"Morning, Fred. I was just going over some of the information in your report. I'd hoped we'd be further along than what I'm reading here."

"We are further along, Charlie. That's what I'm calling about. I'd prefer not to say too much on the telephone at this point. But I'll be out your way in an hour or so and there are a few things I'd like to go over with you…local stuff some of it, things you might be able to help us with. How about coffee at the *Diné Bikeyah*?"

"I think I can shake loose then, Fred; the cafe in an hour will be fine?"

"I'll be there. Oh, and Charlie, come alone if you don't mind; this might better be kept between just the two of us."

Charlie thought this last part went without saying. *Why would the FBI suddenly make me privy to information outside the general network? Or was this Fred's personal decision? Interesting.*

The Legal Services Investigator was in a back booth and would already have ordered his favorite cinnamon roll if not for Sue's recent comment that he might want to buy his next pair of Levi's a bit larger in the girth. She'd smiled and said it in a flip sort of way, but he could tell she was serious just the same. Since his promotion to department head, and no longer being in the field, he had gradually begun to take on a little extra around the middle. He'd always maintained he'd never let this happen...but there it was. He sighed taking a last look at the picture of the cinnamon roll on the menu cover. When the waitress came he ordered coffee, black.

Charlie was on his second refill when the Senior FBI Agent made his way back to the booth. There was a tone to his good morning, which along with the forced smile, put the investigator on his guard.

"So, Charlie," the agent held up a finger to attract a waitress as he spoke, "did you get a chance to finish reading that report?"

"Yes, I did. Why? Was something left out?" His smile told the agent he was well aware there was.

"That is, in part, what I came out here to talk to you about." The agent hesitated, as though carefully sifting through the various aspects of the new information, balancing that which could be most important, against that which would be most interesting.

Charlie's patience ran out... "Has there been any word about Louise Johnson?"

Fred raised his hands defensively then nodded. "In a sense, yes. Not her whereabouts, as yet—but our forensic accountant out at the trading post did discover some rather thought-provoking information. The Johnson's have apparently been 'cooking' their books for years now. He's pretty certain they had two sets of ledgers. The real set, of course, was conveniently missing. Whether they were taken at the time of the murder, or are still hidden away by the Johnsons is unknown. It's doubtful their clients were ever getting a fair shake; at least they hadn't been for a long time, I'm afraid." The FBI man didn't try to hide his frustration, but brightened as he noted, "Our man found them to be more than a little careless when it came to the actual bookkeeping. He found a scratchpad, and though it had a number of pages torn out he suspected forensics might be able to pull some impressions from the underlying pages, and they did. He's still waiting for some bank records to come in as well, but even at this point there's plenty that just doesn't add up.

"The Johnsons…?" Charlie shook his head. "I hate to hear that, but I have to admit I'm not too surprised. I suspected after our meeting with Lucy that those folks were being allowed a pretty free rein in her business affairs."

"Yes, I think that crossed everyone's mind at the time. I truly believe that meeting was Lucy's first inclination something might be amiss, but I'm sure she could see it after a while. I suspect it goes clear back to Lucy's mother's dealings with the Johnsons. That's probably where it all started. It's just grown over time like greed generally does, and now it's beyond what anyone could have imagined." Fred paused for effect. "It appears, right now—with the limited information our guy has available to him—Lucy might be short as much as fifty-large, and that's with all the numbers not in yet."

Charlie did his best to suppress a gasp. "That much huh? The Begays are not going to be happy to hear that. But it might make Louise's disappearance a little easier to take. What are the odds any of that money might someday be recovered?"

"No way of telling at this point but given the Johnson's austere lifestyle our agent seems to think a good portion of that money might still be hidden away somewhere—it will obviously take a good bit more work to ferret out anything like that. In the meantime, I wouldn't let the Begays get their hopes up. Keep in mind they weren't the only victims...but our guy does think they may prove to have suffered the largest losses of the entire bunch."

Charlie still hadn't really heard anything he'd not already known or surmised, and he sat gazing at the FBI man...obviously waiting for him to go on.

"Before you ask, Charlie, even the ledgers we did recover had only codes in place of buyers' names. Without the key to those codes we may be at a dead end. But that's just another thing that remains in limbo."

The waitress finally brought the agent's coffee and he pulled it to him to stir, though he hadn't added anything to it. He lifted the mug to his lips and blew on it, then set it down without drinking.

Charlie studied the agent and wondered when he would cut to the chase. "You mentioned there might be something I could help you with. What was that all about, Fred?"

The FBI man again raised the cup, tested the temperature with the tip of his tongue, and taking a careful swallow, grimaced at the still hot brew before arching an eyebrow at the investigator. "Charlie, I know you think we have been...let us say...overly cautious in the information we've provided the local agencies; and you would be right in thinking that." Fred swirled his coffee around in the cup. "The fact of the matter is the Bureau is currently experiencing some security problems. We've had to put a couple of cases off limits until we get it figured out. What I need to know, Charlie: are you still adamant in your original assessment of Billy Red Clay as Liaison Officer? You were one of his original supporters in his bid for the job, and your confidence weighed heavily in his selection." He held up a hand before Charlie could reply... "We know we've not always been as up-front with Billy as we might have been. And that he may be feeling slighted. It's just that we've had to curtail certain information to the most generic info in recent reports— mostly due to this security thing the Bureau's experiencing—no reflection on Billy or the job he's doing." The agent sat back in his chair mentally bracing himself.

Charlie was quiet for a moment then nodded. "Fred, I can assure you Billy Red Clay is as trustworthy a person as you'll find in law enforcement. He's been upset lately, thinking you've lost confidence in him as Liaison Officer." The Investigator didn't look away when he said, "He'll be happy to learn that's not the case, and I'm sure he'll be happier yet to hear he's not 'under the gun,' as he puts it. I don't know anyone more capable of handling that position. Fred...you can't go wrong with Billy."

The agent broke into a smile "I was hoping you'd say something like that. Billy's well liked among our people in the Farmington office and he's done a good job over these last months. I'll have a chat with him later today." With that Fred Smith picked up his hat, and with nothing further to say, gave a parting wave of his hand and made his way to the cash register. The Investigator noticed the FBI man had picked up the tab. Frowning, he wished then he'd ordered the cinnamon roll; he couldn't recall anyone at the Bureau ever picking up the tab before.

Charlie watched through the front window as the federal agent crossed the parking lot. It seemed Fred carried himself a little straighter than when he came in. The investigator could only hope their talk about Billy Red Clay had lightened his load.

Fred hadn't indicated exactly what sort of security problem the Bureau was having—leaving Charlie to assume it might still have something to do with cases right there on the reservation. It was a thought that left him thinking Fred might have other suspects as well. He wondered if Carla was one of them.

12

The Calling

Carla settled into her morning—going through a list of prominent collectors that might have an interest in the work of Lucy Tallwoman. For the next few days she would have the use of the office next to Fred Smith's. A small office with no window, but an accommodation she appreciated nonetheless. It beat working out of a hotel room and had the advantage of a secure phone and Teletype facilities. It would only be available until Fred's junior agent returned from a training seminar—already scheduled before all hell broke loose in the Johnson murder. She'd have a few days yet, sufficient to wrap up her end of the investigation. Louise Johnson's disappearance had thrown everyone a curve. Some thought the woman might be on the run now, though there was precious little proof of that one way or the other.

Carla had just hung up the phone when Fred stuck his head in the door. "Have everything you need?"

"Yes I do, thanks. I appreciate it, too."

"Carla, do you have a minute? I've just had word from the Albuquerque office regarding a killing down there. They think the guy is a gallery owner you might know something about."

She frowned. "Come on in, Fred. I'm ready for a coffee break anyway. Couldn't sleep last night...party going on next door."

"That's an oilfield town for you...it's a 24/7 business...and no sleep for the wicked." He grinned. "I'll grab a couple of cups...be right back."

Carla started to protest, but he was gone. She cleared her desk, pausing a moment to stare at the vacationing agent's family photo. He was a nice looking young man with a pretty wife and two handsome children. She felt a momentary pang of regret. But then Fred was back balancing a tray with two cups and the fixings.

"Cream and sugar I'm guessing?"

"Yes, thanks."

Fred pulled up a chair and watched as Carla dumped a half-spoon of sugar in one of the cups and creamed it to caramel.

The Senior Agent took his black.

"So, who's this person they think I might know?" She took an unladylike slurp off the top of the still steaming cup and grinned.

Fred smiled. "His name's Raul Ortiz, scion of the redoubtable Santa Fe Ortiz bunch, longtime pain in the... side...of the local authorities. The family's sketchy reputation goes all the way back to the early nineteen hundreds—or so I'm told. One or the other of them came across our radar a couple of times when I was a newbie starting out down in Albuquerque."

Carla nodded. "I ran across Ortiz as a Bureau consultant on an art theft case...this was some time back." She pursed her lips in recollection. "I was able to track the pieces back to several of his people. Every one of them went down without a whimper, and without incriminating any of the higher ups either. About par for the course from what I later discovered. Raul himself has never been charged with anything beyond a parking ticket." She grimaced. "Even those tickets never came to court. Whatever else Raul was, he was no amateur. Whoever took him out was not your average player."

Fred Smith wagged a finger in the air. "Ah, but there's more…earlier that same day an ex-cop, Big Ray Danson, was found dead in a Lincoln Town Car outside an Albuquerque motel. Not just strangled, but rather death by garrote. Not a pleasant way to go, from what I understand."

"Ouch! I would guess not. Any idea who was responsible for that little coup? The same person as Raul's killer maybe?"

"Good guess. Our people down there say there could very well be a connection. Big Ray's car was registered to an LLC owned by…guess who?"

"Raul Ortiz?"

"Close. His brother Bobby, who of course, had reported the car stolen only hours earlier."

"How convenient."

"Yes, it was. You would think such clever people would be smart enough to make an honest living without putting themselves through all this drama."

"Ah, but that might take all the fun out of it, you know…going by the rules and all. I read that somewhere—in a criminology class, as I recall. When you stop and think about it, it's really the only thing that makes any sense." Carla shook her head.

Fred chuckled and allowed she might be right. "So, what did you wind up learning about Raul?"

"First, let me preface the answer with a little background. On the East Coast, there's a small but very active group of collectors that have become responsible for the bulk of the high-dollar sales in the Southwestern Art world. We call them The Factors. They pretty much dictate the price of what's going through the auction houses. As a consultant for several New York galleries I've come to know some of those people, and learned a lot in the process, mostly about the mechanics of marketing and, of course, a few of the many subterfuges that go along with it. Like any big-money pursuit, the art world has long been known to attract a certain shady element." Carla stopped and had a sip of her coffee. "Raul Ortiz was a name that popped up often enough to rate a closer look. He seemed to know everyone in the business. It turns out his real expertise was acquiring hard to find antiquities—with or without the provenance to make them legal. He's one of those 'shadow' characters the authorities know are involved but can never seem to charge with anything that will hold up in court. He was also known to provide skilled professionals, specialists, not particular in how they applied those skills." Carla gave the Senior Agent a knowing look.

Fred nodded but didn't interrupt her story.

A hard-edged glimpse of satisfaction flitted across the woman's face. "From what you say, something finally did catch up with him. He was due…and that's a fact."

The comment caught Fred off-guard. He nodded thoughtfully but kept his thoughts to himself, and later left Carla's office thinking he had learned something—but maybe more about Carla, than Raul. The woman had the rare ability to leave statements open to a certain ambiguity of interpretation. In his opinion she probably *would* have made a good lawyer.

13

Desperado

So now it had fallen to him. There was a time, in the beginning, when Archie did this sort of work on a regular basis, not trusting to farm it out. But now Percy thought he was above that—should no longer be involved in the rougher end of the business. He had become indispensable, was the way Percy had put it. That's why Raul Ortiz had been engaged to provide an operative. Archie had protested the move from the beginning—saying the stakes were too high—he would prefer to do it himself, but the Factor had been adamant.

So, here they were with a job half done, and even that done poorly. Regardless what Percy might think, there was now only one thing to be done about it. On such short notice there was no one else to call on. Archie was well aware he might be pushing his luck with the Factor by taking this upon himself, and that bothered him.

Percival Vermeer was known to take great pains, in exhausting every reasonable alternative before unleashing his hounds. In the end, however, he *would* have his way, no matter what. He liked to think he was the one masterminding each little stage of a project, but that was just Percy. Eventually it always came down to Archie. The Factor simply didn't have the street smarts…or the belly, for what they were up against now.

Archie Blumker had known Clifford and Louise Johnson for a while now, and had approached them on Percy's behalf on several different occasions. The trader was an odd duck and trusted only clients he had worked with for years—most of those transactions probably involving a good bit of under-the-table cash—not unusual in the Indian trade.

Archie had used up every resource at his disposal. Though this was something he was usually very good at, he had so far drawn a blank when it came to locating Louise. The frustration was beginning to wear on him. Finding people who didn't want to be found had long been his forte: Raul Ortiz could attest to that…had he still been around to do so.

The good news was, Archie saw little reason to suspect foul play in Louise's disappearance. To all appearances she had simply gone missing and considering what happened to her husband he could well understand that. She was alone now, vulnerable, and most likely afraid; she would not be inclined to trust anyone. Louise Johnson needed a friend, and should he find her, Archie intended to be that friend. Being the pragmatist that he was, however, he admitted there was a very real possibility the woman knew exactly what she was doing and for whatever reason had simply made a run for it. From all accounts she could certainly afford it, and whether she had the coded list or not, she might never willingly turn up. In that case he would prove to be her worst nightmare.

When he first met Louise, he had gone so far as to speak privately with the woman, hoping to draw her out as a possible conduit to Clifford. Archie was not without charm when need be and expended considerable energy in that direction. The woman would only say her husband kept the particulars of his business to himself, especially when it came to clients. Her story was she did the books using coded information, for which only Clifford had the key. Archie, not destitute of hope, had his ace in the hole and as every gambler knows that can make all the difference should the stars align.

His other assignment was going somewhat better. It hadn't been hard to locate Lucy Tallwoman's camp and he had spent the early part of the morning out on a high point above their new house. It had been a rough climb coming in from the ragged end of the hogback—several miles from the highway—almost straight up for the first mile or so. His topo-maps had shown an easier way in: going cross-country from the west, but that way was most likely deep in mud from the recent rains and probably hours longer if it could be done at all.

Archie kept himself in excellent physical condition but was gasping for air as he topped the ridge and began easing out above the Begays' place. Everything appeared to be quiet down in the camp. Testing the breeze, he figured he would be downwind of a dog. He was almost certain they had one. He'd not seen a family *without* a dog in all his time in this country. He cautiously picked his way toward a venerable old shaggy bark cedar, considerably taller than the scatter of smaller junipers around it and on the very brink overlooking the camp. Close to the trunk he found himself fully concealed next to a conveniently low-slung limb, a perfect rest for his binoculars.

It was still dark when he had started out from the Chevy, but now the sun was peeping over the mesa east of the highway. He watched through his glasses as an old man came from the *hogan* behind the house. Holding his arms to the first bloody rays of the sun he appeared to be singing. Archie thought he could hear him, something in Navajo, just a hint of the song, bits and snatches of it carried on a chilly breeze. He couldn't be certain but thought it some sort of greeting to the sun.

The sheep stirred in their pens and the previously missing dog appeared, barking as he ran to threaten the leaders away from the gates. The black and white male stopped every few yards, turning back toward the old man with a yip, urging him down from the *hogan*. The canine was well aware the old man wouldn't come before having his coffee, but that didn't keep him from trying. The old man disappeared inside, leaving the dog waiting at the pens, one eye on the silent house and growing more anxious as the minutes passed. In the dog's mind, it was important to reassert control over these sheep each morning. They were animals notorious for their short memories.

Archie stayed at his post nearly half an hour, watching. A younger man and two children, a boy and a girl, left the main house and got in a diesel pickup to head down to the highway and the school bus stop. Another truck was left in the yard and Archie rightly surmised it belonged to Lucy Tallwoman. His own truck was well hidden behind a shale hillock and well down the highway—not likely to be seen by anyone on their way out.

Archie thought it interesting these people still lived in much the same way they had for nearly a millennium: herdsmen, small family compounds separated by the great distances required for stock to survive in so harsh a land. For most there were few modern conveniences even in these modern times. Archie had to smile at the television antenna guyed off the chimney of the wood stove. A thin curl of smoke rose in the morning air to drift his way. There was a certain curious charm in it all that tugged at his sensibilities. *Will these people ever assimilate—become like everyone else?* He hoped not. There were few enough natural humans left on the planet.

He watched through the binoculars as the old man came out drinking his coffee, and then saw him wait at the side of the house until the others left. Archie knew Lucy's father lived with them and felt certain this was him. The old Navajo was dressed in a light jacket and carried something in a small pouch slung from a shoulder, his lunch perhaps.

The old man signaled to the dog as he opened the gates and watched as he forced the sheep from their bedding grounds—nipping at the laggards but seldom barking. Then it was up the trail to the hogback to the west. Eventually the sound of their bells and calling of the lambs faded to silence broken only by a soft soughing of the wind.

Archie rested there at the tree, taking it all in, committing the camp to memory as best he could. Leaning against the cedar his attention was drawn to a small hole, no bigger than a tennis ball, in the rough trunk of the tree. It was just about eye level, impossible to miss really. He wondered idly if it might not be home to some small creature, though what that might be he couldn't imagine. He eyed the cavity as he considered the possibilities, *a chipmunk maybe, that would be about the right size.* He couldn't recall those little ground squirrels frequenting holes in trees. But then who knew what an enterprising chipmunk might do given the proper incentive. The sun was in his face now, warming the scent of those young cedar and piñon left up here. He could see where many of the mature trees had long ago been cut down and likely pitched off the edge to be gathered down below for firewood.

Hearing the sound of bells Archie looked to the north and concentrated. The band of sheep had changed direction. Were they coming closer? He listened intently and far off though it was, he was certain now they were headed his way. He had thought the old man might be taking them farther upcountry but apparently not; he was instead bringing them across a switchback and in Archie's direction. He sighed, took out the gum he had been chewing and idly stuck it near the hole in the tree, then slinging the binoculars over his shoulder he turned and silently worked his way back the way he had come. It wouldn't do to be spotted so early in the game.

~~~~~~

The dog eased the band into the clearing back of the point and settled them loosely bunched on the fresh grass. Paul T'Sosi favored the dog with an approving glance before making his way to a favorite resting spot.

From there both the home place and the flock could be watched. He approached the vantage point with a careful eye to the path, rocky and strewn with downed limbs.

Almost to the old cedar tree, Paul was surprised to come across fresh tracks leading in from the south. Prints he didn't recognize and different from the ones he'd spotted previously. He knew the footwear of everyone in the family—an old habit people in that country form early on—to help them keep track of family members. He bent to touch the edge of the impression. It was not yet crumbling or anywhere near dry. Someone, a man by the size of the prints, had been there maybe only minutes before. Raising his head, the old man frowned and cautiously investigated the way forward.

There were only two reasonable ways to reach this place; the trail Paul had come from the camp, and an abandoned branch off an oil field road to the head of the sand wash and that far to the West. That would leave a long hike in rough country to reach the hogback. After the recent rains that particular route would be out of the question. There was yet an unlikely third option; a barely discernable trail that pitched off the south side of the ridge, an old and dangerously steep trail, now all but forgotten. That trail had washed out over the years and only someone unfamiliar with the country would choose it.

Following the tracks out to the point, it was plain the person had stood there beside the cedar for some time, fidgeting, studying the camp. Paul spotted a piece of chewing gum, still glistening with moisture, and stuck near the woodpecker hole in the trunk. That hole had been there as long as he could remember and was now rotted down deep inside the tree. Again, the old man searched about and listened, but could hear nothing over the tinkle of bells and snuffling of sheep. Even more cautious now he followed the tracks back to the south edge of the point and saw where the man had skidded his way down past the first ledge. *In a hurry,* he thought. Paul nodded to himself. *He must have heard the sheep coming.* Obviously, this was someone who had no business here.

Paul moved further along the edge to a place offering a better view. Down where the scrub oak began, he caught just a flash of a person disappearing into the brushy draw that led to the highway. As he had surmised from the track, it was a man, and from the quick look he'd had, apparently white. The person was moving fast considering the condition of the trail. That surprised him. Paul T'Sosi stayed there watching for some time. After another twenty minutes, and seeing nothing more of the person, the old man eventually made his way back to the point where he leaned against the tree and contemplated the camp before returning to the sheep. He stopped for a moment to consider his options: trying to make up his mind if he should let the animals feed or start for home without wasting any more time.

Thinking was more difficult for the old *Singer* these days, and in the end, he let the flock eat a while longer and only after sorting things out in his mind, did he come to the realization he would have to tell Thomas Begay everything…and soon, too. There wasn't much time. He looked up to the sky, judged the wind, and then signaled the dog to start the sheep off the ridge toward home.

The dog, unsure what to make of all this, nonetheless, followed Paul's command and started its gather. The dog knew the sheep had just begun filling their bellies and it wasn't easy convincing them to leave such easy pickings—they were still hungry—greedy for more of the fresh young grass.

~~~~~~

On his way back down the ridge Archie paused once or twice to check his back trail. His view was limited from this angle, but he saw no sign of anyone and could only assume he hadn't been seen. Still, every now and again he had that irksome feeling he wasn't alone. Archie had no way of knowing he had been watched from the time he drove up.

Almost to the bottom now he stopped in the shade and rested as he pulled out a small notebook to fill in a few details of the camp: things he didn't trust to memory. Then with a last swipe of his pen, and a tired sigh, rose to check his surroundings, and make certain he was undiscovered. He could see his Chevy truck from here, and after watching a short while became satisfied everything was as he left it. There was very little traffic that time of day and he took his time approaching the Chevy. No one in sight and no tracks near the vehicle. As he pulled back up on the highway, he couldn't help being satisfied with his morning's work.

~~~~~~

After a long hot shower and short nap, Archie dressed in his last clean shirt and jeans and went to inquire about a good place to eat…and maybe a well-deserved cocktail to boot. A gin and tonic would be good, should they stock his brand…not everyone did out here this wasn't New York, after all.

The desk clerk looked him over and recommended the new restaurant in town, "Italian," he said. "It's getting rave reviews, and if you are quick about it, you might beat the crowd." He grinned. "That's one thing about Farmington, she'll give a new eatery a fair chance."

14

Zuppa di Mare

Thomas Begay had done his best to steer his wife away from her obvious determination to rely on Carla Meyor for marketing advice. But given Lucy's stubborn streak and fascination with the more worldly woman he had to be careful how he expressed this.

"Well, you know," Lucy said, "Carla has worked with some of the biggest galleries in the country and she knows a lot of important people. I'm pretty sure she could put me in touch with qualified buyers."

Thomas turned away as he rolled his eyes. "Yes, you've mentioned that a couple of times now. I don't doubt she knows her stuff; I'm just wondering where her best interest lies—you or the FBI?"

Lucy bit her lower lip rather than answer. Why Thomas and her father had this distrust of Carla was beyond her. *Neither knows anything about the woman— other than her interest in both me and my mother's work. How could that be a bad thing? I'm calling her and that's that.* The recent happenings had left Lucy feeling she had, for too long, allowed others to do her thinking for her.

Later that day Lucy called Carla at her office, told her what was on her mind and asked if she would be agreeable to a short meeting in Farmington that afternoon. "Maybe right after work?" she said, "An early dinner if you would be up for that?"

"I'll be ready—it's been a tough day." Carla was intrigued and somehow pleased Lucy had thought of her. The FBI woman said she knew of a new Italian restaurant just off the main drag. She'd heard good things about it and had been meaning to give it a try.

Lucy Tallwoman was in a very different mood as she went to her closet for the new outfit. It was the one she'd been holding back for a special occasion. Her friend Sue had helped pick it out and it was what Sue might have chosen for herself. While not at all the type of thing she ordinarily wore it was, as Sue had mentioned, the sort of thing Lucy *should* be wearing if she meant to mingle with agents or buyers.

When she came through the living room Paul T'Sosi was in his recliner—the television blasting a Western. His eyebrows arched in surprise as he canted his head to one side and regarded her for a moment, then nodded and smiled.

"That's your mother's *Concho* belt, isn't it? New clothes, too, huh?"

"I got these to wear to your doctor appointment in Albuquerque next month…can't have those people down there thinking we're a bunch of reservation hillbillies." She turned awkwardly to show off the long denim skirt and white blouse with dark blue piping. New western boots peeked from the hem of the skirt and her mother's best belt—small silver *Conchos* set with Morenci turquoise added a stylish Southwestern flair. "Like it?"

Her father was used to seeing her in more traditional dress but was quick to agree it suited her, and made it plain he meant it, too.

~~~~~~~

Carla Meyor looked up from a menu to see Lucy Tallwoman glancing through the side glass before opening the restaurant door. Lucy immediately spotted Carla and headed back to the table, obviously impressed. By Farmington standards the restaurant would be considered quite elegant. Carla remembered when the supper club at the airport was the epitome of classy dining for the oilfield town. She was fairly certain Lucy had never been in that place…or on an airplane.

Carla was already nodding approval as Lucy approached the table, "Looking good!" She eyed Lucy Tallwoman up and down then grinned. "Wow, right uptown. It suits you, Lady…"

Lucy, pleased, grinned back and pulled out a chair. "Do you really think so? Sue Yazzie helped me with it—she's better at this sort of thing. She used to work in an office you know."

Carla raised an eyebrow. "She chose well. I'm impressed."

The waiter was there in an instant, filling water glasses as he announced the specials.

Lucy waited for Carla to order, and then putting her own menu down, said, "That sounds good to me, too. I'll have the same thing." She noticed the glass of wine by Carla's plate, and with a sweep of her hand, avowed, "I'll have whatever she's drinking." She'd watched enough television to know the basics but was without the slightest practical experience to back it up.

Carla nodded at the waiter. "A Pinot Grigio for my friend, as well." Obviously, Lucy Tallwoman had turned a leaf.

The two women went on to discuss the problem of Lucy regaining her lost marketing niche and how Carla might be able to help with that.

The FBI Agent smiled, and assured Lucy. "You will be amazed at how easy this might prove to be. You are who you always were. Nothing's changed. It's just a matter of letting the right people know where you are and that you are handling your own marketing now." Their food came and after a few minutes Carla asked Lucy how she liked it.

"It's good. I'm surprised I guess. The only Italian I've ever eaten was the spaghetti they used to serve once a week at the Episcopal boarding school. They did their best but I don't have many good memories of that place, and their spaghetti was sure not one of them. This is good...whatever it is?"

"Episcopal boarding school, huh. I was raised Episcopal myself. That must have been interesting?"

"It had its moments, I suppose." The two women considered one another for a moment longer without speaking.

"This is Eggplant Parmesan," Carla smiled. "It's always been a favorite of mine from the time I was a kid. It was my father's favorite, too. I make this a lot when I'm home."

"So, your father worked at the BIA dorms in Aztec when you were young? I think I might have mentioned... Thomas and our friends the Yazzies all went to school there...not really their choice, but that's how it was back in the day. Thomas has often mentioned that the white kids thought it was a great place to go to school, but then of course, *they* got to go home at night, didn't they?"

Carla lifted an eyebrow. "Like you said, it was what it was. Those were different times back then...I would be first to agree that doesn't make it right."

"No, that doesn't make it right, and I'm not sure what could make it right even now."

Carla changed the subject. "What about that Harley Ponyboy? He's an amusing little guy—I couldn't help noticing him the other night at the party. Did he go to school with the others?"

"Harley wasn't from around here back then; he only went to school when they could catch him...which wasn't often. He's from up around Monument Valley. It was another world up there at the time he was growing up. He came from old-school traditional people—they would hide him out when the government agents came around. When he was older, he moved down here to find work and then became friends with Thomas. They were both drinkers for a while but not now, not Thomas anyway. Harley's still off and on, though he hasn't gone to the bottle in a long time."

Carla rearranged the food on her plate, took another bite, reflected back on a time she seldom had reason to think of. "My father worked at several different BIA affiliated schools over the years. But I mainly grew up in Durango."

Lucy Tallwoman was not sure what caused this to register. In an instant it had disappeared, as though filtered out or blocked, and she thought no more about it. "So, you aren't married, Carla? No children?" She blushed, "I mean, I know not everyone is married, at least not out in the real world."

The woman smiled at this. "No, I have no children …never married." She touched her cheek. "I'm not sure which of us is living in the *real* world." She tilted her head to one side as she said, "I understand Caleb and Ida Marie are Thomas's children from another marriage? No children of your own?"

Lucy looked down at her plate, then up. "I had a daughter, her name was Alice, but she is no longer with us."

"Oh, I'm so sorry…I've often thought if things were different…I might have wanted a daughter myself."

"Well, it's not like you don't have time yet." Lucy was smiling when she said this but there was a touch of sadness in it, too.

"Oh, I doubt that's going to happen now. I'm a 'career agent', as they say in the Bureau. I suppose I'll always be one. Working for the FBI isn't really conducive to leading any sort of normal life. There *are* those who seem able to manage it, of course, but that's not me."

Lucy Tallwoman, not certain now where the conversation was headed, changed the subject. "I'd like to get your recipe for this eggplant dish some time. My bunch aren't open to many new foods, but I think Thomas and my dad might like this. The kids…well, I'm not really sure." She was thinking, *Jesus, I guess I really don't get out much these days...* She seldom even left the reservation unless Sue Yazzie invited her on some contrived mission—shopping usually, or a quick trip to Farmington for lunch. Lucy brought her thoughts back to the conversation…trying to concentrate on what Carla was saying…something about a New York gallery opening the next week.

15

Fate

Archie found the side street, and after spotting the restaurant, did a double take at the pickup parked out front. He was halfway down the block before admitting to himself he may have just seen Lucy Tallwoman's truck. The late model Ford parked in front of the eatery was a dead ringer for the one he'd seen earlier that morning down below in the camp. But only as he shot a glance in his rearview mirror, did he become absolutely certain. There was the skewed and weathered sticker on the front bumper: "You're in Indian Country." Earlier that morning he'd been unable to read the smaller print, now he whispered it to himself, "KTNN voice of the Navajo Nation."

He parked the Chevy well down the street. *What are the odds...?* He slid his pickup into an empty space and took a moment to study on it, then smiled. *No reason not to have a look, Archie...no one knows you around here.* Still smiling as he entered the restaurant, he immediately spotted Lucy Tallwoman at a front table, riveted to what the woman across from her was saying.

Approached by the hostess Archie pointed to one of the small tables toward the rear.

As the man passed their table, Lucy Tallwoman, caught up in the conversation, seemed not to notice. Carla, however, managed a covert glance. She was trained to be aware and without missing a beat, thought, *so this is the infamous Archie Blumker...I thought he'd be taller...otherwise; he looks exactly like his file photos.*

Archie, choosing a chair facing toward the front, accepted the menu but barely glanced at it before asking a question. He then immediately gave the hostess his order without waiting for the server—passing the menu back to the woman without looking up. She frowned, scribbled something down and handed it to the first passing waiter. Surprised, he immediately turned back to the kitchen and then returned with a large tureen of something, which he delivered to the table before taking the man's drink order. Raising his eyebrows at the hostess, the server then crossed to the bar and in only moments returned to the table with an icy mixed drink ...tall and clear...with a twist. It was the best the house had to offer.

Lucy Tallwoman, facing toward the rear of the dining room, inadvertently glanced the new diner's way a time or two and once caught him watching her. He held her gaze a moment then looking down at his dinner, devoted his attention to the Zuppa di Mare and didn't look her way again.

No more than a casual curiosity, Lucy was sure.

As the two women chatted back and forth, laughing now and again at some little something, Carla took out her compact and checked her makeup as she talked. After only a moment she asked, "Is the man at the back table someone you know?" She pretended to dab at her nose as she studied the diner in the mirror.

"No, I don't think I've ever seen him. I noticed him looking this way and figured he's just curious...you don't see many Navajos in restaurants like this...not around here you don't." Lucy chanced another quick look at the man and was certain he wasn't anyone she knew. He seemed absorbed in his dinner now—not interested in anything else.

"I remember this sort of thing growing up in Durango. People there consider themselves liberals nowadays, recent arrivals most of them, but back then you saw it all the time. I understand what you're saying, but things are changing. It won't always be like this." Her voice took on a pensive note. "You are the sort of person who might hurry those changes along should you take an interest."

Lucy contemplated the woman sitting across from her. *How are we so different, you and I? I can't even imagine what you are talking about?*

Carla held Lucy's gaze as though channeling her thoughts; leaning forward she held up a finger. "In many ways we are the same, you and I. It is only circumstance that has set us on different paths. Circumstances change. I'm thinking you could have a bigger voice in your people's affairs than you might think—this could be just the beginning for you."

16

The Surprise

Back in his room Archie immediately noticed the flashing red message light on the phone. He took his time mixing a drink and turned the television to the local news, muting the sound as he took a long sip. Kicking off his shoes he stacked the pillows and leaned back to follow the silent screen. Occasionally he would turn an eye to the blinking light but remained stubbornly determined to finish his drink before looking into it. It had been in the back of his mind he might hear from Percy tonight. Other than leaving a contact number, he hadn't reported in for several days. That would not ordinarily have been a concern but the Factor had seemed anxious about this operation from the very beginning. This had the ever-suspicious former cop thinking there might be more to this particular project than he was told.

Archie savored the icy beverage a few minutes longer then reached for the phone with a sigh. But before he could pick it up there came a knock at the door. He slipped the automatic pistol from the nightstand and tucked it into the back of his waistband. Draining the last of his drink, he eased over to the door on stocking feet to peer through the peephole. There was no one to be seen. The security chain went up and the door cracked for a better view. Whoever was out there had been well tutored.

Archie said quietly, "Step into view please. I like to see who I'm talking to."

The answering voice was calm and obviously female. "I was told you were a cautious man...and a dangerous one, too."

Archie mentally shifted gears, relaxing slightly. *Not that a woman couldn't be treacherous,* he mused, *but it did reduce the odds.* When she moved into view, he instantly recognized her as the person he'd seen earlier having dinner with Lucy Tallwoman.

"Percy sent you," was his instant assessment.

"Yes...he did."

Archie unlatched the security chain and with an amused twist of his head, ushered her inside. He moved across the room to lift the phone receiver...then put it back down and watched as the light went out.

She smiled. "I thought perhaps you hadn't seen the message light."

Without returning the woman's smile he replied, "I was resting."

"Well then, I'm sorry to interrupt. Unfortunately I was told you and I need to talk...tonight. Percy said it would be all right."

At his direction, Carla moved past him and settled herself in a chair at the far side of the table where she boldly looked him over and quickly made a mental determination, *This is a person who makes certain he is in control at all times.* She would have expected nothing less from a man she'd been told never got excited or lost focus.

She glanced around the room, "Percy was right again," She said. "You know who I am."

"I do now. You're Carla …Percy's spoken of you enough over the years. There's a picture of you as a young girl on a shelf above his desk." Archie paused, and downing the last of his drink, murmured apologetically, "I didn't recognize you this afternoon…because of the age difference from then to now, I suppose. I had the impression the Factor thinks of you almost as the child he never had." Archie rose and directed her attention toward the little refrigerator in the corner. "Can I get you a drink? I think I'm going to have another."

She waved the suggestion away and went on. "I was fortunate enough to be one of the few recipients of a Vermeer Foundation grant, first to study law…and later art. It was a generous and ongoing endowment." She looked him in the eye. "I worked hard to justify it." Carla turned away from the shrouded window as though she'd seen something unpleasant beyond the drapes. "My own father was a distant relative of Percy's. The Factor never really cared for him though he did somehow feel responsible for my mother and me…a sentiment that continued after her death."

Archie pursed his lips and shook his head. "I didn't know that…but it explains a lot. Is Percy still in touch with him…your father, I mean?"

"No, my father's dead, and a long time ago."

"Ah, well I'm sorry to hear that."

"You needn't be. He wasn't a particularly good person. He wound up taking his own life when I was in high school. I seldom think of him. My mother later remarried, one of my father's distant cousins oddly enough, and my new stepfather became the highpoint of both our lives."

"And so, it's only now you've been called upon to provide a service? He must think me in serious need of help?"

"He *was* disappointed in how the Clifford Johnson affair played out. He said it wasn't like you to let things get out of hand."

Archie grimaced. "Everyone was disappointed in the end. Even those responsible expressed considerable regret. That liability has, however, been neutralized as far as possible."

Carla raised her eyebrows and touched the tip of her tongue to her lip. "So, it *was* you…"

Archie shrugged and brought the conversation back to her. "Percy holds you in the highest regard. He mentioned you were working with the FBI…art recovery I believe. He was quite proud of that. He said you might make a valuable member of our team one day, should that be your choice."

"I owe Percy Vermeer a great deal." Carla paused, and then for a moment turned pensive. "Still, I consider whatever might pass between you and I to be confidential…you needn't worry on that account."

"Oh, I'm not worried, Carla, I'm well aware where your loyalties lie—either of us speaking out of turn could have consequences." Archie narrowed an eye. "Now then, what does Percy believe you can help me with?"

"Well, it seems there are recent developments… Information you might not be aware of."

Archie smiled. "Well, I'm not surprised. I *have* been rather 'out of pocket', as they say out here."

She nodded. "Exactly, and we understand that. The crux of the matter is Percy has reason to believe there is another faction, working behind the scenes, to consolidate control over certain segments of the Native art market. Might even be a global enterprise, he thinks. He's certain they are involved somehow with Raul Ortiz, and possibly responsible for several recent attempts to coerce collectors, galleries and even auction houses, to give them preferential consideration. Some of these overtures were quite aggressive—a few involving violence of one sort or another." Carla hesitated before going on. "This appears to be a well-orchestrated consortium, with long ties to foreign financial interests."

Archie sighed beneath a furrowed brow. "You'll forgive me for saying so, but Percy does sometimes jump to conclusions. Does he have any idea who they are?"

"Only rumor—little pieces of information, all hard won I might add—but from sources he considers reliable. He's become convinced their plan has already been put into motion, a plan that might leave him out of the picture entirely." Carla hesitated. "Percy believes, at this juncture, these people plan to compromise several prominent Native artists, insure their exclusivity, so to speak."

"Compromise? As in, eliminate?"

"He's convinced they might go that far."

"And he thinks Lucy Tallwoman might be one of the people in harm's way?" Archie pressed the issue, his curiosity aroused.

Carla directed a cool glance his way. "He made that quite clear in our last discussion."

"Well that puts a different perspective on things doesn't it?" From his brief time with Big Ray Danson, and then Raul Ortiz, he'd come to believe something quite different. Both men, even under pain of death, had vehemently denied any intention of deadly force. It was, of course, possible Raul was unaware of these other client's goals, and only meant to retain some sort of relationship with the trader to facilitate his own hidden agenda. Archie knew from experience that this other client might well have a hidden agenda. It was all beginning to make sense…in a twisted sort of way.

"Percy has become quite concerned for the safety of Lucy Tallwoman and her family." Carla herself sounded worried as she went on, "He learned only yesterday that these *interlopers*, as he refers to them, have already amassed a considerable collection and from very well-known artisans, too. Much of it, I might add, through the auspices of Raul Ortiz."

"Go on… I'm slowly getting your drift, as Raul, himself, was fond of saying."

Carla put her hands flat on the table and leaned forward for emphasis. "Should these artists no longer be producing new pieces—the desirability of their work would increase dramatically. At least that's what Percy thinks is behind it."

"So, Percy's saying he's certain this faction would go so far as to do away with people out here?" Archie wanted to be very clear on the man's thinking. He had never been opposed to killing should there be good reason for it…but then, it wasn't the sort of thing one could call back either. In his view such an action required certainty of purpose.

"It's not unheard of, Archie. Even at the Bureau there are those who tend to consider it a possibility…though granted a remote one, at least to my mind. Still, it's crossed their minds, and is certainly not inconceivable."

Archie scratched his head with one finger and unconsciously rearranged the lock of hair in front. He wasn't a vain man but did concede some aspects of his appearance might be key to his image, and image could be everything in his line of work. As quick as this thought occurred to him he put it aside. It made him uncomfortable.

"What, does Percy propose I do about these people?"

"We…he said *we*… could decide—but left me with the impression you'd know what to do."

Archie heaved a sigh and took a prolonged sip of his second drink. "I see…well, I'll look into it. Perhaps, should you hear anything from your sources at the Bureau, you could give me a heads up…if it's not too much trouble."

Carla nodded in such a way he felt she was not particularly enthused with the suggestion—but there was absolutely no doubt in his mind that she would let him know.

17

Serendipity

Charlie Yazzie studied his burgeoning in-basket with a guilty eye and almost decided to forego lunch. It had been a wilder weekend than usual on the *Dinétah* making for even more arrests and complaints than generally was the case. This Monday morning might prove to be the heaviest day of the month. The responsible thing to do would be to stay with it; try to make a dent in the still growing stack of reports.

Only two hours later, however, the Investigator lifted his head to eye the clock and have second thoughts about lunch. Hunger was punishing him. The old people had a saying: "Denying hunger is one of life's finest tortures." This is how Charlie interpreted it. When said in old Navajo, of course, it was not nearly so poetic. Hunger was torturing him all right. It was gnawing at him like a hungry dog. Watching the minute hand on the clock inch its way toward noon, it occurred to the Investigator he might, if he hurried, slip in before the lunch crowd over at the *Diné Bikeya*. The posting on the office bulletin board that morning was lurking at the back of his mind; the special today was white beans and ham-hocks…with cornbread. It was a dish his grandmother had been partial to. He hadn't cared for it so much as a child, but of late, found his mind turning to it occasionally. It *had* been a long time.

He was just taking his coat down off the hook when the intercom buzzed. He was thinking he hadn't really wanted a line of coat hooks in his office but his wife thought coats hanging on the backs of chairs looked unprofessional. As the former office manager, Sue had developed certain personal predilections in office décor. It was his opinion the coat hooks made the place look like a barbershop.

The buzzer became more persistent, and Charlie looked through the glass to see the receptionist relentlessly poking the call button. He turned back to his own machine and held down the answer key, saying in as nice a way as possible, "What is it Arlene? I was just leaving for lunch..." He could see the woman squinting back at him through thick horn-rimmed glasses. *Those are new* he thought and judged them less attractive than her previous ones.

"Uh... Sir... maybe you could just stop by the desk on the way out? It'll only take a second, Mr. Yazzie. It's not something I want to announce for everyone in the office to hear." This caused everyone in the office to turn an ear that way. Arlene was one of the better receptionists they'd had of late and, by all accounts, the most discreet. He nodded at her through the glass, got his coat, and was at her desk before she realized he was no longer in his office. She took her finger off the button and peered up at him as though the new eyewear had deceived her. Leaning across her desk she assumed an air of confidentiality, and half-whispered, "My mom called and wondered if she might have a word with you after lunch? She'll be through work over at the school cafeteria about one-thirty she said. She could easily stop by then."

The Investigator stared at her a moment and then remembering who her mom was, sighed and offered a wry smile. "This isn't about that parking ticket Frances got last week is it?" He was whispering, too, by now, "I thought Officer Red Clay already took care of that?"

"Well maybe...she hasn't really heard much on it yet. But she didn't pay the fine either—like Billy told her not to." Arlene shrugged. "She's not in jail yet, so she figures that's a sign he's working on it."

"I'm sure she's in good hands with Billy." Charlie looked toward the door... "So, what *is* it your mother wants to talk about, Arlene?"

"Well, sir, she wouldn't say what it was exactly. She just wants to tell you about something that happened the day they found Clifford Johnson's body. She says she don't want anyone putting a spell on her for spreading rumors, but thinks she ought to let you know. I guess she's thinking it's payback for helping her get out of that parking ticket Hastiin Sosi gave her."

Charlie rolled his eyes and glanced at his watch. "Fine, you tell her to drop by after lunch then. But mention I'm busy today, Arlene, I doubt I'll have much time to talk."

Arlene smiled and followed him to the door, raising her voice in parting. "She's not a long talker, Mr. Yazzie, she'll be quick about it. You know she appreciates you helping her fix that ticket."

Charlie looked around to see if anyone was listening. Several obviously were. Shaking his head and frowning he hissed, "Please don't say *fix* the ticket, Arlene, that's not what this was about."

The woman put a finger to her lips and made a downward motion with the other hand, whispering, "Mums the word, Sir," and nodded him out the door.

A cold front had moved in during the pre-dawn hours. The sky, still brilliantly blue, carried the usual harbingers of an early Fall, air so clear and crisp he could see the trickle of steam rising from the power plant on the San Juan. The river, still low despite recent rains. *Almost time to shut down the irrigation headers,* he thought. At the truck he stood a moment, feeling something was amiss, then remembered the sunglasses on top of his head and settled them across his nose. Raising his head to a freshening breeze he took a deep breath and noticed a whiff of coal in the wood smoke from the government housing along the highway. He breathed out and felt a twinge inside—his grandfather died on a Fall day just like this one. He recalled the old man smiling as they moved him out to the brush arbor. He said it was time; he wanted to see the sky, but they knew he wanted his *chindi* to be able to fly free and not hang around to cause people trouble or force the *hogan* to be abandoned.

At the *Diné Bikeyah,* parking spaces near the door were already beginning to fill. Seeing an oilfield truck backing out Charlie positioned himself to slide into the spot, lifting a finger to thank the driver. The burly white man at the wheel glanced his way in the mirror, rubbed the three-day stubble on his chin, and drove off.

The booth he liked best was open and he made a beeline for it. The call from a corner table caught him midstride and he looked over to see Fred Smith and Carla Meyor in the process of ordering. They waved him over and he squeezed by the waitress to take a chair.

Everyone smiled at everyone else and it took no more than a minute or two to complete ordering. Charlie was the only one of the three interested in the special.

"So, how's your day going, Counselor?" Fred gathered the menus, then passed them off to the waitress with a quick smile.

"Busy, busy." Charlie replied, "More than a typical Monday morning, I guess." He was watching Carla from the corner of his eye. She sampled her coffee before raising an eyebrow in greeting. He nodded to the woman and turned back to Fred. "What brings the Bureau out here this morning...couldn't find a decent restaurant in Farmington?"

Carla smiled at this, but Fred didn't. He unrolled his silverware and inspected each piece in turn before answering. "We've been over at the trading post, going over the forensic report, at the scene. We'll probably be there most of the afternoon—checking out a few concerns the accountant had as well. He's just winding up his end." Fred shrugged and went on. "Whoever pulled off the Johnson murder was no amateur. The trader was not the victim of some passing opportunist, that's for sure. The thing was planned and carried out by someone who knew exactly what he was about." He held up a finger. "But even the best occasionally leaves something behind." He gave a smile of satisfaction. "Whoever it was apparently parked behind the trading post, on the far side of Johnson's pickup. You'll recall it rained the day before; the ground back there was still a little muddy. Our guy was able to get a good impression of the tire tracks. It was a black Lincoln Town Car. Albuquerque plates."

"Wow! They could tell all that from the tire tracks? I'm impressed..." Charlie was grinning.

Carla chuckled silently and sipped again at her coffee.

Fred looked past the Investigator and couldn't help smiling himself. "No, as it turns out, our people down there in Albuquerque already have the car impounded in a double murder investigation. The mud in the fender wells was from up here, right here at the trading post, in fact. The driver, who was found dead in the car, had ties to a well-known Albuquerque crime family. Whether or not it was the driver who did the Johnson murder we've yet to determine; the Lincoln apparently got passed around a good bit."

Fred let this sink in. "We've had our eye on the Ortiz bunch for some time—international dealers in Native American art—also known to provide 'professional quality' people with special talents...for a price, of course."

The thought occurred to Charlie that Lucy Tallwoman might be unintentionally caught up in something far more dangerous than she had been made aware of.

Carla, watching Charlie, assumed he might still be a little puzzled, and interjected, "The forensic person, already working on the Lincoln, happened to be the one who processed the tire molds from up here. The car was wearing very expensive tires. The tech says he doesn't see many of that brand, so it didn't take him long to put it together. Serendipity, I guess."

Charlie never ceased to be amazed at the science-rich proficiency of the FBI labs. It was no wonder they were considered the best in the world. He nodded to both agents. "Now I *am* impressed." Still he couldn't help thinking to himself *all they lack is a tracker like Harley Ponyboy.*

The food came and the Feds looked askance at the steaming white beans and ham hock special the waitress put in front of Charlie. The Investigator noticed and grinned back at them.

Fred tied into his *huevos rancheros.* As a local boy he was aware the dish wasn't just for breakfast in this country. It was on all three meal-menus at the *Diné Bikeyah.*

Carla only picked at her chicken salad, and Charlie thought her preoccupied during the whole of the meal. She caught him looking her way once or twice and figured he might still be trying to place her from their time at NMU; his attention caused her to put her head down and concentrate on her food.

~~~~~~~

Back at the office Charlie barely had time to reorganize his workload before the intercom alerted him. Looking to the outer office he saw Arlene's mother, still in her school cafeteria uniform—standing at her daughter's desk. He frowned down at the in-box and then shaking his head looked up and signaled Arlene to send Francis on back. He thought he remembered the woman's last name being Benally—one of the ten most common names on the reservation—along with Yazzie, Begay, Nez and a few others. He smiled at the observation, thinking now how ordinary his name really was.

The door swung open and he attempted a smile as Frances came in. He indicated the chair across from his desk and greeted her in Navajo.

The woman sat herself on the edge of the chair, keeping her hands clasped nervously in her lap. She replied in kind, then immediately got down to business in English. "My daughter says you're busy, Mr. Yazzie, so I'll try not to take up too much of your time this afternoon." She straightened in the chair slightly and lifted her chin in a forced show of confidence. "It's about that morning they found trader Johnson over there at the trading post. As I may have told you last time, I have to be at work by five in the morning and that Saturday I was a little earlier even than that. Anyhow, just as I turned at the four-way...the one just before the trading post...that's where I turn to go to the school. I happened to look over and see a car parked back there behind the building. It's not that far... When my lights hit it I could see who it was plain as day." The woman paused to catch her breath.

"A big black car, Frances, with a large man at the wheel?" Charlie thought this was interesting and would tie in with what he'd just heard at lunch. He picked up his pen and began taking notes on a yellow legal pad.

Arlene's mother looked confused for just a second. "No... Why would you think that?" She raised her hands and declared. "It wasn't that way at all. It was Louise Johnson in her blue Chevy. She looked up when she saw my lights. She looked surprised—I could see her plain as the nose on your face. I pass by there every day on my way from work and there her Chevy was, right there beside her husband's pickup truck. I had just never seen her there so early before—just her, sitting with the overhead light on, like the door might be open a crack like she was waiting for someone." Frances assumed a blank expression. "I just thought it was strange, that's all."

Charlie looked at his notes and clicked his pen in and out a few times. "And this was a little before five o'clock Saturday morning? I didn't know anyone worked in the school kitchen on a weekend?"

"I wasn't working in the kitchen that Saturday. I clean classrooms on weekends…just to make ends meet. They hold remedial classes up there on Saturday mornings so I have to get in and out early. Maybe Arlene told you…I'm by myself now…it takes everything I can do just to get along. When I first moved here Arlene had to help me out a time or two. I hate that. The reason I didn't move in with her and her husband to start with is I didn't want to be a burden on them. You know how it is with mothers-in-law in the same house as their daughter's husbands."

Charlie was silent for a moment. He knew all right, his case files were filled with such arrangements gone bad, not as often as it once had been, but still happening nonetheless.

"Frances this is important. Are you absolutely sure it was Louise Johnson you saw in that car last Saturday morning? Your lights were only on her for a second; could it have been someone else? There are a lot of blue Chevrolets in this part of the country."

Frances pulled herself together, sucked in her breath, and narrowed her eyes at the Investigator. They could hear her in the outer office when she declared. "It was HER ALL RIGHT!"

Charlie held up a calming hand. "I'm sure you know what you saw, Frances, I believe you…I do." He nodded as a validation, of his confidence in the woman. When the Investigator went on, it was in a more conciliatory tone. "Frances, was there anyone else with Louise that you could see?"

"Not that I could see, but my lights were only on her for a second or two." And her interior light went off pretty quick, too."

"Frances, I have to ask you to keep this to yourself, for now." His expression turned deadly serious when he said. "This could be very important down the road. Tell absolutely no one, do you understand what I'm saying, Francis? What about Arlene, does she know?"

"No, Arlene don't know and I won't tell her neither." Frances Benally appeared suddenly frightened by the investigator's tone. She bobbed her head and again swore she wouldn't say anything.

Charlie got the impression she would do as she promised and reached over to pat her hand. "In time, Frances, I will let you know what comes of all this. I want you to know you did the right thing in coming to me."

Twenty minutes after the woman left his office Charlie was still trying to muddle his way through what he'd heard—it still didn't make sense. *If Frances is right and Louise Johnson was at the trading post that morning, it must have been before the killer was there…or at the same time?* For just a moment Charlie thought he should call Fred Smith to run this by him. It would be interesting to see what he could make of it. He was already reaching for the phone when he changed his mind. *By rights, I should go through the Liaison*

Officer. By going around Billy Red Clay I could be alienating a damn good friend and officer.

Charlie batted this around for some minutes before coming to the conclusion there were few options, none of them perfect. This was going to require a light touch, and in the end, someone might still get their feelings hurt. By late-afternoon his mind was still so filled with the events of the day he had hardly made a dent in the stack of reports. What he'd first thought might be a simple robbery attempt had now evolved into something much more complicated. At a little after four o'clock, a shadow fell across his desk. Looking up he was surprised to see Carla Meyor standing in the open door; glancing toward the reception desk, he wondered why Arlene let her pass without letting him know.

The FBI Agent caught the look and hooking a thumb toward the front desk apologized, "Sorry about that; I waited up front for a bit but there was no one at the desk. I could see you back here and decided to just come on back."

"Not a problem at all..." Charlie smiled. "I was looking for an excuse to take a break, and here you are. Please, Carla, have a chair—Arlene must have stepped out for a minute." He glanced again at the front office and saw the receptionist already settling herself back in at her station. Seeing her look his way with a tilt of her head and a questioning expression, Charlie waved a hand to let her know it was all right, while stating for the record, "Arlene is probably the best office manager we've ever had." He was quick to add, "At least since my wife left the job."

"I'll make my apologies on the way out." Carla, too, gave Arlene a quick wave." Turning back, the smile disappeared, replaced by a more contemplative gaze. "The fact is, Charlie, I thought it time I should explain a few things…about our time at the University…I mean."

"Oh…?" Charlie sat back in his chair and gave the woman his full attention.

She opened her handbag and pulled out a photocopy, obviously taken from an old yearbook. She looked at it and then almost reluctantly it seemed, pushed it across to him.

He took the photo, a heavy-set young woman with stringy brown hair and sallow complexion, eyes overshadowed by large heavy framed glasses. A grimace probably meant as a smile tugged at the corners of her mouth as she slumped toward the camera. Charlie studied the picture for several moments and shrugged his shoulders. "Sorry, I have no idea who this is."

"That's probably because you don't associate it with my current name." The precursor of a grin was breaking over Carla's face.

Charlie came upright in his chair and took a long look at the woman then made a second inspection of the photo. Yes, there it was—the eyes were unmistakably the same—the one thing that changes very little in most people. "Well…if you're serious…and it appears from the look on your face that you are, I would never have guessed this to be you."

"It's not me anymore, Charlie, but it was once. Even my name was different then. It was Foldiere, Carla Benét Foldiere. I went by Benét through my first year at UNM. When my mother remarried it was to my birth father's cousin; she met him through a rare Vermeer family function. Unlike my father he was a kind and gentle man who was well thought of by Percy

Vermeer. Though I was already in high school Carl was generous enough to adopt me and I took his name. By doing so, I became eligible for a considerable educational grant available even to distant family members and, in my case, further sanctioned by Percy himself. Unfortunately, my stepfather was not part of our lives very long. He was killed in an automobile accident not long after my mother's death." She couldn't help frowning at the look on Charlie's face as he toggled back and forth from the picture to the attractive woman now before him. Carla looked down for a moment and then pursing her lips, said, "There are a lot of people who don't remember me from those days. I've only been to one class reunion and that was enough to convince me that I made no great impression back then."

"But you did attend my remedial tutoring sessions your first year?"

"I did indeed, but only for a few sessions. I was usually way in the back and seldom had questions. There was no reason you should have remembered me."

Charlie smiled thoughtfully at the Federal Agent. "Nonetheless, I'm sorry I didn't remember...and even more sorry I pretended I did. That was inexcusable..."

"It's human nature not to be caught out, Charlie, you'd be surprised how often...it's a natural reaction."

Charlie nodded his agreement. "That aside, I'm glad you stopped by. I've spent a lot of time worrying over this and I'm relieved...sort of." He smiled as he looked across the desk at her. "By the way, Carla, I meant to ask at lunch and totally spaced it—has the Bureau heard any more on the whereabouts of Louise Johnson? Tribal has scoured the reservation for word of her and…nothing. I know the Bureau has a long reach and thought there might be something else, somewhere."

Carla thought for a moment as though choosing her words. "Not really. There's the usual unconfirmed sightings, of course, but nothing you could hang your hat on as yet." The agent, obviously good at channeling people's thoughts, eyed him as though she thought he might have some hidden purpose in inquiring.

Charlie quickly picked up on this. "I just thought I'd ask, no real reason beyond curiosity. It just seems unusual, a prominent businesswoman like Louise Johnson disappearing without a trace?"

"I agree. We have several people working on it, but so far, no luck.

"I'm sure that end of the investigation is in good hands with you folks. I'll be anxious to hear what you come up with."

The Agent nodded her assurance indicating she would let him know.

On his way home that evening, with a folder of reports yet to finish, Charlie still was not sure why he didn't tell the agent about Frances Benally's visit. He rationalized this to himself as wanting the information to come from Billy Red Clay—with a view to shoring up the Liaison Officer's admittedly tenuous position. They would have to let the FBI know eventually, of course, but he thought it could wait until Billy got the message he'd left him earlier.

Glancing down at the yearbook photo of Carla Meyor beside him he nodded to himself. *She'd purposely left that lying on the desk.* Good! *Maybe it would help bring about a ceasefire with Sue.*

18

The Amalgamation

It was almost midnight when Archie's phone beeped to indicate a message. He rolled over with a groan to check the time. It took a moment for his mind to make the adjustment—it was nearly two A.M. back east—it would not be Percy Vermeer at this hour. That left Carla, the only other person who had the number. Flicking on the lamp he gave himself time to come fully awake. The flashing red light was just enough to illuminate his unshaven face in the mirror on the closet door. He paused at the image, haggard, older now than he realized. He reached for the phone and grunted into the receiver.

"Sorry...but you said to let you know should anything new turn up." She sounded almost cheerful.

Archie imagined a smile on the woman's face. "Louise Johnson... Right?"

"Yes... They found her car at a sleazy motel a couple of hours from here. Grants, New Mexico."

"Still no idea what's become of her though?"

"Not really...not for sure...there was an empty pill bottle on the nightstand. It remains to be seen if that was a factor. It's hard to say how this is going to wind up. She may have decided to make a run for it, and this was part of her plan...or who knows...she could have been abducted.

"How long since she was last seen...anything on that?"

"Not long, four or five hours, from what I saw in the preliminary" There was a short silence. "It seems she had a visitor earlier in the evening; apparently not unusual for that particular motel. According to the night clerk the person didn't stay long and it's not sure when the car left, probably no more than a half-hour or so.

"A man?"

"Yes, a man, he thought. He couldn't see the plates but thought it looked like a rental. Being discreet is apparently part of their business model. Louise may have gone willingly or...there's the chance she may have been taken."

Carla yawned. She'd been up all night. "I'll keep you posted," she murmured before hanging up.

Archie smiled and replaced the receiver. Percy's information had been correct after all, apparently there *was* another interest at work. That was going to complicate an already complicated situation. He looked again in the mirror and lifted his chin...there was no denying it, he was, in fact, getting old.

He woke at four and again at six, unable to sleep after the call. This wasn't like Archie; he normally slept well regardless of the situation. He felt no real sense of urgency—he had a pretty good idea what he was up against now. He shaved and dressed, then called down to the desk to inquire if the breakfast bar was open?

He positioned himself with a view of the outer lobby and set his roll and coffee down with the determination to relax a few moments before tackling the day. It might be his last opportunity for a while. He glanced at the complimentary newspaper on the table, folded the front page, and propped it against the napkin dispenser. The Johnson murder was front and center. He glanced at the date and saw it was yesterday's paper. A picture of the murdered trader and his wife, obviously taken in happier days, took up a quarter of the page. Archie put his tongue to his teeth and made a tsk, tsk, tsk. *Too bad the pair had not been more amenable to Percy's earlier proposals...all this could have been avoided.*

Percy, he was sure, would be saddened by the news, though Archie felt certain it would only make him more determined...that was just Percy.

Archie stretched and contemplated the roll on its saucer. It was the last one on the tray and he had taken it against his better judgment—he wasn't in the mood for cold cereal. He was a man who enjoyed his amenities, and this didn't fit the bill. Probably it was his continual deployment to the backcountry that was causing him to feel a bit jaded. He might even be losing his edge...that could be serious. The Factor had, several times of late, mentioned Archie's eventual retirement, assuring him there would be an ongoing and generous stipend along with their undying gratitude for his valuable service over the years. Percy made it clear the time to call it quits would be entirely up to him. Archie had never really thought about retirement, but he was thinking about it now. The problem was he didn't know what he would do with so much free time. He thought he might like to take up fly-fishing—this though he'd only ever caught the one fish. The trout he'd hooked up by Jemez.

He looked over the top of his paper as he took the last sip of the now lukewarm coffee and then picked at the crumbs left on the saucer. A Federal Express man pushing a package-dolly crossed the lobby to the front desk. Archie instantly felt better, these could be the things he was waiting for, things he might need and hadn't been able to bring with him. When the lobby cleared, he made his way to the desk and asked if he had a delivery.

The manager sat his readers lower on his nose, squinted up at Archie, finally smiling his recognition. "Ah yes... Mr. Jones, I believe. We do have something for you this morning, overnighters, both of them." He disappeared through the doorway behind him and quickly returned with the parcels. As he hefted the larger one up on the desk, exclaimed, "My, that's a heavy one." He glanced at the declaration label. "Survey instruments...eh? Well, I hope there's nothing broken? Would you like to open it and see if it's all right...while I'm here to witness? We seem to be having a lot of that lately." He glanced expectantly at Archie, as though checking for damage would be the logical thing to do.

Archie had actually been expecting only one package and regarded the smaller packet with curiosity. Finally, he became aware of what the manager was saying and looked up for a moment. Archie lifted the larger of the two and stood it on end against the desk. It was addressed to Ed Jones, San Juan Field Services...but in care of the motel. He smiled at the bold blue stencil declaring it 'Survey Equipment'. Archie shook his head. "I'm sure it's fine. These particular instruments are pretty much bullet proof."

Archie nodded his acceptance. The smaller package, in a special delivery tear-proof envelope, was also addressed to Ed Jones, but from an altogether different sender. Signatures were required and Archie signed for each with a flourish.

The motel manager watched him go with an odd look on his face, and then jotted something on a paper.

Back in his room Archie snapped the security chain in place and leaned the long box against a chair. He knew what *it* was, and who sent it.

Taking off his jacket Archie directed his attention to the envelope. Fishing a small penknife from his pocket he sliced open the flap. Inside was a folder of dossiers complete with carefully documented photos. He glanced at the title "The S-4 Report". He had no idea what that meant. He set himself down at the table and began reading. Thirty minutes later he sat back in his chair, rubbed his forehead a moment and again sifted through the photos. He took particular note of the detailed inscription on the back of each one and committed to memory as much of it as possible. Nibbling thoughtfully at his upper lip Archie slipped the packet of photos into his pocket and replaced the folder in the envelope.

The report had been prepared by Percy's private staff and encoded in terms no outsider was likely to decipher. It was not at all what Archie might have hoped it would be... He realized now that things were much worse than he had anticipated. There was no doubt this material had cost Percy a great deal, and not just in money, either. In a briefing, only days earlier, an intermediary had mentioned one of their foreign-service people had been compromised. Archie had worked with the woman from time to time and held her in high regard. She was well versed in international intrigue and an expert in the sketchier side of the art world—she would be missed. The loss weighed on Archie even now. The Vermeer Foundation demanded the very best people in their field, the sort of people who were neither easy to find...nor to replace. This might explain Carla being here.

The Factor did not condone retribution in such instances, but despite his policy to the contrary, it sometimes happened. While he didn't personally require satisfaction in that regard, he knew Archie Blumker would demand it. Percy seldom interfered with the man's personal sense of duty—his loyalty, once given, was absolute. Archie's methodology was always meticulously conceived and precisely executed. Percy felt he had little to fear from any retribution Archie might deem necessary. His organization was, of necessity, a tightly knit group. And it was Archie that held them together. Percy Vermeer understood what made him tick, and knew Archie wouldn't be Archie without his more primordial impulses.

Now, sitting quietly in his room, Archie went back over the report in his mind...again and again. There was now a glimmer of understanding of Carla's oddly fortuitous arrival. He removed the folio from the package and began rereading with a view to narrowing the field of operatives. The names wouldn't matter, those would change as required. Even appearances could be altered to some extent. It was the carefully compiled personal information that would be key. There were detailed descriptions, mannerisms and special skills listed. Those were important. According to the report, only three people were known to be working for the opposing consortium as free agents, and just two of them with the level of expertise required. He doubted more than one would be sent. Maybe only one...but he would be the best money could buy, and like Archie himself, would have the advantage of unlimited resources.

It took him over an hour to sift through the possibilities and pick the most probable operatives. They were impressive; youth aside, there was already enviable track records...something not taken lightly even by the likes of Archie Blumker. He couldn't help dwelling a moment on his own reflection in the mirror. He did somehow look older, just in these last weeks if that was possible, and for the very first time ceded he might now be past his better days. There comes a point when wisdom gained is no longer a match for the resilience and stamina of youth. Faster, smarter, tougher was the name of the game. Disquieting as the thought was, Archie forced himself to brush it aside. It was not the mindset for so formidable an undertaking as this. He did still hold a few cards and while no one of them would give him a deciding edge, taken all together they might suffice. His main advantage at this point was that he knew both the country and the people.

At least two of those on his list were from Europe. They would be out of their element. There is more to this game than intrigue and mayhem. He knew that for a fact. Prior knowledge of the playing field was essential to his way of thinking. He would beat them on experience.

19

The Awakening

Lucy Tallwoman had reached a determination. Her continuing association with the more enlightened Sue Yazzie, coupled now with the more sophisticated Carla Meyor's new friendship, had brought her to a completely different level of self-awareness. Carla's entire outlook on life went beyond anything she had ever imagined for herself. In the end these were the things that decided her once and for all. *I am through being that person who has no goal or life beyond this house and my weaving.*

Sue Yazzie had long recognized Lucy's hidden abilities and often had counseled her to think of expanding her outlook on life.

It is time my life took a different direction. The children will soon be grown, my father gone—what then? Carla's interest in her growing fame as an artisan was further inspiration to use that recognition as a steppingstone to higher goals. Goals that might make a real difference for her family, and possibly, even her people.

Lucy Tallwoman's thoughts were racing as she sat at her loom, fingers flying, almost without conscious direction. *Why, there was already one woman on the tribal council, a woman of common background, too, and much like herself. Why couldn't she do something like that?* The idea was so mind bending it caused a catch in her breath. She stopped, let her hands fall to her lap, and gazed out the window. *Why am I thinking like this? I am not an educated person...I have no qualifications.* Then, she chided herself, *neither has that other woman on the Council.* That one, in fact, has no credentials, beyond a wide social circle and the support of a large clan. And look at her! she was already making her mark. The woman campaigned for only the one thing—advanced health care for the reservation— apparently that had been enough. Lucy narrowed an eye at the horizon. There was more than one desperate need on the *Diné Bikeya.*

~~~~~~~

Thomas Begay stood by the corrals quietly watching as Paul T'Sosi tried to separate a lamb from the gang of youngsters it ran with. It had a hurt foot and seemed thin to the old man. He wanted a look at it. Already the animal was trying to lie down. Sheep are easily discouraged when life doesn't go their way and most are born quitters. Once one decides it's sick enough to lie down it can be down hill from there. Paul, seeing he couldn't catch the ailing animal, finally threw up his hands and came to the fence breathing in short bursts, his face grey with dust.

"We need to get that lamb up to the shed and see what we can do for it," Paul said between gasps.

Thomas pointed his chin at the injured animal. "I'll catch him up when I feed, Paul. What are you doing out here so early anyway?"

The old man eyed his son-in-law. "I was out taking a little walk to greet the sun when I noticed this lamb not being right."

"I been seeing you heading up the hill every morning at daylight, Paul. What's that about?" Thomas didn't look at the old man when he asked this, but it was plain he expected an answer.

Paul moved closer to the fence grasping the top rail for a moments support. "Someone's been watching us from up there." The old man looked over his shoulder at the ridge behind the house, "First one, and now another one…different tracks this time…watching us from the big shaggy bark on the point." After a moment the old man recovered his breath and continued, "I almost caught up with that one but he made off before I got a good look at him. He wasn't a big man but he could move fast. The other one came the day before, I think, a smaller person by his track. Both of them came up the old trail along the ridge. I don't know…maybe they are taking turns watching us. Why would someone go to so much trouble to keep an eye on us?"

Thomas Begay stared at the old man for a moment, then shook his head. "I don't know, Paul. I think she has your breakfast ready though, you better go on up to the house. I'll have Caleb catch up that sick lamb." He paused, and sounded determined when he said, "Harley and I will look into this business up on the hill. It's nothing for you to worry yourself about, Paul. We'll take care of it."

Later, after Paul had eaten his breakfast and returned to the corrals, he supervised Caleb as the boy caught up the lamb and the two of them took it to the shed.

"Did that friend of yours give you those coyote gitters, Grandfather? Lucy said you and Harley were in town yesterday."

"I got 'em."

"Was there a good many of them?"

"There was enough. He said he had more, should we someday need 'em."

~~~~~~~~

Thomas took Lucy aside and told her what the old man had said about someone watching. "I don't know if Paul saw anything up there on the hogback or not, he might have imagined it for all I know. But I called over to Charlie's place. Harley's been staying over there the last few days while he works up their pasture. Charlie can't seem to find time to do it himself." He chuckled, "He still hasn't figured that tractor out." Thomas rolled his eyes toward the hogback. "Harley will have a look up there and see what he can find, if there *is* anything to find." He said this last as though he somehow doubted Harley would find anything. "One thing I do know is the old man has no business climbing that hill. He's getting to where his balance is off. The least misstep could cause him a fall that could be the end of him."

Lucy nodded thoughtfully and then agreed, "I suppose you're right, I'll talk to him." Privately though, she was worried that telling her father he couldn't leave camp might further impact an already fragile self-image.

"I don't like it," she said, finally. "But when he comes back in the house, I will try to ease into it and maybe see what's on his mind." What Thomas told her hit home. Charlie had advised caution and to stay inside—hold off going into town for a day or two. "Fred Smith at the FBI has reason to be uneasy with your situation. He'll let us know if something changes."

As the sun passed its zenith and headed toward the mesas to the west, Thomas poked his head in the door. "Charlie's coming... He's got Harley with him."

Lucy stood under the shelter of the porch and watched as her husband walked out to meet the truck. She didn't follow. This would be up to the men. Harley got down from the Chevy first, but Charlie remained looking toward the hogback, then shook his head and got down himself. The three of them stood behind the truck and talked, casting the occasional glance over the cab and up to the ridge above camp.

Lucy watched for a moment, then turned and went inside to put on a pot of coffee. *These men know what to do. They can handle this* she thought.

~~~~~~~~

Harley Ponyboy listened intently as Thomas filled them in on what Paul T'Sosi thought he saw up on the ridge, making it clear he had some doubt. He wound things up by saying "I decided to give Harley here a chance to look things over before we go tromping around up there and maybe confuse whatever sign might still be readable."

"That was the right way to think, Big Guy." Harley's uncanny ability to work his way past muddled indicators was well known, but in this instance less might be more. He nodded. "I'll go up there alone first and try ta figure out what's what before things get all torn up. If Charlie has to call in the FBI, they're going ta mess it up for sure. They always do." He cast a calculating gaze at the point above camp. "We can decide what ta do after we know more…it shouldn't take long…at least I don't think it will."

Thomas frowned at the thought of Charlie calling in Federal Agents. *Hell, if the situation is like the old man says, the people spying on this camp might even be the FBI.*

Thomas turned to the tracker and nodded. "Okay, Harley, we'll do it your way…that's why we called you in on this, I guess." He turned to Charlie with a toss of his head toward the house. "Let's go inside and get some coffee." He beckoned across the way to Paul T'Sosi who stood silently watching.

The old man had just come out of the lambing shed where Caleb still worked on the injured lamb. At Thomas's signal he waved back and then he too, headed towards the house. Paul turned before reaching the porch to follow Harley's trudge up the hill; He remained staunch in his belief Harley Ponyboy would prove him right. *Then, by God, we'll see how crazy I am.* The old man was fed up with everyone thinking he'd lost it.

Inside, Paul, along with the other two, arranged themselves at the kitchen table sipping the coffee his daughter brought—none of them speaking, each with his own line of thought on what Harley might find on the ridge.

Lucy Tallwoman, at the stove, watched the three through the steam from her own cup, waiting to see who would be first to speak. She caught her husband's eye and for a moment thought he would say something, but Charlie Yazzie spoke before Thomas had a chance.

Looking across the table at Thomas Begay the Investigator thought he saw those old familiar signs of rebellion. "You weren't thinking of taking on this little problem by yourself, were you?" He knew how Thomas figured things and thought he'd best get out ahead of that curve. "That's the last thing you need to be thinking." Over the years, the two friends had been through a lot and each owed the other...neither was shy about saying what was on their mind.

Thomas looked up at the ceiling through nearly closed eyes and mentally withdrew. That, in itself, was a bad sign, and everyone in the room knew it. Lucy shot him a hard look. She knew her husband wasn't a talker. He was a doer, generally giving little thought to any consequences his actions might cause.

Looking around the table with a frown, the lanky Navajo uncrossed his legs and rose to move to the window. He stood, not seeing anything beyond what was already in his mind—even that seemed fogged in a red mist. "We'll see what Harley says." He went to the stove for a refill.

Charlie sighed. "Fair enough but keep this in mind; there's lawmen out here with long memories. They're not likely to cut you any slack should you go out of bounds on this thing. The old days are gone. You have a family, kids, to think of now. Those are responsibilities that no one else may be able to handle."

Old Paul T'Sosi raised his coffee and eyed his son-in-law across the rim. He knew Thomas wasn't listening to a word Charlie said. That was part of the reason Paul told him about the interlopers in the first place. Eventually this would be up to the head of the house, and that wasn't him anymore. His daughter was strong willed and would do her best come what may, but in the end, there might be things only Thomas could take care of.

The three men sat at the table for over an hour, waiting for Harley Ponyboy, chatting quietly among themselves, mostly about horses and sheep—none willing to bring up what was really on their mind.

Lucy, eventually tiring of *man talk*, left for the other part of the house where she sat at her loom to ease her worries in the comfort of what she knew best.

On their way back and forth to the coffeepot each of the men would pause to gaze out the window for any sign Harley might be on his way back down. The dog may or may not bark; he'd known Harley since he was a pup. Charlie happened to look toward the corrals as he passed by the window and saw Caleb Begay and his sister. They had taken it upon themselves to move the sheep east of the camp to graze for a bit before dark. The recent rain had started the grass nearly everywhere. *Good for them,* Charlie thought, *they'll grow up to be good people.* The longer he knew these kids, the surer of this he became.

Another half hour passed before the muffled sound of Harley stomping the mud off his boots came from the back entrance, causing them to look toward the kitchen door. Thomas glanced around the table, sat up straighter in his chair and tightened the grip on his cup. Harley would know something one way or the other.

When Harley opened the door from the mudroom and saw three sets of eyes on him the little man blinked but without changing expression. He had what looked like a short piece of pipe in one hand and stuck it in his hip pocket as he moved to the stove where he poured himself a cup. He turned to the table and nodded as Thomas kicked out a chair for him.

Pulling the cylinder from his pocket, Harley sent Paul T'Sosi a questioning glance as he laid it on the table.

Charlie canted his head and eyed the pipe with suspicion. "And that would be…?"

Thomas was shaking his head as he stared at his father-in-law. "Paul, you didn't…"

The old man rose from the table without a word or a glance and left the room.

Harley watched him go with an unhappy look on his face then sighed as he sat down and tested his coffee, even before adding milk and sugar. "It's a coyote *gitter*, Charlie, and it's damn lucky for me I knew what it was before I pulled it out of that knothole."

Charlie sat back and scratched the back of his head. "I didn't think there were any of those left. They've been illegal for years as far as I know." The Investigator had never actually seen one, but had heard the stories.

Thomas eyed the *gitter*. "That damned thing isn't armed is it, Harley?"

Throwing a small beaded swatch on the table beside the pipe Harley grimaced. "Not anymore, it's not." He pointed at the beadwork. "That's the trigger that was left hanging out of the tree-hole it was in. No

Diné would have touched it—thinking it an offering of some sort. Even the kids would have known better than to bother it." He averted his eyes as he spoke. "But, I'll bet you, most whites wouldn't have been able ta resist pulling it out for a look."

"How did *you* know what it was, Harley?" Charlie wouldn't have had a clue...but he wouldn't have messed with it either.

"I probably wouldn't have recognized it...if I hadn't been with the old man last week when he picked up a box of them from someone he had meet him at the Co-op. There were five or six of these things in an old wooden case. I could see Paul didn't want me to know what he had, so I just let on like I didn't know what they were. But I knew all right. I wish now I hadn't taken him ta town in the first place, but I did, and there it is." Harley's voice dropped to a whisper and the other two had to lean in to make out what he was saying. "It took me a bit ta ease it out of that woodpecker hole without it going off; I made sure I was standing up-wind as I pulled it out. I really didn't think it would work as old as it was. I set it off with a long stick and it surprised me when it went off.

Thomas sniffed, "Pretty smart old man, I guess, anyone up there spying is going to wind up under that old cedar. It's the only real cover. He chuckled to himself and elbowed Charlie. "Even you, Charlie— that's where you first came up on our camp in the dead of night." He smiled, "It was old man Paul who spotted *you* back then and called you out."

Charlie smiled in spite of himself nodding at a memory he'd hoped was forgotten.

Harley had heard the story, of course, and smiled along with them.

"What else did you find up there?" Charlie was deadly serious now and so was Thomas. They settled in to hear what he found out...and then decide what they were going to do about it.

Harley, keeping his voice low, said the sign pointed to two separate people, besides Paul, being up on the point recently. Probably, the outsiders were there no more than a few hours apart. "From what I could see both watched and studied the camp for a good bit. They came and went by the same route." Harley paused and again tasted his coffee, making a face as he realized he still hadn't doctored it. "As you might guess, the old man was the last one up there; his was the last tracks going out to the point." Harley forced a grin. "That may be why there was no dead people waiting for me under that tree." He stopped for a moment as he went back over everything in his mind, making sure he had left nothing out. "I expect Paul was right about those two. And he might have had a good chance of getting one of them, too...if I hadn't found that *gitter* first."

Charlie's question was, "I wonder how he thought he'd get rid of a body if someone did fall for his little trap?" He couldn't picture the old man dragging a body out of there by himself, not to mention getting rid of it.

With a halfway smile, Thomas cleared his throat, "I suppose that's where I would have come in." For a brief moment he tried to imagine helping his father-in-law dispose of a body. Thomas was traditional minded enough to abhor the very thought of grabbing hold of a dead person. It had him shaking his head as he fell into a more contemplative frame of mind. The fact of the business was—family *was* family. Clearly, he would have done what he had to do to help old Paul T'Sosi cover the misdeed. He looked over their heads to stare through the window as he murmured, "People disappear on the *Dinétah* all the time. Always have. You both know that."

Charlie glanced over at him. "Lets just be glad it didn't come to that. I don't know what kind of case I could have made for either of you...not one that would have done much good I'm afraid."

Thomas threw him a serious look. "The bottom line is there were two different people up there on that ridge and on separate occasions, too. Whether they were connected or not, we don't know, but I have to think one or the other of 'em *will* be back at some point. Those two were obviously up to no good—you can count on that—we already know there's someone out there willing to kill." He spread the fingers of his right hand and studied it for a few seconds. "I know how Paul must have felt, worried about Lucy and the kids and all. I doubt he would have even thought of something like this had he been in his right mind." No one had an argument for that.

Charlie rubbed his forehead as he sometimes did when he was getting a headache. It didn't happen often, but it was happening now. He started to say something but thought better of it and lowered his head for a moment hoping it would go away.

Harley who hadn't said much up to this point lifted an index finger to the two. "Right now it looks like we either bring in the Feds...or we handle it our own damn self...it wouldn't be the first time."

Charlie appeared uncomfortable with this line of reasoning. But Harley was right; it wouldn't be the first time.

20

The Decision

There was no doubt whatsoever in Archie Blumker's mind, about where all this was headed. Nor was there any doubt who would have to fix it—if it could be fixed. He seriously doubted Carla was equipped to take charge of the situation. FBI training aside, this job would take more than a course in *Covert Intervention*, or whatever the boys down at Quantico were calling it these days. Percy Vermeer, on the other hand, seemed to have an unquenchable faith in the woman, but then Percy had never been in the trenches. The man didn't have a clue as to how the nuts and bolts went together. The question in Archie's mind was—did The Factor intend him to assume responsibility at this point? That's what he would normally do. Or, was he to await instructions from Carla? That was the impression she'd left at their last meeting. The woman had obviously been groomed and manipulated from her school days with an eye to just such a time as this. Who really knew what she could do should push come to shove? One thing he was pretty sure of…things were going to get interesting.

On his way down to the truck, Archie rolled the problem around in the back of his head. He couldn't help returning to the Vermeer Foundation report; he'd spent the entire morning memorizing every word of the file. The photos were indelibly imprinted in his mind, for what that might be worth; should he run into any of these people, they would most likely look nothing at all like their photos. The organization was not unknown to him and he'd long been aware their interests lay in the same area as the Vermeer Foundation. Still, he had never once crossed paths with them and now, in a rare moment of self-doubt, he wasn't sure he wanted to. As he re-ran the information in his mind, he couldn't help wondering *who* they'd sent. Surely it can't be who Percy thinks it is, *the man with no name,* as the report refers to him.

Archie's heard rumors of this particular operative for nearly ten years, a long time for a person in this line of work. He thinks to himself, *he must have some age on him by now.* The thought makes him feel better. His professional pride won't allow him to think he's not up to this. The niggling fact remains, however, the man has already taken out two of Vermeer's best people, the last one a good friend of Archie's. *They were every bit as good as me.*

An unknown operative that comes from nowhere, and by all accounts has never failed. What's to be made of that?

Returning from lunch, Archie was about to turn into the motel when he recognized a familiar car parked just up the street, no more than a half-block away. He smiled and without hesitation drove past the vehicle with hardly a glance. He does, however, see Carla brush aside an errant curl of hair, the signal to back off. The woman must suspect she's being watched. *What? she can't risk even a call from a public phone booth?* This could throw a wrench in the works. He's certain she's received the same information packet that he did and has no doubt they are dealing with a rogue operative. More than likely one of Carla's own from the FBI, who has her under surveillance. This could be a game-changer and might well put the ball back in his court.

Archie knows better than just circle the block. He keeps on course for the next major thoroughfare, where he angles off and stops at a neighborhood bar and grill. Taking his time over a frosty mug he plays the ancient pinball machine, something he hasn't done in twenty years…and it shows. A pair of small-town pool hustlers at a back table look up from their game, nudge one another and hide smiles. Archie realizes he has been manhandling the machine, bumping it at just the right moment to deflect the steel ball in the proper direction. That was the style in his younger days. Such a tactic took considerable skill if one was to avoid setting off the tilt alarm, which would shut the machine down and inevitably raise the ire of the proprietor.

The two men at the pool table grin at one another and look toward the bartender who's frowning across the room at Archie. The ex-cop finishes his play with a high score and, as he leaves the establishment nods to the pool sharks without shame. One salutes him with his stick, and Archie wishes he had time to give them a lesson in the finer points of that game as well.

Back at the motel, and still on guard, Archie is fairly confident he wasn't tailed but surmises there might yet be someone waiting…watching. Archie's very good at blending in—no one could say he isn't a local oil-field hand waiting for a call from some tool pusher. There are several of those staying here. He walks past his room toward the end of the hall and the ice machine. Filling a bucket, he retraces his steps to the room, cautiously glancing at each door he passes.

This time Archie checks and sees the tiny piece of clear plastic still in the bottom edge of the door where no one ever seems to check. It is exactly as he'd left it. Smiling, he unlocks the door, key in one hand, cradling the ice bucket to his chest with the other. Carla sits across the room resting her elbow on the table, a 1910 model FN automatic in her hand, business-like even by today's standard; the little Belgium pistol looks elegantly deadly even in her small hand. It occurs to him *this is the exact model that killed Archduke Franz Ferdinand of Austria in 1914, ultimately setting off one of history's bloodiest wars.* With this still in his mind, Archie crosses to the dresser, takes a bottle from the top drawer and wonders how Carla came by the pistol, he hasn't seen one in years. He brought the bottle and ice to the table without a word.

Carla saw him looking at the pistol and laid it aside. She'd left her larger service revolver in her room, preferring the less obtrusive little automatic for walking around protection. The Agent turned up two glasses and then set them back on their paper doilies. Holding one finger high on the glass nearest her she waited for him to pour, took a healthy swallow, and then smacked her lips.

The woman is a one-off, no doubt about that. "No one followed you?" Archie poured himself about half the amount and sipped it as he looked across the table at her.

"Not that I saw…but then I probably wouldn't have, would I?" She was breathing more easily now and didn't appear embarrassed to admit this, "It was more of a gut feeling than anything else, I suppose. I get those now and then—I've learned to pay attention."

He nodded and wiped his lips with the back of his hand. "I had one of those myself, yesterday morning early. I thought I was just getting old and scary. He glanced toward the window. "Where's your car?"

"In the little shopping mall three blocks from here." She smiled. "I shopped awhile and then called a cab. A maid was coming out the back door and I told her I was locked out. She probably thought I was a hooker but let me in anyway."

"You got Percy's info packet?"

"I did." Carla reached over to scoop a few more ice cubes into her glass, and Archie poured her a splash more.

"So are *you* in charge down here now," he asked.

"Is that what you think?"

"It occurred to me."

The two stared at one another for a moment, Carla being the first one to blink. "I'm not in charge," She said this with a finality that surprised him.

"Then, exactly why are you here?"

She swirled the ice in her drink sloshing a few drops across the table. "Why, just doing my job—I'm your backup Archie—that's why I'm here."

Archie took a deep breath and another sip before saluting her with his glass and nodding amiably. "I'm guessing you have something new to tell me?"

"A couple of things actually. There's a Navajo Investigator involved in the Johnson murder case; you may want to watch out for him. His name is Charlie Yazzie, with the tribe's Legal Services Office. He has a good rapport with the Bureau, but keeps his own agenda as well." She smiled thoughtfully. "He hangs out with a couple of old friends that occasionally work for him. One of them is Lucy Tallwoman's husband, Thomas Begay, the other, a tracker named Harley Ponyboy. They are close—almost like clan. They look out for one another apparently." Carla thought a moment, considering how to go about the second piece of information.

"And the other thing?"

"Investigator Yazzie informed us through channels that there is now reason to believe Clifford Johnson may have had two visitors on the morning he was killed. The first you already know, an ex-cop from Albuquerque named Ray Danson." She waited…idly wondering if he would own up to killing Big Ray.

Archie nodded noncommittally and sat back in his chair. This news confirmed what Ray Danson had maintained right along—the man had indeed been straight with him. Archie felt no remorse at hearing this. Big Ray got what he had coming, as had Raul Ortiz. They had chosen a risky profession and suffered the consequences. It happens.

"Do they know who the second person was that morning at the trading post?"

"Only that he was probably with Cliff Johnson's wife, Louise. Cliff was most likely dead when they left."

Archie cursed under his breath and tightened his grip on the edge of the table. It had crossed his mind, several times, that Louise might have something to do with her husband's death. He'd already guessed the woman wasn't happy with the trader. What angered him most was that someone else had been smart enough to work that angle first. He thought he would have more time.

"That's not all. Our agents confirm they've found a Farmington storage unit registered in Clifford Johnson's name...a big one...climate controlled. The owner said Cliff had it for years. Last night someone with the keys to the gated entry, and the unit itself, drove a box-truck in, transferred the collection to the truck, and was gone in a matter of forty-five minutes or so. The storage company doesn't maintain a fulltime presence on site but does have a local security firm check the premises every few hours...24/7. It was well executed—maybe no more than one or two people involved. The rent-a-cop said there was still dust hanging in the air when he discovered the unit open." Carla watched his expression, as she said, "The Johnsons have long been known to have a large and valuable personal collection of Native art and artifacts. They'd been salting the stuff away for years and knew better than to keep it at the trading post; Cliff was robbed there once before. Their live pawn *was* kept there, of course, in a huge old safe Cliff bought years ago, but it wouldn't have held even a small part of their own collection."

Archie went slant eyed as this registered. "Someone must have had better powers of persuasion than Ray Danson. Or me," he added ruefully. Archie was thinking of his many conversations with Clifford Johnson, trying to work out some sort of agreement for the Vermeer Foundation. Even his attempts to form some sort of alliance with Louise Johnson had been fruitless.

Carla guessed what he was thinking. "I wouldn't feel too badly about it. I've read the autopsy reports—

the information didn't come easy for whoever wound up with it."

"Ray Danson and I were *both* under orders not to leave any collateral damage in the wake of our negotiations. Both of us thought that sort of thinking a mistake at the time, but that's how Percy wanted it. I imagine he's rethinking that part now." He swirled the ice in his glass and looked over at her. "Percy's not always right, you know. You might want to consider that going forward."

Carla gave a tiny sigh. "Percy prefers to do this sort of thing in as unobtrusive a manner as humanly possible...when he can. He just didn't realize how urgent the situation had become."

"Yes, well we both misjudged the time factor on this one, I'm afraid.

Carla gave him an odd look, which he interpreted, incorrectly, as disagreement.

Archie wondered if she really considered herself his backup.

21

The Storm

Up on the Canadian border, a remarkably rapid shift in the Jet Stream was sending an arctic air mass hurtling south with unprecedented speed. The front was reportedly accompanied by extremely low temperatures. Dubbed the Arctic Express it had stockmen across several states hurrying to gather livestock and bring them in closer to home. Fortunately, most of those cattle and sheep had already been brought down from the high country, mostly thanks to regulatory grazing mandates.

It had been a long and hot summer in northwestern New Mexico, morphing seamlessly into a warmer than usual autumn; just the sort of pattern that can precede a swift change in that country. There had been little rain. Just enough, in fact, to leave people in the far reaches of the *Dinétah* praying for more.

By sunup, most folks were surprised to see a dark bank of clouds boiling out of the northwest and already on the edge of the state line where it was pummeling a wide swath of Colorado and Utah. Reports on KTNN's Daybreak Weather declared a change was on the way. "Due to several unforeseen weather anomalies," the announcer said, "the system could be severe and blow in sooner than anticipated." The weatherman's tone didn't sound overly concerned, but then he was in a nice warm studio and didn't have to rustle around in the snow for firewood or hustle livestock to better cover.

~~~~~~~

Legal Services Investigator Charlie Yazzie was satisfied the FBI would find his newfound witness credible. There was no doubt now, at least in his own mind, that Frances Benally had seen exactly what she said she saw the morning Clifford Johnson was murdered. Thinking of the sad disappearance of Louise Johnson, Charlie couldn't help but believe that same person might be responsible for both tragedies. The question uppermost in his mind now was…would it end there? On the surface one would think so, but there was something askew somewhere that caused him a measure of uncertainty. Harley Ponyboy had tracked *two* men suspected of spying on Lucy Tallwoman's camp and followed sign leading to two separate vehicles. The one, he'd thought was a pickup; the other a car, both had the generic sort of tire-tread patterns typically found on cheaply shod rental vehicles. Why did these two people come separately? Was one even aware of the other? And more important, what were they after? Both Thomas Begay, and Harley Ponyboy, postulated theories for this—all so far fetched as to beggar credibility.

Thomas suspected someone was out to discover how his wife's weaving differed from others so it could be duplicated. Harley, for his part, thought someone might be waiting for her to finish her latest piece and then steal it right off the loom.

The one thing both agreed on was that it definitely had something to do with Lucy Tallwoman—partially because of Clifford Johnson's death note, the full sum of which was Lucy Tallwoman's name. The second sticking point was, now that it was out in the open, the inordinately large amount of money the trader was getting for Lucy's work. It was easy enough to see how that alone might engender jealous reprisals from those not so fortunate. In the end, however, none could say with any real certainty what was behind either of the shocking incidents.

~~~~~~

By the time Charlie Yazzie left his office that afternoon the temperature had dropped thirty degrees, headed for the cellar. According to the afternoon man at KTNN, the *Dinétah* might be in for a rough few days. This time he was sounding a little more concerned by the forecast.

In the parking lot, Charlie thought of his Aunt Annie Eagletree as he hoped Harley and Thomas had her stock down off the mountain. They'd been working at it every chance they got for weeks now and he thought they should have things pretty much sorted out. He called Thomas earlier but with no answer. Harley finally had a phone in his trailer, but it only worked about half the time.

Charlie fumbled for his keys, hands already freezing cold. He looked up to see Tribal Policeman

Billy Red Clay pulling in. He blew on his hands and waited.

Billy rolled down the window, frowning as a sand-filled gust peppered his new sunglasses. "Looks like we're in for some weather, huh?"

Charlie pulled up the collar on his jacket and nodded. "Looks like it... That's what the radio says." He moved around the front of the truck and got in on the passenger side. Billy had the heater on full blast and the Investigator held his hands to the dash vent as he asked, "What's up Officer?" He appraised his friend in the moment's silence, thinking *Billy Red Clay isn't here to pass the time of day.*

Billy pulled off his sunglasses, grimaced at the dust, and blew the lenses clean before laying them on the dash. "First of all, I just wanted to thank you, Charlie, for running that info from the Benally woman through me first. You could just as easy gone around me and direct to Fred Smith."

"I could have, but you're the Liaison Officer, Billy. It's your job to keep the Bureau informed, on Tribal's side of things." The Investigator smiled, "We all need to be following protocol and right on up the ladder, too." Rubbing his hands together in front of the vent Charlie pretended not to notice Billy's expression as he turned away.

The Tribal cop looked back for a moment and nodded. "The Bureau thinks this throws a whole new light on the case."

"That, or it confuses things beyond what they were already confused."

"But, *you* feel sure there were two different assailants there that morning?"

"Yes I do. Francis Benally is a credible witness in my book and I believe when Fred's people review their findings they may discover evidence to that effect."

Billy thought this over. "So, this means we have two bad guys still running around loose?"

"There's that possibility, but as far as I can see the two may not have been acting together. Which reminds me... Old Paul T'Sosi believes their camp is being watched. He says a couple of people have been up on the point spying on them. Harley spent some time up there and thinks the old man is right. Your Uncle Thomas, of course, is all primed to do something about it." Charlie went quiet as he looked over at the young policeman, and then, "I went over the downside of that with him, but you know your Uncle. Talking never does any good with Thomas once he gets something set in his head. We'll need to keep an eye on those folks; maybe you could drop by there in the morning on your way in and see what they're up to. Thomas has a legitimate reason to be upset, but he and Paul both have a reputation for going overboard when it comes to something like this. In fact, I think the old man might be egging Thomas on. It's not often those two agree on anything but when they do, it can mean real trouble."

"Do you want me to mention anything to Fred? I can't believe the Bureau would be up there poking around without letting us in on it, they know we're connected to those people. I can't imagine they'd go behind our backs."

"No, I'm like you, Billy, Fred Smith might jump in if we ask him, but I doubt it's been them snooping around up there."

A gust of wind shook the car, causing Billy to look out the window and nod toward the northwest. "Looks like it's coming, all right…" A curtain of white was moving their way and at the rate it was traveling, wouldn't take long to get there.

Charlie glanced at the approaching weather and wondered if he would have time to reach home before it hit. He sighed, shook his head before reaching for the door handle and flexed his fingers in the warmth of the heater vent a last time before stepping out of the car. "I'll call you later, Billy. Those folks up at your uncle's should be good for now. I doubt anything's going to be moving in this weather."

Halfway home Charlie hit the storm head on. After only a mile or two he decided to stop, get out and put the front hubs in. It was just a matter of time before he needed them. By the time he was back behind the wheel his fingers felt like they were about to freeze again. Almost home, the Investigator estimated there were four or five inches already on the ground. Still, he didn't have to shift into four-wheel drive until he started up his own lane. He'd seen the big drifted-in tracks of the school bus at the stop and was relieved to see they had obviously beaten the worst of it. Should it keep up, he doubted there would be school tomorrow. He parked the truck and sat there a few minutes, watching it snow and thinking of all the people in the outlying areas…some without power, or even basic supplies. Most years brought snow to the reservation but seldom so early…or so much. He suspected drifts were already beginning to block rural roads; it might take days before road crews could re-open them.

When Charlie came in the door, both kids ran to him, excited to tell about the school bus and how it almost skidded off the road. Charlie swore silently under his breath. He'd warned Sue; May Nez, at 22 years old, was too young and inexperienced to be driving a busload of kids in the wintertime. He looked up and frowned as his wife came in from the kitchen. She'd heard the kids and knew what was up with his frown.

"It wasn't May's fault, Charlie, she's a very mature girl for her age. It was that dog of the preacher's—ran right out in front of her. My God, she was barely able to miss hitting it."

He took a deep breath, eyeing the children, who were obviously waiting to hear what he would have to say about that. A gust of windblown snow rattled the windows. Slowly shaking his head Charlie held up his hands in resignation, and then turned to go wash up for supper…mumbling to himself as he went. *That's exactly what I meant about the Nez girl not having enough experience for the job—it's not like she was driving a load of turnips.*

At the dinner table the children glanced their father's way whenever the conversation turned to the bus ride home; Joseph Wiley made sure that happened at least twice before his mother told him to hush up about the bus. The boy frowned down at his dinner and kept a watchful eye on his father hoping to see some support, if there was any support.

Charlie went on chewing his food without tasting it, not saying anything—thinking to de-escalate what might well turn into a *situation*.

They had almost finished eating when the phone rang and Charlie, happy to leave the table, headed for the front room. They had two phones now, one in the kitchen, and a new one in the living room. Sue thought they needed an extra phone for whatever privacy it might afford Charlie when business came up, or when she and Lucy Tallwoman were discussing matters, the children didn't need to hear. Like her mother used to say, "little foxes have big ears and carry long tails."

"Yazzie residence..." Charlie had to say it twice before the weak answer could be heard above the storm-induced static.

"Charlie, is that you?" Thomas Begay's voice sounded like it was coming from the depths of a well. The Investigator had to cover his other ear to make him out. "I think we'd better... together in the morning... can even get into town."

"Is it still snowing hard up there?" Silence... "I say...is it *snowing* hard?" Charlie realized he would have to almost shout to be heard.

"It's a whiteout, Charlie!" Thomas was fading in and out and thought it likely he would lose the connection altogether. Thomas's voice came booming in for a moment. "Here at the window I can't see more than a few yards and then only between gusts." The static built to a roar and neither man attempted to say anything for a few moments.

When the noise finally died down enough to hear, Charlie still could catch only bits and pieces of what Thomas was trying to say. "Are you people going to be all right up there?" He was shouting now.

Thomas shouted back, "We're okay for now, plenty of firewood left and we have an electric heater plugged in…if the power don't go off." Suddenly Thomas could be heard like he was in the next room. "It's not like we've never done this before. Lucy just went to the store yesterday, so there should be plenty to eat for a while." Then as quickly as the line had cleared up it went completely dead.

Charlie still had a dial tone so figured it was the Begay's line that went down. Not many people lived out that way, making Charlie think it could be awhile before things got fixed. He looked out his own window and could not even see his truck. He couldn't imagine why Thomas wanted to get together in the morning—something that probably wouldn't be possible anyway.

Back in the kitchen Sue was at the sink washing dishes and little Sasha was doing her best to learn how to dry. The little girl, not tall enough to reach the sink, was standing on a stool, bellied up to the counter so nothing had far to fall. Joseph Wiley, bent over his homework, glanced up from the kitchen table as his father came in. He was still hopeful his father would say something in his defense.

Sue asked, "Who was on the phone? I thought I heard you say 'Thomas' a couple of times… The wind's making so much noise I wasn't sure."

"It was Thomas, all right, sounds like they're getting snowed-in up there."

"Oh? They're okay though, huh?"

"I think they'll be fine, but their phone's gone dead. I guess, Thomas wants to meet up in town tomorrow; I don't know what that's all about; I didn't get a chance to ask. He doesn't even know if he can *get* into town in the morning. It might take half the day before plow trucks get out that way—even then, I doubt there will be phone service." Charlie walked up behind Sasha and peered past her out the frosted window. "If it keeps up like this, I may not be able to get into town tomorrow, myself."

Sue went to click on the radio and tuned it to KENN in Farmington just as the weather came on. Charlie turned to listen.

"An early winter storm is currently centered over the Canyon Lands and forecasters say another front is following close behind. This could set up a pattern for more of the same over the next few days. Travel advisories are out for the entire Four Corners area. Officials say roads are becoming snow packed adding to the dangerous conditions. They warned that drivers could become stranded as major roadways drift closed."

Sue's face clouded as she moved to turn up the radio. Looking back over her shoulder at her husband she pursed her lips and said, "Well, that's not good."

Before Charlie could answer the radio went dead momentarily, then came back on with a crackle. "It is now confirmed. There will be no school tomorrow for the entire county. Nor will day schools be open on the Navajo reservation. Stay tuned for further reports as they come in." Sue turned down the volume, but not before Joseph Wiley gave a rousing cheer. Little Sasha, as usual, was quick to mimic her older brother. School closures were rare in that country and were considered a great gift, as far as most children were concerned.

Sue looked at her youngsters and sighed, it would be a day of mixed blessings for the Yazzie family. "Well, at least the Begays are used to it, living that far out of town and all." But Sue was thinking of their friend's downed phone lines, *there goes our morning chat, I guess.* It was the rare day she and Lucy didn't talk on the telephone, now that they both finally had one. At least that *had* been the pattern before Carla Meyor came along. It seemed, of late, that her friend had become more focused on a somewhat different path...talking about local Chapter happenings...politics and such. Things her friend hadn't spent much time thinking about before Carla.

Sue was the one who had, for years, encouraged Lucy to widen her horizons and become more involved socially. Now that she had, Sue didn't quite know how to take it.

~~~~~~~~

Paul T'Sosi rose early and went to the *hogan's* small window where he scraped a hole in the icy rime. Where once there had been a view clear to the highway and beyond, now the back of the new house was all he could see, and even that now shrouded in snow. It was only a short distance to the back door of the house but the path appeared to be blocked by a waist-high drift. The old man contemplated the increasing barrier between him and the kitchen, and hot coffee. It wouldn't be easy, forcing his way through. Putting on his coat and old woolen hat, Paul stood at the window and squinted through the falling curtain of snow. He had let the fire in the old sheepherder stove die nearly to embers and was thinking he ought to rebuild it and stay inside for a while longer to see what developed. That would require the last of his firewood. Then, too, there was still the matter of coffee...that was in the house.

As he stood there weighing his alternatives Paul thought he saw a movement at the back door of the house. Caleb was rubbing a clear spot in the door's little glass. The boy looked out to see his grandfather peering back at him from the *hogan*. When the boy smiled and wiggled his fingers at the old man, he could see relief on his grandfather's face.

Paul watched as a crack appeared, and the door was repeatedly shoved up against the drift allowing Caleb to squeeze outside in his heavy coat. The boy stood there obviously at a loss for something he could use to clear a path. Then he saw Paul motioning toward the end of the house and spotted the shovel Thomas had left the previous afternoon, before the weather convinced him it was a losing battle. The boy nodded at the old man before edging along the side of the house where the snow was not so deep. Breaking the shovel loose from the ice, he began clearing a path to the *hogan*.

Paul T'Sosi watched intently as his adopted grandson worked his way toward him. The boy was growing into someone that could be counted on to take a hand. The old man thought that was important and smiled at the thought.

Thomas Begay was watching from the stove as he made the morning coffee. He watched from the kitchen as his son put on his heavy coat and signaled to his grandfather. Thomas felt indebted to those helping the boy grow into a man…it was the Navajo way and he was grateful. The entire family must pitch in if a child was to stay to the *Beauty Path*. If his Uncle John Nez lived closer, he might have been an even more important part of Caleb's coming of age. As it was, John made it a point to check on the boy when he was in the area counseling him in whatever way he could. He had done the same with Thomas Begay when he was a boy, and a willful boy at that...one that might not have turned out even as well as he did, if not for his Uncle John.

It was only a few minutes more until the boy and his grandfather came into the house, both grinning and shaking off snow in the mudroom. The two men and the boy gathered around the kitchen table as equals and with their mugs of steaming coffee, laughed at the predicament brought on by the weather—secure in the knowledge that, together, they were equal to it.

22

The Stretch

By six o'clock Archie was dressed and, on his way down to the breakfast bar. He grabbed a couple of rolls and his coffee as he watched the television news above the buffet. People seemed excited about the weather. He smiled as the weatherman warned everyone to stay inside and keep warm. Back in New York, winter storms like this were common enough. People there were accustomed to staying inside in such weather and didn't need to be told. But then few of them had stock to feed or water tanks to thaw. Behind him an older, well-dressed man with a cane, stood smiling, though obviously impatient for his breakfast. The man nodded at Archie as he glanced past him at the buffet, as though worried Archie might be picking through the best of it. He appeared relieved to see the attendant approaching with a fresh supply, and quickly moved aside for the woman. As Archie edged his way past the elderly man, he recalled the man's room was only a few doors down from his own. He had several times passed him in the hallway and the old gentleman always nodded pleasantly enough.

Back in his room, Archie walked over and clicked on the TV. Putting his breakfast on the table in front of the window, he stood there for a moment staring at the snow, still coming down wet and heavy. He smiled to himself *a good time to take a lay day, rest up and get my mind straight. This is just beginning.* He had barely finished buttering his second roll when the phone rang causing him to frown. He hesitated hoping it might stop…but it didn't. He gulped his coffee on the way to the nightstand and sat by the phone a moment offering the instrument one last chance to be quiet. Finally he tossed the Styrofoam cup in the trash and picked up the receiver, listening intently for just a moment before answering. "…Yes?"

"Archie…."

It was Carla. "You're not at work, I would guess?" She wouldn't be calling from her office.

"No…still at the hotel. They haven't even started clearing the parking lot yet, looks like I'm going to be stuck here the better part of the morning…possibly longer than that.

Archie leaned back against the pillows. "Same here. Weather guy says it's not going to quit for a while either." He was sure the woman had a better reason to call than the weather, and waited. She seemed reluctant…uncertain how to begin.

"You've heard something… Right?" Archie had a pretty good idea what this was about. He'd been expecting it.

"Yes, I have," She finally admitted, hesitating a moment before going on. "And it's not good…"

Archie waited.

"Agent Smith called this morning, first saying I shouldn't worry about coming in until the roads are cleared." She paused again but this time for only a second. "What he really wanted me to know was that the rental truck involved in the storage unit heist turned up—involved in an accident down in Albuquerque. A convenience store owner called it in to local police, saying the driver appeared to be hurt. But as the investigating patrol unit arrived, the driver jumped out and limped off on foot. The cops ran him down and reported the man seemed delusional, possibly strung out—anxious to talk his way out of jail time—or so they thought. It didn't take much for the man to give permission to search the vehicle...and guess what? It was full of trading post loot taken from the Johnson's storage unit. We had a statewide bulletin out right after the robbery, of course, but hadn't expected it to be this easy. Professionals seldom drop the ball like this."

"So, you don't think the driver was involved in the actual killing?"

"Right now, we don't think so. This particular driver was a low-ranking member of the Ortiz family; it's still not clear if Raul Ortiz had set himself up to broker the shipment or just supplied a hired hand to bring the stuff down to their warehouse for safekeeping." Carla sounded even more convinced when she said. "I'm sure any operative involved in the Johnson murder would be too smart to get caught out like this."

Archie suppressed a curse. "It's pretty obvious now that Raul was playing us off against these people from the start."

Carla agreed, "It would seem so, I have the feeling the trader's murderer is still hanging around up here, and that means he's not finished." She paused. "The Begays could be in more danger than they know, especially since it's gotten around that Lucy

Tallwoman's name was somehow linked to the trader's death. Someone might have reason to think she knows something she shouldn't. Of course, Senior Agent Smith still suspects there's a leak somewhere."

"That could explain where the operative is getting his information."

"There's no one on the Bureau's radar in this case that we can put a finger on at the moment, but that doesn't mean someone's not lurking around to tie up loose ends."

"Percy has known about these people for some time now, Carla, I suppose he has been waiting to see how far they would push us. That said, the last thing he wants to own is the notoriety of an all-out war. Personally, I think it may be too late to avoid one. "

Carla yawned. "Well, he should be more in line with our thinking by now."

Archie couldn't let it go. "Percy has, from the beginning, maintained we should look out for Lucy Tallwoman—he's been protective of the Begays all along, for some reason."

Carla shifted the phone to the other ear and purposely changed the direction of the conversation. "Archie, I spoke with Lucy Tallwoman this morning. She called me, mentioned their phone went down last night but is back on this morning. The Begays are sure someone's been watching their camp—someone besides you, I mean. She says they're *certain* two different people have been up there on the ridge, spying on them. Thomas Begay and her father apparently intend doing something about it. I told her that might be a mistake and did she want the Bureau to send someone out when the weather cleared? She said no, they would handle it."

"I mentioned the tracks I ran across on the trail above the Begay camp. I had a feeling then I was being watched. Whoever else was up there may have an agenda that's very different from ours."

Carla waited for Archie to weigh in further, hoping he would have some specific insight in regard to the Begays, something she could work off of, but either he didn't or, if he did, he intended keeping it to himself.

A heavy sigh from Archie's end gave the impression he wasn't overly concerned. "Nothing's going to happen today, Carla. All the outlying areas are snowed in, and will be for a while, I imagine." He knew she was waiting to hear what should be done, but he couldn't quite bring himself to share...not just yet.

After he hung up the phone, Archie again went to the window and watched the snow flutter down from a grey and increasingly dreary sky. He finally admitted to himself it was smart of Percy, not to bank on just one person. Maybe Carla Meyor *was* being groomed to take his place...maybe that's why Percy mentioned his retirement recently. There was no doubt having an ear in the Bureau would prove a huge advantage going forward. Still, Percy should know that depending on an inexperienced person could be something they would come to regret.

Archie got down by the bed on one knee and pulled out the long box with his tools. He could wait for the storm to pass and the roads to be cleared before taking up a position above the Begay camp, let the man come to him. The problem with that strategy being, it could take time. And there was the risk the operative might somehow get by him, or even intercept him. After considering all the logistics of the thing it became clear the more rational way to proceed might be to find the person now and take the fight to him. Archie was pretty much convinced that only one operative had been sent. It wasn't likely such a person would be camped out somewhere. No, he would be right there in town, just as *he,* himself, was. There were not that many places…it could even be there at his motel…or Carla's maybe. He wondered if the woman had thought of that.

For Archie, there was the nagging premonition the operative had *already* spotted him, followed him back from the Begays' camp perhaps. That was something to consider. Unpleasant as the prospect was, it might indeed be better to force the person's hand right here and now and possibly on more advantageous terms.

Archie had been at this business a very long time and there was one thing he knew for a fact; the direct approach was often the best approach. It might not work for everyone, but it had often worked for him. He had long ago learned the element of surprise could be a deciding factor in almost any critical maneuver. From the beginning, he'd felt this operative seemed prone to rush things. No matter how good the man might otherwise be, patience was apparently not his long suit, and that in the final analysis, could prove his undoing.

~~~~~~~~

Carla watched the hourly weather reports with a growing sense of resignation. She was, it seemed, stuck in limbo and with plenty of time to think. *Archie Blumker might well be the expert when it comes to a street-smart evaluation of the players in this game.* She was finally forced to give him that much but, still, she thought, there are things he doesn't know. *Blumker still needs me more than I need him. It's true he's clever, possibly even more than Percy let on, but he doesn't have access to the resources of the Bureau. I do.*

Despite all this internal posturing Carla remained unsure, mentally debating whether or not she should have been more forthcoming with Archie. She had purposely left him unaware of her growing intuition that Senior Agent Fred Smith might have reservations about her. This was a wild card and one not to be taken lightly; if she was right, Archie and she both could be compromised.

Carla's thoughts eventually spiraled into a vortex of self-doubt… *What about Lucy Tallwoman?* There was now more than just the growing bond of friendship between them. There were long forgotten ties few were aware of. Old Paul T'Sosi had immediately shown some sense of it when first he'd laid eyes on her, some familiar something about her. Her appearance maybe, or some inherited resemblance. Something had obviously triggered a long-forgotten bitterness in the old man. His impaired state of mind apparently made it impossible for him to recall exactly what it was just then, but he might eventually…and then what? *Neither Lucy nor Paul has any idea who my birth father was, but should they eventually put two and two together, it could very well be a game-changer.*

Carla had been just a young girl when Lucy Tallwoman had fallen under the spell of the white music teacher in that last year at boarding school. Even Carla's Bureau file didn't have that information, only that her father ended his own life when she was still in high school. *Few are left now who know the backstory—that Lucy's deceased daughter, Alice, was my half-sister.* The fact was, Alice had long been a hidden part of both their lives. Thomas and Charlie Yazzie knew bits and pieces, of course, but she doubted it was enough for either of them to put the story together. These were painful things Carla hadn't thought of in years and now they were back to haunt her. Should she go to Lucy with this now...or just let it lie and hope for the best? There was the slim hope the information might strengthen their bond, but more likely it would forever destroy whatever ties she had managed to forge. Percy Vermeer knew the story and, she suspected, somehow felt guilty for the actions of his relative. That may well have been the reason he was protective of both her and Lucy Tallwoman.

23

The Enigma

After examining her deposition for a third time, The Legal Services Investigator remained mystified at Frances Benally's report. It still seemed odd to Charlie that Clifford Johnson's wife was present in those early morning hours preceding the trader's death. Not that he didn't believe Frances. He did. The FBI had already suggested Louise might be involved in the crime. They'd learned the trader went in to work in the wee morning hours the last day of every month, to catch up on his bookkeeping, but more likely, they thought, to adjust hidden accounts unfettered by prying eyes, including those of his wife.

Charlie had a hard time believing Louise Johnson had a part in her husband's death; the two had been together a long time and according to neighbors seemed to get along well enough. On the other hand, Louise was considerably younger than Cliff, and an intelligent, handsome woman in the bargain. It was not inconceivable she might have tired of Cliff's penny-pinching and secretive management of their resources.

Only the day before, Billy Red Clay had mentioned questioning a number of long time customers of the

Johnsons' trading post and found more than a few thought the couple's relationship had soured of late.

Charlie was still thinking of Billy Red Clay's report when his private line rang and the officer was on the phone. Only a few people had this number and Charlie intended to keep it that way.

"Hey, Charlie, hope I'm not interrupting something? I was wondering if I might drop by later—talk to you in private if you can find a minute?"

"Sure... What's up, Billy?"

"Uh... I'd rather not say until I get there...paranoid maybe? The grader went by a few minutes ago so the roads should be clear to your office by now...when's a good time?"

Checking the clock the investigator decided, "Let's say in about thirty minutes if that works for you; I should be leaving about then anyway...I'll meet you downstairs in the parking lot."

It was obvious: whatever was on Billy Red Clay's mind, he preferred it to be just between the two of them. Charlie had barely hung up when the receptionist buzzed his intercom. "The Bureau is on line two, Sir, Fred Smith I believe."

Charlie raised an eyebrow and thought, *what the hell?*... then threw a questioning glance at the blinking red light before picking up.

"Yazzie, here...is that you Fred?"

"Yep, I tried your private line...busy...I just wanted to run something by you if you have a moment?"

"What's up?"

"It's Carla Meyor, I understand she came to see you the other afternoon?"

"Well, since you know that, I can only assume she told you...or you're keeping track of her...which is it?"

The agent hesitated. "Well, she didn't tell me."

"I see... So how can I help you Fred? I'm sure you have good reason for asking about Carla, but I have to tell you straight out, there wasn't much of any importance discussed. Mainly just small talk, school days and such."

"Charlie, did Carla happen to mention the Vermeer Foundation in any context at all...in relation to school, or?"

"Fred, I'd have to think about it. She might have. It may have come up in conversation. What exactly is the Vermeer Foundation?"

"I wish I knew, Charlie. I have people working on that as we speak. All I know at the moment is that it's a 'non-profit' headed by a man named Percy Vermeer of New York state. A well-known collector of Native art and antiquities. I should know more by this afternoon. I just thought she might have said something."

"Fred, is Carla under investigation?"

"Not really Charlie, not at this point anyway. I'm just curious about a few things, I guess—call it an overactive imagination if you like." Fred chuckled, but Charlie had the impression he was more serious than the attempt at humor indicated. He definitely seemed concerned about Carla, or maybe something in her past.

"Fred, you did know, of course, that Meyor was not her name. She was adopted, somewhat late in life from what she told me." Charlie heard papers rustle and knew Fred Smith was leafing through a file.

"Yes, Foldier was her birth father's name...and yes, the Bureau did know that. I see here the man later took his own life. Well, that's a shame."

"Maybe not so much a shame as you think. He wasn't a very nice guy according to Carla. I got the feeling there was more to the story than that but didn't press her for details. As to your question about the Vermeer Foundation; I recall her saying both her father and stepfather were distant or shirttail relations of the Vermeer's...second or third cousins apparently. But as unlike as cousins could possibly be from what she said." Charlie supposed he may have overstepped the bounds of personal confidentiality but this *was* the FBI he was talking to. He wasn't Carla's lawyer or legally bound in any way. That, however, didn't prevent a twinge of guilt.

"Okay, *that* I didn't know, but I should have more info on that later this afternoon. The Albuquerque office has taken a special interest in Carla Meyor, Charlie. I suspect they are pulling out all the stops on this one. The Vermeer Foundation has managed to stay under our radar for some time. Their organization has only recently come under scrutiny, following some tax problems which wouldn't go away." Fred Smith was clearly a little agitated and growing more so as he continued. "By the way... there *is* the off chance someone here in our office is the source of that leak, the one we'd previously *thought* was coming out of Tribal. All this is still just supposition at this point. But make no mistake we intend to get to the bottom of it, and pretty damn quick, too. Needless to say, Charlie, all this is strictly confidential. I wouldn't mention any of it to the Begays as yet, not until we are on firmer ground…but I'm sure you understand that."

After the FBI man hung up Charlie sat back in his chair and raising his eyes to the ceiling rethought the entire conversation. He'd never seen Fred this riled up. He became more and more certain the Agent had already uncovered more of Carla 's agenda than he let on.

Carla had been a question mark in the back of his mind from the beginning, just not in this particular context. The woman was an enigma; there was no doubt about that. Looking up at the clock Charlie went for his coat. Downstairs he watched through the glassed front entry for Billy—all the while wondering how deeply embedded Carla might be with the Vermeer Foundation.

~~~~~~~~~~

The snow had temporarily eased off, leaving only a skiff of new powder to cover the freshly plowed roadway. Billy Red Clay's long hours running wintery highway patrols, left him certain there was an icy glaze below the inch or so of white powder. He adjusted his speed accordingly but despite the cautionary tactic was surprised when the unit went sideways as he turned into the parking lot. The young officer was wearing an embarrassed grin as he pulled up to the nearly deserted building and waved through the windshield.

Charlie moved around to the passenger side and waited as Billy tossed his coat in the back and hit the unlock button. The car was warm inside…too warm, Charlie thought as he unzipped his jacket.

Billy was first to speak, "So, have you heard anymore from Uncle Thomas and that bunch up country?"

"No, I have not. Sue called and said their phone has been 'in and out' all day. I figured to give him a call later on this evening if I can get through."

The two sat there a moment as Billy turned off the windshield wipers and adjusted the heater before getting into what he'd come for.

"You may already know some of this, but in case you haven't seen the latest report...that rental-truck load of trade goods from the Johnsons' trading post turned up in Albuquerque. That should have been on your FBI update this morning?" Billy smiled as he gave Charlie a knowing glance. "San Juan County's finest, Sheriff Dudd Schott and his department, are handling the theft up here. They were supposed to keep the FBI...and us, in the loop. But as you know, county law doesn't always 'remember' to give Tribal a shout, rarely, in fact. Luckily, I called the Undersheriff this morning on other business. I've known him a while now, a nice enough guy actually... We had quite a little chat. He knows the Booking Officer in Albuquerque who was a friend of the truck's driver, back when they were young, I guess. Almost like a brother from what the Undersheriff says. Anyhow...the Booking Officer says his friend got roped into that deal without knowing what was involved."

"Did this 'friend" know anything about the Johnson murder?"

"According to the Booking Officer, his friend claims not to know a damn thing about any murder.said he was just sent to pick up the truck. He did say the person who handed over the load was a real scary dude who, now…get this…told him he had to stay in Farmington to take care of some 'unfinished business.' The driver's job was just to deliver the load to the city. He said he had no part in the heavy stuff." Billy smiled. "Hard to say how much of this is true, of course, but Sheriff Dudd Schott apparently bought into it. He hasn't said anything to any of the other agencies as far as the Undersheriff knows. Maybe Dudd's hoping he can round up the bad guy by himself…take all the credit. Not a hard thing to believe if you know the man."

Charlie screwed up his mouth and squinted one eye at the policeman. "So, the murderer of Cliff Johnson, his wife, too, most likely—is still running around loose up here?"

"That's how it looks to me, Boss. You're the only one I've spoken to about it as yet." Billy gave the Investigator a wry grin. "At this point I expect your guess is probably as good as mine."

"When were you going to tell Fred? You're the Liaison Officer."

"I was hoping I wouldn't have to tell him *anything*, Fred's waiting to hear from the Feds in Albuquerque right now. They may already have come up with most of this, and if not, I'll fill him in then…especially about Dudd Schott withholding information."

Both men grinned and Billy Red Clay gave his friend a thumbs-up.

"Do you suppose I could make a couple of calls from your office? Our radio tower must have iced up again, or something. I can't get out on the two-way. I just have to get ahold of maintenance on the outage, and maybe call home so my mom won't worry."

Charlie smiled.

Back up in the office, Billy made his calls and the two men sat for a moment before heading out.

"I'm serious, Billy—about telling Fred. I wouldn't wait too long. This thing is starting to come loose. You do not want to be standing in front of it when the FBI gets moving."

Billy Red Clay nodded his head and had already stood to go, when the Legal Services Investigator saw his expression change. Following his gaze, he saw FBI agent Fred Smith striding past the front desk without so much as looking at the receptionist. *Determined*, was the word that came to mind. The two Navajo glanced at one another, one as much surprised as the other.

"...uh oh," Billy managed before Agent Smith was upon them.

Charlie raised an eyebrow at Fred as he came barging through the door. "What's going on, Fred?" The Agent's behavior warned him there was a problem...a big one.

The FBI man opened his mouth and looked first at Charlie and then back to Billy. "I thought that was your unit out front." He started to say something else but catching himself midstride thought better of it and instead just started over. "I don't suppose either of you fellows know they just found Louise Johnson's body?" He was looking hard at Billy Red Clay.

Billy, with the inscrutable expression peculiar to his people, shook his head in a way that denied it, but didn't bother to come right out and say so.

Charlie had known the Tribal Cop since he was a boy and knew he was hard to rile—but he *had* seen him lose it a time or two. He motioned the young policeman back down in his chair. Charlie's years of experience with Billy's Uncle Thomas, made him once again aware how alike the two could be, more so than either of them cared to admit. Charlie stared a moment at the Federal Agent before waving *him* to a chair as well. "Have a seat Fred..." And then more gently... "Where did they find Louise?"

Smith sat himself down rather heavily, as though suddenly tired. He appeared to regain his composure before exhaling. "In a U-Haul load of Indian collectables down in Albuquerque. Thought to be the merchandise from the Johnson's storage unit. Police were almost finished unloading it when they found the body rolled up in a rug. That pretty well clinches her connection as far as they're concerned."

Charlie canted his head slightly as he mouthed, "That is a damn shame, Fred. No one deserves that...regardless what part she might have played in the thing." The investigator was quick to amend the statement. "Assuming, of course, she played any part at all."

Smith slumped back in his seat and studied both of the men before going on. "Actually, Louise Johnson is not the reason I'm here."

"No?" Charlie couldn't imagine any more justifiable reason for the agent's brusque visit than what he'd already heard.

Billy leaned back in his chair as well and gave the Agent a long stare before looking away. He only turned back to the Federal Agent as he saw him scan the outer office, then frowning, reach over and push the door shut.

Fred paused a moment to dwell on what he was about to say, then offered Billy Red Clay an apologetic grin. "I see now I may be a little overwrought. There could have been more on my plate this morning than I was able to digest." He laid both hands flat on the table. "I want *both* of you two to know how much I've appreciated your help these last few days… More than that, your personal commitment to furthering interagency transparency and cooperation is beyond anything our organizations have experienced in the past. The Bureau knows we have a ways to go yet, but I want to tell you—we're working on it." Fred turned slightly toward Billy as he said these things and the policeman backed off, touching the brim of his hat in acknowledgment he nodded his appreciation.

The two Navajo edged their chairs closer and Charlie scanned the outer office himself before reaching down to unplug the intercom. He suspected the FBI man was about to say something provocative.

"As you may know, the Bureau's Farmington Office has been experiencing an information leak. Turns out it may be internal…one of our own people involved." Clearly it pained the Senior Agent to admit this, and he was quick to point out it still was not certain who the guilty party was—but that there was little doubt it was someone in the office. "But I'll get back to that part of the story later on," he said quietly.

Charlie had more than a vague notion who the Senior Agent had in his crosshairs, and it wasn't Billy Red Clay, but he could see Smith was unprepared to say more at this point. *Fred must have very little hard evidence. Farmington's Bureau Office being as small as it is, the field of suspects has to be limited.*

Fred spoke in a quiet, almost self-effacing manner that he thought the two Navajo would relate to. Letting slip the hint of a smile, he said, "While it may surprise you men—I too, had friends growing up," then smiled outright. "One of whom, as it happens, is now the manager of a local motel. Craig Benson at the Thunderbird." Fred tapped his fingers on the edge of the desk. "And that brings me to the real purpose of my being here this morning. Craig called me a few hours ago with something extraordinary. Let me preface this by saying the man may be a little excitable at times, but his word is unimpeachable. He and I were at the Academy together down at Quantico. He washed out late in the program, pressure finally got to him, I expect. Still, he remains absolutely dedicated to the precepts of the Bureau. I would stake my career on what he told me. That may, in fact, be exactly what I'm about to do." He stopped and looked from one to the other before admitting, "Quite frankly, I could use your help."

This brought the two Tribal lawmen to attention.

The agent surveyed the outer office a last time… "What I'm going to tell you can go no further; there are major players involved, and of the sort we seldom run into out here."

This unexpected turn took Charlie by complete surprise and he could see Billy Red Clay was reserving judgment as well.

Fred lowered his voice and began speaking in a measured tone, one meant to eliminate any possibility of misunderstanding. "Craig has, for the past several days, taken it upon himself to keep a certain person under surveillance, one of the motel's guests actually. His suspicions were aroused by several incidents: packages addressed to a now defunct local engineering firm with which he was familiar. And after taking the trouble to do a little extra digging, found the name the guest was registered under belonged to a person who had been dead a number of years. My friend is convinced there is something questionable going on, but didn't feel justified in calling me until he knew more. Then, too, he figured there were some of his actions I might not condone." Fred paused for a moment to be sure his listeners were still with him…seeing they were he went on. "Feeling certain his suspect was about to make a move he decided to follow him, and became convinced the man was about to be contacted by a confederate. At the last minute the suspect was apparently warned off. He aborted the meeting and my friend knew the opportunity had been lost. He tailed him to a local bar and eatery, and after watching a while, returned to the motel and checked the man's room before he could return. Under the bed, he found a box containing a rifle set up for long distance work." Fred paused giving the pair a significant glance before going on. "There were silencers in the box, as well as several military issue hand grenades in their original packing. The numbers on the long gun had been expertly removed—a federal crime in itself—as is possession of both the silencers and grenades. All this taken together…my friend felt he finally had something I might be interested in, and decided to give me a call."

Charlie loved high intrigue. It brought back thoughts of his short involvement with the DEA only the year before. It had been a welcome and exciting break from what had become a desk-bound interim in his career at Legal Services. He had for a while, in fact, toyed with the idea he might even be interested in a position Drug Enforcement had open in Albuquerque.

"A new career in a different world," he'd told Sue. After a serious sit-down with his wife and a lot of soul searching on his part, he'd turned the job down, deciding he could do more good right there on the reservation. Though the idea hadn't panned out, it had left a taste for the action and excitement the life might have to offer. He could understand what had motivated the motel manager to mix in. The man probably thought this might be his last chance to be a part of something he could now only dream of.

"So, what did you have in mind that Billy and I might help you with, Fred?" Charlie was serious, but at the same time wondered why the agent would need their help at all? When he asked as much, Fred Smith seemed hesitant to answer for a moment.

"Well," the FBI man said quietly, "The truth is, you boys are my only real option at this point." The Senior Agent shook his head. "I don't know who to trust in my own office—and the last people I would care to call on would be the local agencies in Farmington. This is a Federal investigation, of a crime committed on Indian lands and under the jurisdiction of the Federal Government. The FBI can be legally assisted by Navajo Nation law enforcement personnel should it be required in the pursuit of a felony committed on the reservation."

"What did you have in mind, Fred?" Charlie was inclined to go along with it, whatever it entailed, and knew Billy Red Clay would jump at an opportunity like this...whatever it was.

"I don't suppose you boys would be interested in confronting a suspected professional assassin and possibly being shot at in the process, would you?"

Billy Red Clay squirmed in his chair and grinned. "Can we shoot back?"

24

The Test

Archie Blumker watched from his window as a plow truck pushed snow to the side of the parking lot. News reports stated San Juan County back roads were slowly being opened—a few highways already cleared with others reported not far behind. He'd had plenty of time to consider what was to be done about Percy's dilemma. He'd spent most of the day studying the portfolio spread out on the table in preparation for the task that lie ahead.

Guests were beginning to stir. One or two could be seen carrying bags to vehicles, starting engines to warm, as they scraped windshields and cleared small drifts left by the plow. Archie was amused to see his portly neighbor from just down the hall standing timidly outside the motel entrance. Finally, using his cane for support, the elderly gentleman felt his way out onto the still icy sidewalk to survey the situation. He seemed confused as to how he might go about extracting his car; the plow had left quite a snow bank blocking it. After watching a few moments Archie had about decided to go down and offer to help. He frowned as he saw the old gentleman lean out past the edge of the sidewalk, apparently looking for a way down the sharp incline. As Archie looked on, the man apparently decided not to chance it, half turned, but misjudged the placement of his cane, which slipped on the icy cement pitching him forward. Archie watched in dismay as the old man's feet went out from under him, then stared in disbelief as the elderly man contorted mid-air, to come lightly to his feet in a crouch at the foot of the drop off. Though nearly hidden between two cars Archie had a clear view of the entire thing. He had never seen anything to equal it. The old man, not appearing so old now, gathered himself, glancing about to see if anyone had taken notice. After a moment, and apparently satisfied he was unobserved, he shrugged his shoulders and straightened up to run a hand through his hair and adjust his scarf.

Archie blinked, leaned forward in disbelief—had he only imagined the astonishing recovery? He watched intently as the man, now again old, brushed at his clothing with shaky hands and limped cautiously back up the incline to the sidewalk…then to the lobby, depending heavily on his cane, as an old man should.

Archie mentally re-ran the incident several times, still having a hard time trusting his own eyes. Then, slowly it began to dawn on him. Moving away from the window, he removed the packet of photos from his jacket pocket and examined them again for perhaps the sixth time; finally, holding one out, he tapped it with a forefinger and thought, *ah, yes Archie, there he is…of course, the most unlikely of the lot!* He studied the photo as though seeing it for the first time. Given the advantage of hindsight, the eyes and other more subtle facial features were now quite apparent. *Yes, it was him all right.* Allowing his mind to reassess the operative's photo in this new light, it was clear he was a man probably only in his thirties, if that. Who would have thought him to be the overweight, age debilitated person in the room two doors down? From their few chance encounters there was absolutely nothing Archie could recall that would have given the man away. *So, this is the man with no name?*

The notation on the back of the photo supported what he'd seen—there, just below the martial arts credits: Accomplished gymnast and once nationally ranked Canadian skater. Certainly not the average operative, but then, there were no *average* operatives.

Archie prided himself on a certain ability to see through the more common subterfuges...but not this time. He chuckled, shaking his head in admiration at the photo. *They should have added world-class actor, and master makeup artist, to that list.*

Archie had no physical skills he thought remarkable, and as far as acting, could only play one character, himself. Even that sometimes proved to be a poor effort. Overall, he considered himself quite ordinary, with the exception of two things. he was singularly obsessive in his pursuit of a goal...and ruthless in carrying it out.

From the hallway came the muffled chime of an elevator. He hurried to the door, and pressing his face hard against the cold metal, put his eye to the peephole. He was unable to make out more than a fraction of that door belonging to his neighbor. He dare not open his own even a sliver. This was a person who would be watching. He had already underestimated the man once; a second time might be his last. He was now obliged to admit the possibility of being out-classed. No matter, there was always a workaround of one sort or another.

The entire profession, if it could be called that, required less actual skill than most thought. In Archie's view success was mostly just a matter of stubborn determination…with perhaps a dollop of luck from time to time. What bothered him about this man down the hall was his chameleon-like ability to morph into something he wasn't, which made it likely he had other undisclosed talents as well. Already Archie figured engaging him physically might not end well. In one way they were very much alike—this person would instantly kill him if he could. That was a given. Archie's intricate planning, coupled with his long experience and attention to detail, might serve to level the field. Or, he could just walk down the hall and shoot him.

In the end this is what the ex-cop chose. He was a reliable hand with a gun, not as good as he once had been, but still felt he could make a workmanlike job of it. Thinking these things, and feeling the first fine tentacles of excitement, he threaded the silencer onto the barrel, slipped in a full clip, and jacked one into the chamber. It always made him smile when a movie-cop waited until the last possible second before loading one in.

Nerves of steel—that was the thing—and Archie had that in spades.

25

Crossfire

Fred Smith led the way through the lobby and on to the reception area. The hotel manager was waiting and nervously ushered the three men to his office. Barely able to contain himself Craig Benson informed them the suspect was still in his room. Pointing to the surveillance monitors above his desk he slowly scrolled through the security cameras to the floor in question. "That's it…third door down on the left—309." He shook his head. "As far as I know he's still in there." The former FBI hopeful was visibly excited, his voice thin and high pitched.

Charlie thought *Surely Fred doesn't intend this guy to be in on this…regardless of past training.* He shot Billy Red Clay a glance, and saw him wink back without expression.

Senior Agent Smith assured the hotel man they would attempt to keep the operation as low key as possible. He made it clear his old friend was to stay in the office and monitor the arrest on camera. Only in the event something should go seriously wrong should he call for assistance. "Craig, we don't anticipate anything we can't handle," Fred assured him.

The manager, looking somewhat disappointed at not being included in the actual takedown, nonetheless, agreed. He pointed to yet another monitor and pulled up a photo of their suspect taken from the desk security camera the day before. "This is your guy."

They gathered around, and Charlie was surprised to hear Fred Smith suck in his breath and go wide-eyed at the sight of the image. "That's Archie Blumker! He showed up in the Vermeer Foundation report, and was on a 'person of interest' watch list from Albuquerque this morning. I had no idea he was in the area." For a moment the Federal Agent seemed deep in thought...then pointed at the screen. "When did he check in?"

"Not until a day or so after the Johnson murder. I took the liberty of checking his rental's paperwork, he hadn't even left Albuquerque until after the killing." He knew what the FBI man was thinking.

Fred was about to reply when Billy Red Clay reached across to point at the screen monitoring the third-floor hall. The elevator up-arrow lighted and as the door opened all four men watched as an elderly man with a cane haltingly made his way off the elevator, then looking neither left nor right, tottered down the hallway.

"Who's that?"

Benson answered immediately, "Just a guest, he checked in shortly after our guy."

The Federal Agent nodded, immediately dismissing the old man. "Let's not get in a rush, we'll give the old fellow time to get to his room." Fred timed the sequence in his mind. "Billy, if you'll take the east stairwell...and Charlie, you take the west. I'll go up on the elevator, disabling it as I get off. We should have him boxed in at that point." He turned to the manager. "I'll need the key to the control panel and a master room key."

"I was pretty sure you would," Craig pulled both keys from his pocket and handed them over.

The FBI Agent shook the keys as he turned to Charlie. "I'll give you men five minutes, exactly, to find your places. Billy's in uniform and you, Charlie, may as well be. You'll want to stay inside your stairwell doors until you see me step off the elevator. No need alerting him in advance."

Billy Red Clay, checking his service revolver, nodded to Charlie and the two left for the third floor.

Fred watched them go with an air of confidence. Marking the time, he and the manager continued watching the painfully slow progress of the old gentleman in 306, now almost to his room. After checking both ways down the hall, Fred watched frustrated as the man fumbled with his keys. Dammit! He appeared to be having trouble seeing in the dimly lit hallway. Finally sorting things out he was able to let himself in.

"How many other guests are on the third floor?" Fred's voice was barely above a whisper.

The hotel manager didn't hesitate. "There are none. The storm pretty much shut us down last night. Only Blumker...if that's his name...and that older gentleman in 306, are left up there."

"Good." Fred turned his attention back to the monitor and surveyed the now empty hallway. They waited another minute or so and then, looking at his watch, the agent turned to the door with a last pointed look at his friend. "Craig, it's important you stay here you know…continue your surveillance."

"You can count on it, Fred."

The Agent *was* counting on it; should things go south this man would be their only backup.

~~~~~~

Charlie Yazzie arrived first at the west stairwell. Out of breath and edgy, he moved to the small glass looking out onto the hall. Carefully peeking at the edge of the portal, he could see to the far end. Billy Red Clay either had not yet arrived or was keeping out of sight. Billy had the longer distance to go and Charlie figured it would take him a little more time. Turning his attention to the elevator, he watched the lighted up-arrow ticking off floors. At number three, it stopped but the door didn't open. Charlie decided Fred was having trouble disabling it…maybe there was a problem with the key. He pulled his .38 and looked again to the other end of the hall where he now saw Billy behind his window palms up in question. As the elevator finally opened Fred stepped out, weapon already drawn.

Gunfire immediately erupted from room 306 and the FBI man was hit twice in quick succession. Charlie first thought it was Fred opening fire and was already out the door to cover him when he saw the agent stumble and fall backwards.

Billy Red Clay was instantly on the shooter. He got off a wild shot and in return took two rounds, himself—one to the shoulder that spun him aside and left him slumped against the wall. The second bullet grazed the side of his head dropping him to the floor.

Charlie saw now where the shots were coming from, and diving for the floor came up firing, emptying his revolver at the half-open door of 306. A bullet instantly slammed into the wall beside him and another clipped his left hand. Charlie crouched and fumbled to reload as blood made the revolver slippery, making it difficult to eject the empties.

The old man in 306 stepped out into the hall, an automatic pistol in each hand. He took dead aim at Charlie Yazzie.

Instinctively the Investigator threw up his bleeding left hand in a futile effort to ward off what was coming. Momentarily paralyzed with pain he squinted between his fingers only to see the shooter blink and with a surprised gasp, sag back against the door. Charlie hadn't heard the shots, but saw the two holes appear in the old man's shirtfront. Blood spurted and ran down his chest and he lowered his head, to watch in disbelief as the floor pooled with blood. Making a last desperate effort to raise his pistol the man flinched as a third and killing round struck. Sighing, the operative looked up to gaze into Archie Blumker's eyes.

Without lowering the silencer-equipped automatic Archie nodded a final salute before swinging his own gun on Charlie Yazzie.

Still frozen in place and defenseless, the Navajo Investigator could only stare back thinking, *So this is Archie Blumker...then this is it...*

Shaking his head slightly as he looked at Charlie, Archie appeared unable to decide if killing him was worth the trouble. "Scoot that pea-shooter over my way, if you don't mind, Cowboy."

Charlie, now on one knee, glanced in desperation at the few bloody cartridges he'd dropped while attempting to reload.

Archie shook his head more forcefully. "Don't even think about it...there's not a chance in hell that's going to happen." There was a deathly silence. "Of course, I may decide to shoot you anyway...that's something you may want to factor in."

Charlie sent the empty .38 skidding away and rose painfully to his feet, automatically putting his hands above his head. Blood streamed unnoticed down his left arm. "All right..."

"A wise decision." Archie smiled as he picked up the gun, studied it a moment, and then stuck it in his waistband. As he came even with him, he motioned the Investigator back against the wall. "You'd best see to your friends now—one, I think may be hit pretty bad." Archie cocked a thumb back over his shoulder and said, "That dead man over there would have killed you all, you know. He was an excellent shot." Archie then walked past him to the stairwell and without turning, was gone.

~~~~~~~

Charlie already had pillows under his friend's heads, when the hotel manager rushed in with washcloths and towels to staunch the flow of blood. It was no more than ten or twelve minutes later that Charlie heard the sirens coming.

Though Billy was still out, Charlie could see his wounds looked worse than they probably were and he was able to concentrate on Fred Smith.

The FBI man was conscious. He had lost a lot of blood yet still was able to speak in an audible whisper. "I didn't think it would come to this... I had no idea what we were up against. Or, that there would be two of them... It was a bad call." His voice broke as he turned his face away and fell silent.

Charlie could see the agent was fading fast, probably already going into shock. While he knew the injured man probably couldn't hear him, he nonetheless, whispered, "It wouldn't have mattered, Fred. We weren't up to either one of these two...they were way out of our class."

The hotel manager placed cold towels on Billy Red Clay's forehead. The young Navajo cop began to moan quietly and Charlie watched as his eyes fluttered open for a moment.

The manager went down to explain the situation to the arriving city officers. He'd seen most of what happened for himself and was pretty sure his recording machine would have most of it on tape.

Charlie had wrapped a small towel around his hand and was still trying to help the others when the Ambulance crews arrived. Charlie told him the FBI agent was the more critical of the two. The head EMT, hooked Fred up to an IV while instructing another to take his vitals. All this, before the Federal Agent was even on the stretcher.

When Charlie asked how they thought Fred was doing the Medic shook his head. "I don't know what's holding him up, Bub. He's about bled out. I'm afraid to give him anything for the pain." By the time they loaded Fred into the ambulance he was unconscious.

As the second crew worked on Billy Red Clay, the young cop began coming around. He asked Charlie if Fred was going to make it, but the Investigator could only shake his head, too choked up to say more.

26

Survivors

Carla hung up the phone and went to the door. Glancing through the peephole, she unlatched the safety chain and let Archie in.

"We have somewhat of a problem." The ex-cop didn't raise his voice or sound the least worried. Archie had snatched the small "ditch-bag" from his truck and now set it on the chair beside him. Other than that, it was just the clothes on his back and a good memory for coded account numbers.

Carla nodded. "I thought there might be a problem. I've been watching a 'Breaking News' bulletin on T.V. There's a video clip of your motel...surrounded by cops. It didn't take me long to figure out what that was about." She pursed her lips. "How bad was it?"

Reflecting on this for a moment he murmured, "I'm afraid your Senior Agent took a bad hit, and there were two others with lesser injuries: a Tribal cop, and another Navajo with a badge on his belt. I still can't figure out how they came to be involved?" He took a deep breath. "The good news is, no more worries about the operative who took out the Johnsons." Archie looked at the little refrigerator in the corner. "You wouldn't have anything to drink, would you? I could use a kicker about now."

Carla went to the fridge and came back with two miniature airline bottles. "This is it, I'm afraid," She poured them into separate glasses and passed one to Archie. "Who were the two Indians?" she asked, swirling her scotch dangerously close to the rim.

"I didn't have a chance to ask," Archie smiled, "but their little war party probably saved my ass. They took the brunt of the action before I knew what was happening—good thing too—a few minutes more and I'd have been walking straight into it. The bastard was waiting for me. He and I had the same idea at the same time." He mulled this over... "The man was as good as I've ever seen. If he hadn't been distracted, I believe he might well have killed me." He lifted his glass in a quasi-toast and murmured, "He was no quitter...that's for damn sure."

Carla, too, was thinking... "When I called in to the office for my messages this morning, there was no mention of anything like this in the works."

"Ah, well, that explains why you didn't give me a heads-up this morning." Archie tried not to grin. "You don't suppose they're on to you...do you?"

"That's a real possibility," she smiled. Looking up she swallowed the scotch and sat her empty glass by the newspaper. "Fred knew he had a leak, and almost certainly suspected me. He couldn't have known for sure—but I think it had been working on him for a while." Carla toyed with the edge of the newspaper. "That young cop that got shot was most likely Billy Red Clay. He's the Liaison Officer to the Bureau. The older one, I would guess, was Charlie Yazzie. I mentioned him once before if you'll remember; he's a Legal Services Investigator for the tribe. Agent Smith liked and trusted him." She nodded as though thinking. "Charlie carries a stainless .38 with turquoise set grips!"

Archie reached inside his jacket and placed the Tribal Investigator's Smith & Wesson on the table. "Like this?" he chuckled. "We'll leave it here for him; I imagine he'll want it back."

Carla looked at the revolver, noticed the dried blood, and ran a finger over the turquoise. "He got hit, did he?"

"He was lucky. He might lose a finger, or maybe even two, but that's about it. I probably should have finished him, but was feeling a little obligated, I guess, you know, for them taking the heavy end." Archie was smiling now. "The shooter was most likely headed my way when they surprised him."

"I didn't figure you for a sentimentalist?"

"No? Well, maybe I'm mellowing in my old age...should I take Percy up on his retirement plan?"

Carla turned to the window, surveying the freshly plowed yet nearly deserted street. She said over her shoulder, "Archie, I'm not sure you understand the sort of retirement plan Percy has in mind for you at this point?"

"Really? The two of you have already discussed my *retirement*?" He still was smiling but only with his lips.

Turning to him she placed both hands on the table. "Yes, we did...only a few minutes ago, as a matter of fact. We were on the phone when you knocked." Carla slipped her little FN automatic from under the newspaper and pointing it directly at him she too smiled and took a deep breath before saying, "What do you think Archie... Are you ready to retire?"

For an instant, his drink halfway to his mouth, he considered throwing the heavy glass, but instead calmly finished it off and set the glass on the table. Turning back to the television news story he watched the motel manager, in the parking lot by his pickup—the man, obviously enjoying the attention, was gesturing toward the upper floor of the building, pointing out the fugitive's window.

Archie said over his shoulder, "You're not going to shoot me, Carla." He smiled as he watched the manager raise a hand to indicate how tall the killer was.

"What makes you so sure, Archie, what makes you *so* sure I won't shoot you?" She smiled, "You don't think I'm a company girl?"

Archie turned to her with a grin. "If you were going to shoot me, Carla, you wouldn't be standing there talking about it. And though you may well *be* a company girl... I still haven't figured out *whose* company...have you?"

Carla ran her tongue across her upper lip, looked down at the gun in her hand and eased her finger off the trigger before lowering it. "So, what exactly do *you* think should be done, Archie, you know too much about Percy, the foundation...and me, to let you just walk away."

Archie exhaled slowly and shook his head. "Well, the sorry fact is, by tomorrow morning it won't really matter. Everything connected to Percy Vermeer, and that includes us, will be front-page news. With an FBI Agent shot down in cold blood...whether he dies or not...the Feds won't let up. The entire thing will come down now no matter how much money Percy throws at it... It's all coming down. You and I both know that. At this point, I would suggest the two of us are in the same boat."

"So, what are our options?" Carla lost the smile as she listened.

Truth be told, Archie had been thinking about this for a while now. Regardless what Percy had promised over the years, and no matter how much he wanted to believe it—in the back of his mind he'd always known it could come to this.

"The Vermeer Foundation will come to an end, Carla...but that doesn't mean you and I have to go down with it. I'm thinking we would make a very good team, you and I." He paused to see how this might register. Seeing a tentative smile on her lips he went on. "I have a small cottage—tucked away in a charming little Mexican village—I think you'd like it. For some years now, I've been putting a little by in foreign accounts, as a hedge, let's call it, against an eventuality just such as this. In time, there's the possibility we might even be able to continue our careers...together. I was thinking Europe for that, maybe? With your legal education and art expertise, and my contacts...and, shall we say, baser skills, we could conceivably do quite well." He turned to the window drawn by yet another set of sirens wailing in the distance. "Just a suggestion, of course. You might already have plans, and that's fine too." He gave her time to consider.

As he spoke Carla thought the words oddly out of character for someone like Archie. There was no sign of anger or vengeful indignation toward The Factor, or anyone else for that matter. The things she would have expected from such a man were totally absent. It seemed his entire mental acuities were now focused in a different direction—the way going forward, and what might reasonably be salvaged.

"So, we make a run for it. Hide out in Mexico…or later Europe, and live the good life?" Carla was chasing the possibilities around in her head.

"Something like that, I guess." He could see she was at least considering it.

"What do you think the odds are of something like that working out?"

"Not as good as I'd like, but there's a gamblers' chance I would guess." He stopped to listen again, the sirens closer now. "One way or the other Carla…time is running out. We should go."

Carla regarded him a moment longer, as though seeing the man for the first time. There was no doubt Percy Vermeer and his organization would, more than likely, not recover—just as Archie predicted. The Vermeer Foundation had too long eluded notice…this would be the game changer. Percy himself, in their conversation that morning, made it very clear just how far he would go to preserve his reputation and all that he'd worked for. He obviously perceived Archie as a liability now, one that needed addressing; he'd said as much. Carla couldn't help wondering *who* would be next. Archie was among The Factor's oldest confidants; she'd heard his praises sung for years. She herself would now come under scrutiny…what then?

If there was one thing Carla Meyor *was* sure of, it was this: people caught in a vise are prone to squeeze others…whatever it takes to relieve the pressure. It was just human nature—Percy believed it—and in her short time at the Bureau she'd seen it many times herself. She was being squeezed from both sides and she didn't like it.

~~~~~~~~

As it turned out, it didn't take long at all for Archie and Carla to find themselves of the same accord. Some indefinable bond was being forged that neither could deny. Carla, drawn to the myth-like aura that had long defined the man—and Archie, attracted to a beautiful intelligent woman, who insisted on thinking for herself—despite nearly a decade of Percy Vermeer's manipulative guidance.

As the couple drove west in Carla's rental and now well beyond the Arizona border, they calculated they had at least five or six hours before the Bureau figured out the extent of Carla's involvement and issued warrants to ensnare the rogue agent. By that time the two of them should easily be in Phoenix and on a plane to somewhere else. It wasn't going to be easy; there would be pitfalls, disagreements that come with any new relationship, not to mention adjusting to a new and very different life in another country. In the end, however, they felt their plans were both do-able and by far their best option. That was quite enough for now.

~~~~~~~~

Archie sat at their little patio table stirring local cream into coffee freshly brewed from a highland roast. He smiled and doubted there was a more pleasant place in all San Miguel Allende. The cottage sat just north of town, in a little village close by the lake. He'd purchased the property some years back with the thought in mind he might someday retire there, or barring that, at least use it as a refuge. He'd kept his ownership secret, trusting in the interim to a property management company, a good one, who took care of every detail and had the highest regard for anonymity. The rental provided more than enough to maintain and improve the property, and a little besides.

He closed his eyes for a long moment that he might savor these first hours of the day. He listened to the soft sounds of the housekeeper putting the kitchen in order after a late breakfast. There were birds singing in the tall hand-wrought cage behind him, and there, just by the ironwork gate, he could hear the calls of their wild cousins hiding in the flowering avocado tree. He watched as Carla puttered about the rosebushes adorning the adobe walls of the patio. A man came once a week to do the yard work and had shown her how to prune back the more mature flowers to encourage new blossoms. Archie thought she was taking too much stem, but didn't say anything. It was too nice a morning.

Eventually he turned his attention to the letter, unopened beside his cup. Sighing, he picked it up and inserted the little serrated fruit knife from breakfast. He should have waited until later in the day when he might have a drink before reading it. It was from his brother, of course. No one else could possibly know where they were. Mailed from a forwarding service outside the country, this was a mode of communication he trusted. He could not, however, imagine this letter being good news.

He pursed his lips and narrowed an eye to better focus on the familiar script. It was a fairly long letter and Archie suspected therefore it might be the last. His brother was a cautious man not given to taking chances. Henry had a reputation to protect.

Much of the letter was as he thought it would be, newsy and filled with home—except for the part about Percy, and then later the price on their heads. It really wasn't that much money from what Archie knew of the business, almost disappointing in a way. He would have expected it to be a good bit more. Probably it was set by a vindictive member of the Ortiz family, one of the few not now in jail, maybe. He suspected the whole bunch were short on money, what with the federal attachments on nearly everything they owned. That might explain the paltry sum?

Archie shook his head, smiling as Carla came up the path from her work with the flowers. She'd brought along a few long-stem red and pink roses, which she artfully arranged in the table vase.

"It's a letter from Henry, isn't it?" She didn't expect encouraging news. She suspected they had already used up their share of good luck.

"Yes, yes, it is." He leaned toward the roses and sniffed. "Henry sold my place in New York; it was in his name anyway. I expect it will be a while before we see anything from it though. He'll take his time like he always does. He's the more careful one. That's why he's the lawyer, I suppose."

"Ah, well, I guess there's some security in that line of work, or at least some comfort in thinking there is."

Both of them smiled at this. Carla glanced back, checking her recent work with the roses, before taking a chair just across from him.

Archie passed her the letter, though not sure it was the right thing to do. She'd probably be better off not knowing.

Carla began reading and only a few lines in he heard a catch in her breath. He knew she'd come to the part about Percy Vermeer. Henry told how Percy, devastated by the notoriety and long legal wrangling, had eventually been charged. Despite mounting a brilliant defense, his lawyers unaccountably, lost. On the day Percy was to report to the court he became fiercely depressed, locked himself in his office, put on Bach's Toccata Fugue in D Minor, gradually increasing the volume until the windows shivered. He then took the handgun from his desk drawer…and put an end to the pain.

She couldn't help tearing up at the news.

Archie understood, and though it was exactly the sort of thing he would expect Percy to do, he too, was inexplicably saddened. This, despite the certainty that, had Percy lived their lives would have been at even greater risk. It would have been a more certain peril than anything threatened by the Ortiz family. He was thinking to himself, *just one less thing to worry about,* and watched as Carla continued reading. Only moments later he saw her smile in spite of herself and knew she had come to the part about the price on their heads. Though in truth, it was now only his head on the block. The Ortiz quarrel was only with him, not Carla.

"How could Henry possibly know this?"

Archie smiled along as he held up a cautionary finger. "Oh, Henry has his ways… He has his own sources." Archie became more serious as he went on, "And no, that's not much money, in the States. But then, we're not in the States." He cleared his throat, "I don't think it's anything to worry about but it's best to keep that sort of thing in perspective, don't you think? It will keep us on our toes if nothing else." Archie saw a shadow cross Carla's face but still, slight though the risk might be, was glad he'd mentioned it. He considered eternal vigilance a part of the ongoing price they would pay for this new life.

~~~~~~~

During their self-imposed exile, Carla and Archie had fallen into a cautiously optimistic and even comfortable life in their little cottage at the edge of the village. Posing as a retired married couple and under assumed names, they gradually came to think they might have eluded detection, at least for the time being. They continued to stick close to home for the most part, and for all intents and purposes fit the profile of the many other ex-pat couples in the area. They'd heard no more from Henry Blumker but felt certain Archie's brother would let them know should he learn of any impending threat. Eventually they were lulled into a guarded complacency, taking the occasional walk about the town plaza of an evening, and on market day enjoyed short forays to the local open-air market. Both Archie and Carla spoke decent beginner Spanish and had even picked up a few colloquialisms particular to the region. All in all, they conceded they were as happy as the situation would allow and thought their decision to remain there a while to be a good one.

Walking to the plaza one evening Carla was delighted to discover a wedding in progress—the

Church steps thronged with locals. The lucky couple was from prominent families who had gone all out to provide their children a memorable start to their marriage. A mariachi band was playing and a few locals along with ex-pats and a couple of more cautious tourists made up the beginning of a street dance. Carla found it charming and took Archie's arm, leading him to the edge of the growing celebration. Archie, seeing Carla in such high spirits, allowed himself to join in despite his natural reluctance. The bells began to peal and the marriage party came laughing from the Church, causing the gathered crowd to break into a cacophony of cheers and calls of congratulations as a knot of dancers wended their way past.

Archie never heard the shot, just quietly folded to his knees as though in supplication. Carla felt the tug on her arm and looked down to see him covered in blood, a look of total disbelief on his face. The moment seemed frozen in time. When Archie toppled forward, Carla, just beside him, instantly was aware he was beyond help. She looked up for a split second and was staring into the shooter's face—they locked eyes for an instant before he disappeared into the crowd. Few were even aware what had taken place. As if in a trance, Carla rose to her feet and without any discernable expression of sorrow or grief turned and quietly made her way from the plaza—never to be seen in that place again.

27

The Aftermath

Charlie Yazzie and Billy Red Clay, both bandaged and still lightly sedated, sat side by side in the waiting room. Billy for the third or fourth time, asked, "I wonder how he's doing in there?" Without waiting for an answer, he touched the bulky bandages under his hospital scrubs. The bullet had passed through the fleshy part of the underarm leaving behind a relatively clean and uncomplicated wound. His surgeon expected it to heal without lasting effect. The head wound, while a deep furrow along the side of his scalp, required only scrupulous cleaning, antibiotics, and stitches before bandaging. From his comprehensive set of x-rays the radiologist could find nothing to indicate there might be any future problem. The concussion had knocked Billy out and he was still a little uncertain on his feet—but medical consensus held he was a lucky man...an inch more to the right, and he might have been dead.

Charlie wondered privately if the trauma to Billy's head was the reason he was repeating himself. The Investigator was well aware his own wound was comparatively minor alongside the others...he knew he'd been lucky. His left hand, encased in restrictive bandaging, more on the order of a cast actually, hurt like hell, he said, when asked. The bullet, entering between the last two fingers, ranged halfway up his left wrist to splinter bone and damage important ligaments. The surgeon first thought he might have to take the little finger off entirely. Now, however, it was thought both fingers might turn out to be only a little stiff—possibly affecting his grip—but no more than that.

Sue had been there earlier and would be coming back with fresh clothes for both men as soon as the children got home from school.

Billy didn't want his mother notified, as she had been ill. He preferred telling her himself, later on, when she could see he was all right. Both men refused to leave the hospital until they knew more about Fred's condition.

It was FBI Agent Fred Smith that had everyone worried. When they brought him out of surgery his wife was the only one allowed in the recovery room and she had not left his side since, though it had been several hours. No one coming or going to Intensive Care seemed to know the extent of Fred's injuries or his prognosis. At this point his friends could only hope for the best.

~~~~~~~~

Billy Red Clay snored quietly as he slumped to the side of the lounge, one arm in a sling.

Charlie, unable to sleep, looked Billy's way occasionally, only to shake his head and turn back to his magazine article. The sound of the glass doors swinging open caused him to look up to see the Begay family coming. Thomas led, with old Paul T'Sosi bringing up the rear. The entire group had a grim look about them, determined, apparently, to see for themselves the extent of the injuries and hear directly what happened.

Harley Ponyboy dawdling along behind the main force also appeared miffed...probably just because his friend Thomas was. He came no further than the entrance where he took up a station by the door. Leaning on an elbow at the end of the reception counter, he concentrated his gaze across the heads of those in the waiting room.

Sue Yazzie was late returning, having had to go to the neighbor's house for a babysitter.

Sue, when she was first notified, immediately called Lucy Tallwoman, who instantly declared they would meet her at the hospital. "I'll have to send Caleb for Thomas," she said. "He's gone to stand guard up on the hogback, to keep anyone from sneaking up on us now that the road has been cleared."

Now at the hospital, Thomas Begay, still in his heavy coat and broad brimmed hat—Levi's still wet to the knees from wading snow—went directly to his sleeping nephew and nudged Billy's foot. "How are you?" he asked gruffly, causing a few people to look their way. The Salt People are known for their ability to sleep anywhere and under any conditions; Thomas himself was famous for it. He nudged Billy again, and asked more loudly. "I say..."

Billy opened his eyes to stare at his uncle as though unsure who he was.

During all this Charlie Yazzie, sitting only a few feet away, looked straight ahead but made no comment. He knew Thomas was ignoring him, thinking *him* responsible for not knowing what was going on and leaving him to sit out there in the snow waiting for a killer who would never come.

Billy Red Clay, coming fully awake, frowned up at his uncle. "Here I am, shot all to hell-pieces...and you kick me awake to see how I am?"

"You don't look all that bad to me." Thomas reached out to touch the dressing on his nephew's head. "Does it hurt?"

"It does when you push on it." Billy knew his uncle wasn't any happier with him, than he was with Charlie.

"You should have called me!" Thomas couldn't understand not being notified.

"Yes, all it would have taken was a call and you could have been sitting here with a bullet in you, too." Billy was in no mood for his uncle's indictment and looked away as he said, "Maybe you're right...maybe I should *have* called you."

Thomas's eyes narrowed and he frowned, before turning to glower at Charlie Yazzie. "I damn sure expected more from you. You said you'd let me know what was going on—it was colder'n a frog's wiener up there on that ridge."

Charlie, looked his friend directly in the eye without blinking; knowing full well that would make the man uncomfortable. When finally the Investigator did open his mouth it was with a rueful smile, "I thought there wouldn't be much to it. It wasn't like we knew what was going to happen. I figured Fred was kidding when he said there might be shooting."

Thomas stood staring back a moment, then dropping his gaze, let it wander around the room before coming back to Charlie's hand. Shrugging helplessly, he asked, "What's going to happen with Fred?"

"No one knows that yet…"

Paul T'Sosi had taken a chair at the far side of the waiting area where there was some elbowroom. The old Singer was rocking back and forth mouthing a chant, bits and pieces of an Enemy Way. That's what Harley Ponyboy thought it was anyway, and he smiled as several white people got up and moved away.

The old man recalled the time when Charlie's son, Joseph Wiley, was born. Paul had been at the hospital doing a chant then, too, convinced the baby had need of his prayers.

After warning the old man to hold it down a time or two, the young orderly, a Navajo himself and more than a little nervous to be messing with a Singer; did eventually screw up his courage and escorted Paul from the room. That was some years back, but even now the old man hadn't forgotten it.

Paul was much quieter this time around, hoping to avoid that sort of embarrassment. Already a few white people were muttering under their breath and darting looks his way. A local Methodist minister frowned over at Paul and shook his head. He was there to counsel relatives of a dying man, and thought he should be the one doing the praying.

Charlie raised his head and gazed around the circle, a few of them now chanting along with Paul. His frown gradually softened as he considered these people who had come to express their concern and offer good wishes. These were *his* people, and while they might seem strange to some—he knew this was a show of support and a genuine token of their good will. For the Diné this was in itself, a kind of medicine—a sincere attempt to bring about a higher state of *Hozo* for everyone there. He could not fault them for that. It was the Navajo way. More and more, he was coming to understand that.

28

The Way of It

Lucy Tallwoman was no more inclined to believe her father's new Albuquerque specialist than she had his previous advisors in Farmington. She did, however, convince the doctor to help get Paul signed up for a proposed medical trial he'd mentioned.

"Those people should have an Indian or two in their program," she told him, and then insisted her father would be a good choice. She swore, that she herself would oversee his medications and keep track of improvements, should there be any.

Lucy made a strong argument—winding it up by saying her Uncle John Nez was on the Tribal Council, and that she would soon be, herself. While not true in the strictest sense, the possibility was in the offing. She had declared for the next election and was readying her campaign. Aided and abetted by Thomas's Uncle John she was now convinced it was within her grasp. She made it clear to the doctor there were a good many people on the reservation in need of such treatment and she meant to be an advocate for them. "Also," she mentioned, "the State of New Mexico keeps a close eye on the denial of such privileges to its Native peoples." She said this by way of inferring a Tribal Council

Member had a lot of pull with state lawmakers, which, unfortunately, was seldom the case.

The Doctor, unconvinced though he might be, finally relented, and in view of their long trip down to see him, he said he would "see what he could do."

Lucy honestly did not expect to hear back from the man, but in only a week's time the specialist called to say her father had been accepted into the program and a packet would be sent to his doctor in Farmington for administration and oversight. Apparently, fewer people than they thought had applied and they had been able to squeeze him in. Paul's local physician readily agreed to participate. He was a young doctor just starting out and thought working under the auspices of such a trial might promote his visibility. Paul was to start his treatment regimen the following week and the entire family looked forward to whatever improvement that might bring.

~~~~~~~~

Several weeks passed and shortly after a visit to Agent Smith's home, Charlie called the Begays to say he and Sue were coming to see them.

After the usual greetings Lucy couldn't wait to tell them about her father. They'd been happy to hear Paul now had a treatment option for his condition. They would have told the old man that in person...if he hadn't been napping.

"How is Fred Smith doing?" Thomas was first to ask the question on everyone's mind.

"It's been slow going..." Charlie, not wanting to appear overly optimistic, offered a cautious but honest assessment. "He's home now but not really up and around that much yet. That belly wound has been a little stubborn. The doctor says they may have to go back in if things don't improve soon. Still, they think he's going to come through this."

"He's going to be all right?" Lucy was obviously pleased to hear it, but didn't want to say so for fear it might jinx his progress.

"We hope so. They'll know more in a week or so…when they get that intestinal thing under control." Charlie shook his head and decided to tell them exactly how it was. "He'll probably never be the same in some respects and may not return to work—certainly not in the foreseeable future. The Bureau wasn't too happy he'd taken it upon himself to instigate our little raid. That might weigh into it as well." Charlie pursed his lips and exclaimed, "Fred tried to explain to them he didn't have *time* to go through channels, saying he might have lost the opportunity altogether."

Thomas drew back and folded his arms across his chest. Glaring out the window he muttered, "That might have been for the best."

Charlie frowned and shook his head. The Investigator had made the trip to Farmington every few days these last few weeks, often accompanied by Billy Red Clay, now on the mend and nearly his old self. Charlie, too, was coming along nicely. His physical therapist was convinced he might regain partial use of his injured fingers.

The women left to make coffee. Charlie and Thomas after glancing at Paul T'Sosi asleep in his chair, made their way out to the front porch where they sat in the sun. Warm weather had returned for the present and no one could get enough of it. After the unseasonal storms earlier that month, people had soured on thoughts of the approaching winter.

"Billy Red Clay came by this morning. He said he might be out to see you this afternoon." Charlie eased into it now, recalling the pair's last contentious meeting.

Thomas hadn't seen or heard from his nephew since their harsh words at the hospital. "That would be good. I didn't mean to throw down on him like that. I guess I owe him an apology...and maybe you, too."

Thomas almost never apologized for anything, and Charlie considered this offer a remarkable concession for him. He waited to hear what he would say.

Thomas however said nothing more, as though the admission itself should be sufficient apology and didn't mention anymore about it.

Charlie actually felt relieved—he'd grown used to his friend the way he was and couldn't picture him apologizing...that wouldn't be Thomas. He doubted he would be able to keep a straight face if he did. "In case you didn't know, they still haven't found any trace of Carla Meyor.

Thomas wanted to say *I don't know how in the hell I would know. No one ever tells me anything*—but he didn't say this as he was in no mood for more apologizing. He glanced toward the house. "That will make Lucy sad, she was connected to that woman, you know. She's upset enough over all this other stuff."

Charlie hesitated before saying; "I know how close she was to Carla, even before she knew the woman had the same father as Alice."

Thomas studied on this for a minute. "So... you already knew Carla's father was Alice's father too?" He nodded down the road toward town. "The man was teaching at the boarding school Lucy went to. I knew from Alice a long time ago about her mother getting mixed up with a teacher at boarding school. Alice knew her father was white. But before Carla came into the picture no one really knew who he was, other than Lucy, of course." Thomas looked at the door. "The old man knew…said it came to him in a dream…but the next day, didn't seem to remember it. More likely he just didn't want to talk about it, I guess. I remember him saying once that if he'd caught up with that teacher, he'd have killed him. I never heard him say anything like that before. He never spoke of the man again until yesterday."

It was obvious to Charlie that Thomas, like the old man, didn't like thinking about it. He murmured, "That's a hell of a thing for a person to carry around all these years," He nodded. "Carla came to my office not long ago and in passing, mentioned something about her father. I guess she knew all along Alice was her half-sister. That might be why she volunteered to assist out here in the first place. She was curious about Lucy." He looked down at the porch. "Sue told me more about it when she heard what happened in Mexico. Lucy had told *her* a long time ago what happened at boarding school. I didn't know until recently that Carla was Alice's half-sister."

Later that evening when they were alone in the kitchen, Lucy Tallwoman looked at Sue with tears in her eyes. "Do you really think Fred is going to be all right?" She couldn't help some lingering feeling of responsibility—believing her growing notoriety as a weaver might have caused some jealous person to lay a curse on everyone she knew.

Sue Yazzie put her arm around her friend, all the while thinking to herself, *why do the Diné seem always to credit some spell or curse for whatever bad thing might happen to them?*

~~~~~~

It was nearly six months later that Agent Fred Smith now back at work, was notified by the head office in Albuquerque that the fugitive, Archibald Blumker, had been killed—in a small town in the state of Guanajuato, Mexico.

The next morning another American was found dead in nearby San Miguel Allende. This time the dead man was thought to be a former FBI candidate named Craig Benson, shot down in his hotel room while awaiting transportation to the airport.

No one had been apprehended at the time of Blumker's death but in his nearby home a short note was discovered, from his former companion, rogue FBI agent Carla Meyor. It was addressed to Agent in Charge Fred Smith, at the Farmington N.M. Bureau office. The message read as follows:

First let me say that Archie Blumker, despite what some think, was not all bad. When up against bad people, he could be capable of terrible things, but at other times he was much like anyone else.

I'm sure you realize by now that you and your friends would be dead if not for him. The shooter wouldn't have left witnesses—nor would Archie ordinarily. I can only think some innate personal code may have saved you.

I'm guessing Craig Benson's fantasy of being a Bureau agent spurred him to find us...or perhaps it was the local television notoriety fleeting though that was. It was a pretty piece of work—finding us the way he did. I suspect he hadn't revealed all he learned through his surveillance.

You'll not hear from me again and knowing what I do of the inner workings of the Bureau, I may be hard to find.

Fred laid the message aside and picking up the phone dialed the Crestview motel. As he waited for someone to answer he thought of the last time he'd seen his friend. Craig had come to visit him at the hospital, ranting about the incompetence of the local agencies— obsessing on how they'd let Blumker escape. He would have done things differently, he said, had it been up to him.

When the desk clerk answered, it was to tell him that Craig Benson had quit his job nearly a week before...to travel and pursue greater opportunities.

R. Allen Chappell

Addendum

These stories hearken back to a slightly more traditional time on the reservation, and while the places and culture are real, the characters and their names are fictitious. Any resemblance to actual persons living or dead is purely coincidental.

~~~~~~~

Though this book is a work of fiction, a concerted effort was made to maintain the accuracy of the culture. There are many scholarly tomes written by anthropologists, ethnologists, and learned laymen regarding the Navajo culture. On the subject of language and spelling, they often do not agree. When no consensus was apparent, we have relied upon "local knowledge."

Many changes have come to the *Dinè*—some of them good, some, not so much. These are the Navajo I remember. I hope you like them as well as I do.

ABOUT THE AUTHOR

R. Allen Chappell is the author of nine novels and a collection of short stories. Growing up in New Mexico he spent a good portion of his life at the edge of the *Diné Bikeyah*, went to school with the Navajo, and later worked alongside them. He lives in Western Colorado where he continues to pursue a lifelong interest in the prehistory of the Four Corners region and its people, and still spends a good bit of his time there.

For the curious, the author's random thoughts on each book of the series are listed below in the order of their release.

Navajo Autumn

It was not my original intent to write a series, but this first book was so well received, and with many readers asking for another, I felt compelled to write a sequel—after that there was no turning back. And while I have to admit this first one was fun to write, I'm sure I made every mistake a writer can possibly make in a first novel. I did, however, have the advantage of a dedicated little group of detractors quick to point out its deficiencies… and I thank them. Without their help, this first book would doubtless have languished, and eventually fallen into the morass.

Navajo Autumn was the first in its genre to include a glossary of Navajo words and terms. Readers liked this feature so well I've made certain each subsequent book had one. This book has, over the years, been through many editions and updates. No book is perfect, and this one keeps me grounded.

Boy Made of Dawn

A sequel I very much enjoyed writing and one that drew many new fans to the series. So many, in fact, I quit my day job to pursue writing these stories full-time—not a course I would ordinarily recommend to an author new to the process. In this instance, however, it proved to be the right move. As I learn, I endeavor to make each new book a little better…and to keep their prices low enough that people like me can afford to read them. That's important.

Ancient Blood

The third book in the series and the initial flight into the realm of the Southwestern archaeology I grew up with. This book introduces Harley Ponyboy: a character that quickly carved out a major niche for himself in the stories that followed. Harley remains the favorite of reservation readers to this day. Also debuting in this novel was Professor George Armstrong Custer, noted archaeologist and Charlie Yazzie's professor at UNM. George, too, has a pivotal role in some of the later books.

Mojado

This book was a departure in subject matter; cover art, and the move to thriller status. A fictional story built around a local tale heard in Mexico years ago. In the first three months following its release, this book sold more copies, and faster, than any of my previous books. It's still a favorite.

Magpie Speaks

A mystery/thriller that goes back to the beginning of the series and exposes the past of several major characters—some of whom play key roles in later books and are favorites of Navajo friends who follow these stories.

Wolves of Winter

As our readership attained a solid position in the genre, I determined to tell the story I had, for many years, envisioned. I am pleased with this book's success on several levels, and in very different genres. I hope one day to revisit this story in one form or another.

The Bible Seller

Yet another cultural departure for the series; Harley Ponyboy again wrests away the starring role. A story of attraction and deceit against a backdrop of wanton murder and reservation intrigue—it has fulfilled its promise to become a Canyon land's favorite.

Day of the Dead

Book eight in the series, and promised follow-up to #1 bestseller, Mojado. Luca Tarango's wife returns to take Luca's remains back to Mexico and inveigles Legal Services Investigator Charlie Yazzie to see that she and Luca's ashes get there for the Mexican holy day.

The Collector

Book number Nine in the series brings most of the original characters into play, but centers around Lucy Tallwoman. The murder of her agent causes her life to spiral out of control as unseen forces seek to take over the lucrative Native Arts trade.

From the Author

Readers may be pleased to know they can preview selected audio book selections for the Navajo Nation Series on our book pages. Our Audio books can be found featured in public libraries, on Audible, and Tantor Audio Books and, of course, in many retail outlets. There are more to come. Kaipo Schwab, an accomplished actor and storyteller, narrates the first five audio books. I am pleased Kaipo felt these books worthy of his considerable talent. I hope you like these reservation adventures as much as we enjoy bringing them to you.

The author calls Western Colorado home where he continues to pursue a lifelong interest in the prehistory of the Four Corners region and its people. We remain available to answer questions, and welcome your comments at: rachappell@yahoo.com

If you've enjoyed this latest story, please consider going to its Amazon book page to leave a short review. It takes only a moment and would be most appreciated.

Glossary

1. *Adááníí* — undesirable, alcoholic etc.

2. *Acheii* — Grandfather *

3. *Ashki Ana'dlohi* — Laughing boy

4. *A-hah-la'nih* — affectionate greeting*

5. *Billigaana* — white people

6. *Ch'ihónit't* — a spirit path flaw in art.

7. *Chindi* — (or *chinde*) Spirit of the dead *

8. *Diné* — Navajo people

9. *Diné Bikeyah* — Navajo country

10. *Diyin dine'é* —Holy people

11. *Hataalii* — Shaman (Singer)*

12. *Hastiin* — (Hosteen) Man or Mr. *

13. *Hogan* — (Hoogahn) dwelling or house

14. *Hozo* — To walk in beauty *

15. *Ma'ii* — Coyote

16. *Shimásáni* — Grandmother

17. Shizhé'é — Father *

18. *Tsé Bii' Ndzisgaii* — Monument Valley

19. *Yaa' eh t'eeh* — Common greeting-Hello

20. *Yeenaaldiooshii* — Skinwalker, witch*

21. *Yóó'a'hááskahh* —One who is lost

*See Notes on following page

Notes

1. *Acheii* — Grandfather. There are several words for Grandfather depending on how formal the intent and the gender of the speaker.

2. *Aa'a'ii* — Long known as a trickster or "thief of little things." It is thought Magpie can speak and sometimes brings messages from the beyond.

4. *A-hah-la'nih* — A greeting: affectionate version of *Yaa' eh t'eeh*, generally only used among family and close friends.

7. *Chindi* — When a person dies inside a *hogan*, it is said that his *chindi* or spirit could remain there forever, causing the *hogan* to be abandoned. *Chindi* are not considered benevolent entities. For the traditional Navajo, just speaking a dead person's name may call up his *chindi* and cause harm to the speaker or others.

11. *Hataalii* — Generally known as a "Singer" among the *Diné*, they are considered "Holy Men" and have apprenticed to older practitioners sometimes for many years—to learn the ceremonies. They make the sand paintings that are an integral part of the healing and know the many songs that must be sung in the correct order.

12. *Hastiin* — The literal translation is "man" but is often considered the word for "Mr." as well. "Hosteen" is the usual version Anglos use.

14. *Hozo* — For the Navajo, "*hozo*" (sometimes *hozoji*) is a general state of well-being, both physical and spiritual, that indicates a certain "state of grace," which is referred to as "walking in beauty." Illness or depression is the usual cause of "loss of *hozo*," which may put one out of sync with the people as a whole. There are ceremonies to restore *hozo* and return the ailing person to a oneness with the people.

15. *Ma'ii* — The Coyote is yet another reference to one of several Navajo tricksters. The word is sometimes used in a derogatory sense or as a curse word.

18. *Shizhé'é* — (or *Shih-chai)* There are several words for "Father," depending on the degree of formality intended and sometimes even the gender of the speaker.

20. *Yeenaaldiooshii* — These witches, as they are often referred to, are the chief source of evil or fear in traditional Navajo superstitions. They are thought to be capable of many unnatural acts, such as flying or turning themselves into werewolves and other ethereal creatures; hence the term Skinwalkers, referring to their ability to change forms or skins.

R. Allen Chappell

Filename: The Collector 72718
    print-1 4.23.35 PM.docx

Directory:
              /Users/Navajo/Library/C
    ontainers/com.microsoft.Word/Data/Docu
    ments

Template:
              /Users/Navajo/Library/
    Group
    Containers/UBF8T346G9.Office/User
    Content.localized/Templates.localized/Nor
    mal.dotm

Title:

Subject:

Author: Ron Chappell

Keywords:

Comments:

Creation Date: 5/10/22 9:52:00 AM

Change Number: 2

Last Saved On: 5/10/22 9:52:00 AM

Last Saved By: Microsoft Office User

Total Editing Time: 1 Minute

Last Printed On: 5/10/22 9:53:00 AM

As of Last Complete Printing

    Number of Pages: 289

    Number of Words: 69,690

    Number of Characters: 317,336
    (approx.)

Made in United States
North Haven, CT
06 February 2023

32139155R00163